M. John Harrison

was born in 1945. He published
has subsequently published six novels, three coll———
stories, including *The Ice Monkey*, and a graphic novel in
collaboration with the artist Ian Miller. His last novel,
Climbers, won the Boardman Tasker Memorial Award in
1989. He lives in London.

'Mike Harrison writes with the sort of precision, clarity and
control that most authors only dream about.'   IAIN BANKS

'He has a wide emotional range, and he realises the unreal
by brilliant selection of detail. It is lifelike. It is also written
in the kind of prose which, as when you tap a nail on a
crystal glass, never rings false.'   *Guardian*

'A curious and accomplished writer. Harrison handles his
material with a grace which approaches the mandarin.'

ROBERT NYE

'A witty and truly imaginative writer.'   *Literary Review*

From the reviews of *The Course of the Heart*:

'M. John Harrison is a blazing original. His books are fictions
of elegant delirium, dark and transcendent by turns. *The
Course of the Heart* is his finest achievement to date.
Exquisitely wrought and brilliantly imagined, it is erotic,
chilling and visionary . . . the work of a great imaginer, and
an extraordinary writer.'   CLIVE BARKER

'The complex but unhesitant shuttle of M. John Harrison's
overlapping narratives draws us remorselessly towards the
revelation of a great secret . . . a book truly written and one
which repays whatever we hazard to invest in it.'

IAIN SINCLAIR

Further reviews overleaf

'Mike Harrison is particularly concerned in *The Course of the Heart* with those moments when strangeness irrupts into ordinary landscapes, whether the result is angels on Peckham Rye or children under Saddleworth Moor. He is a strikingly palpable and concrete writer and the book's mystical orientation is combined, unusually and very effectively, with a keen sociological eye. Harrison has taken bold risks, but the risks pay off. This memorable book is the manifestation of a powerfully distinctive vision, at once sleazy and iridescent.'   *Times Literary Supplement*

'Ian McEwan's *Black Dogs* has certain similarities to this, and will no doubt receive twenty times the coverage, but Harrison's book is a stranger, more striking work from one of Britain's most underrated writers.'   *Arena*

'Harrison is a powerful writer . . . the prose is simple, the observations sharp, the imagery arresting. Its evocation of the sensation of emptiness which can grip people in middle age, and of their instinctive fumbling for some deeper fulfilment, is poignant and exact. Harrison is at his best recording the bleak landscape of the soul.'   *Sunday Telegraph*

'Harrison here reaches the level of Peter Ackroyd, Barry Unsworth or Russell Hoban. The lyrical beauty of his descriptive writing lingers in the memory, as does the merest glimpse of the Coeur that he proffers. This is a strange, sad, but beautiful book.'   *New Statesman & Society*

'A brief, complex novel that opens slowly but eventually settles to a layered bloom, out of which tricky structure all manner of pungent stuff emerges in puffs. A novel of emotions, in which smells and sounds encode feelings as information in *Foucault's Pendulum*, for instance, encodes secrets.'   *Time Out*

M. JOHN HARRISON

The Course of the Heart

Flamingo
An Imprint of HarperCollins*Publishers*

To JJ with love

Flamingo
An Imprint of HarperCollins*Publishers*
77–85 Fulham Palace Road,
Hammersmith, London W6 8JB

Published by Flamingo 1993
9 8 7 6 5 4 3 2 1

First published in Great Britain by
Victor Gollancz Ltd 1992

Author photograph by Seamus Ryan

ISBN 0 00 654602 1

Set in Palatino

Printed in Great Britain by
HarperCollinsManufacturing Glasgow

Contents

'Was man nicht erfliegen kann, muss man erhinken.'

Ruckert, *Die beiden Gulden*

'. . . She hath yielded herself up to everything that
lives, and hath become a partaker in its mystery.
And because she has made herself the servant of each,
therefore she is become the mistress of all . . .'

Aleister Crowley

PROLOGUE
Pleroma

When I was a tiny boy I often sat motionless in the garden, bathed in sunshine, hands flat on the rough brick of the garden path, waiting with a prolonged, almost painful expectation for whatever would happen, whatever event was contained by that moment, whatever revelation lay dormant in it. I was drenched in the rough, dusty, aromatic smells of dock-leaves and marigolds. In the corner of the warm wall, rhubarb blanched under an upturned zinc tub eaten away with rust. I could smell it there.

Some of the first words I heard my mother say were, 'A grown woman like that! How could a grown woman act like that?' She was gossiping about someone in the family. I can't remember who, perhaps one of her younger sisters. It was the first time I had heard the phrase. 'A grown woman.' I imagined a woman cultured like a tomato or a potato, for some purpose I would never understand. Had my mother been 'grown' like that? It was an image which ramified and expanded long after I had understood the proper meaning of the phrase.

My mother loved films. She loved the actresses Vanessa Redgrave and Glenda Jackson as much as the characters they played. She was a tallish, thin woman herself, but otherwise nothing like them. Against their grave and bony calm, always breaking out into rage or delight, she could set only the tense provincial prettiness shared by nurses and infant teachers. Her name was Barbara, but she had her friends call her 'Bobbie'. When I was older I found the effect of this as sad as her neatly tailored trouser-suits and deep suntan. She was frightened the sun would make her haggard but she sat out in it anyway, in the garden or on the beach, turning up her face in a static flight reflex of vanity and despair.

The women she liked Redgrave and Jackson to play were queens, dancers, courtesans, romantic intellectuals determined to batter themselves to death like huge rawboned moths inside the Japanese lamps of their own neuroses. Sexuality seemed to be the strongest of their qualities, until, at the crux, they diverted all the sexual momentum of the film into some metaphor of self-expression – an image of dancing or running – and gave the slip to both the filmic lover and the audience. Much more important was to remain at the focus of attention, and for this they were in competition even with themselves. Having captured the centre stage they were ready to abandon it immediately, dance away, and still ravenous, demand:

'No. Not her. Me.'

The year I was twelve, my mother was thirty. I remember her walking up and down on the lawn at the front of the house shouting, 'You bloody piece of paper, you bloody piece of paper,' over and over again at a letter she was holding in her right hand. It was from my father, I suppose. But clearly something else was at stake. 'You *bloody* piece of paper!' Eventually she varied the emphasis on this accusation until it had illuminated briefly every word. It was as if she was trying for some final, indisputable delivery.

Her sense of drama, the transparency of her emotion, un-nerved me. I ran round the garden pulling up flowers, desperate to offer her something in exchange for whatever loss she was suffering. 'Have my birthday,' I remember shouting. 'I don't want it.' She looked puzzledly at the broken-stemmed handful of marguerites. 'We must put them in a vase,' she said.

My role was the role of Vanessa's male lead, Vanessa's audience. I was to follow my mother's retreat through the diminishing concentric shells of her self. The layers of the onion, peeled away, would reveal only more layers.

'A birthday's the last thing I want, darling.'

The letter was left out on the lawn all afternoon, where the rain could pulp it. When my father stayed away for good, she took to saving her skin, carefully applying a layer of honey-coloured make-up every morning, only to remove it even more carefully at night. Liberated perhaps too late by best-selling feminist novels, she wore wide American spectacles with tinted lenses to protect her eyes and emphasise the fine, slightly gaunt structure of jaw and cheeks.

'I am a sadder but a wiser woman,' she wrote to me from a holiday villa in Santa Ponsa, perhaps over-estimating the maturity of a boy seventeen years old. 'We never get to know people until it's too late, do we?'

I was flattered by these sentiments which, unfinished and adult, implied but somehow always evaded their real subject. Long after I had given up trying to puzzle out what she meant, I was still able to feel that she had confided in me.

'But there you are, my dear. As you grow up I expect you're finding that out.'

By then I was already playing truant two or three afternoons each week from the grammar school. I couldn't have explained why. All I ever did was walk about; or sit hypnotised by the Avon where it ran through the local fields, watching the hot sunlight spilling and foaming off the weir until a kind of excited fatigue came over me and I could no longer separate the look of the water from its sound and weight, its strange, powerful, almost yeasty smell. This I associated somehow with the 'grown woman'. She had developed with me. That yeasty smell, that mass, was hers. She didn't so much haunt as stalk my adolescent summers, which were all rain and sunshine and every minute the most surprising changes of light.

My mother, unaware of this, told people I was young for my age; and indeed during my first term at Cambridge I spent most weekends at home, travelling by rail on Friday evening and early Monday morning. The train often stopped for a few minutes near Derby. I don't remember the name of the station. Two old wooden platforms surrounded by larch, pine and variegated holly gave it an air at once bijou and mysterious: it was the branch-line halt of middle-class children's fiction forty years ago. Sitting in the train, you had no idea what sort of landscape lay behind the trees. The wind rushed through them, so that you could think of yourself as being on some sandy eminence away from which spread an intimately folded arrangement of orchards and lanes, of broad heathland stretching off to other hills. Afternoon light enamelled the leaves of the holly. Everything was possible in the country – or garden – beyond. Foxes and owls and stolen ponies. Gorse and gypsy caravans in a rough field. Some mystery about a pile of railway sleepers near the tracks, shiny with rain in the green light at the edge of the woods!

15

I wanted it desperately.

Then the light passed, the wind dropped and the train began to move again. The trees were dusty and birdlimed. All they had hidden was a housing estate, allotments, a light engineering plant. A woman with a hyperactive child came into the carriage and sat down opposite me.

'Just sit down,' she warned the child.

Instead it stared defiantly into her eyes for a moment then wandered off to make noises with the automatic door.

Early in my second term I bought a stereo. I quickly learned to put on the headset, turn up the volume and listen again and again to the same piece of music, each repetition of a significant phrase causing soft white explosions all over the inside of my skull.

Whether the music was the first movement of Bruckner's Fifth or only the Bewlay Brothers, the result was the same. The actual cortex, the convoluted outer surface of my brain, was somehow scoured and eroded by these little painless epiphanies. I half-hoped that if I listened long enough or got the volume high enough, it would be worn as smooth as a stone by them, so that I would never be able to think again. My ideal at that time was to remain conscious – perceptive, receptive – while no longer conscious of myself. I never achieved that. The music always lost its effect. The explosions ceased to scour. My brain began to grow itself again. I woke up to myself, staring out of the window at the green light rippling through the trees.

Girls eighteen or nineteen years old swam down towards me through it, their arms and legs moving in lazy, thoughtless strokes. When I thought about them they were red-haired, smiling, sleepy-eyed as a Gustav Klimt. A year later I lay on the floor with one of them.

It was early June, bright but humid. The air had been like a hammer for days, the streets stunned and dazzled into silence. She lived with some other people, but the house was empty all through the week. Her room, which was at the front and shaded by the great canopy of a horse-chestnut tree, stayed dim and cool for much of the day. For an hour in the morning the shadow of the slatted blinds moved across the sofa with its Indian cushions, on to the fringed maroon and orange rug and then on again, to dwell over her parted legs and scattered underwear. A little after two o'clock a thin, incandescent line of sunshine sliced into the upper part of the room, caught the dusty paper birds of a cheap mobile and flared them briefly into enamel and gold. That was it.

'This room reeks of sex.'

'It reeks of us,' I said.

I had known her for a week and two days. Half awake alone in my own bed I would catch the smell of her, and in a moment of shocked delight, remember her whispering, 'Fuck me! Fuck me!' in the middle of the night. Wherever I was I could close my eyes and visualise precisely the curve at the base of her spine where it seemed to hold its breath before it arched out into the smooth, heavy muscles of her behind. I loved her contact lenses. I loved the way she had to stop in the middle of the street to slip one out into the palm of her hand then lick it up into her mouth like a cat to clean it.

'Perhaps we should have a bath.'

At three o'clock, someone manhandled a bicycle up the steps outside and came into the house. We heard footsteps on the cool tiled floor of the hall. By then we were restless, a little tired, sticky to touch. Whoever had come in knocked first hesitantly then determinedly at the door of the room. A voice I knew asked for me.

'Don't answer,' she mouthed.

'Yaxley's ready to try,' said the voice at the door. There was a pause. 'Are you there? Hello? Yaxley says he's ready. This weekend.'

'Don't answer!' she said, quite loudly.

I sat up and looked at her. I had known her for a week and two days, and I loved everything about her.

'Shh!' I said.

She pulled me down again. 'Go away!' she shouted.

'Are you in there?' said the voice at the door. 'It's Lucas!'

'Hang on, Lucas – ' I answered.

Would anything have changed if I hadn't, if I'd stayed there quietly with my hand between her legs, trying not to laugh?

' – I'm coming.'

PART ONE
In the Wake of the Goddess

1

Misprision of Dreams

Pam Stuyvesant took drugs to manage her epilepsy. They often made her depressed and difficult to deal with; and Lucas, who was nervous himself, never knew what to do. After their divorce he relied increasingly on me as a go-between.

'I don't like the sound of her voice,' he would tell me. 'You try her.'

The drugs gave her a screaming, false-sounding laugh that went on and on. Though he had remained sympathetic over the years, Lucas was always embarrassed and upset by it. I think it frightened him.

'See if you can get any sense out of her.'

It was guilt, I think, that encouraged him to see me as a steadying influence: not his own guilt so much as the guilt he felt all three of us shared.

'See what she says.'

On this occasion what she said was:

'Look, if you bring on one of my turns, bloody Lucas Medlar will regret it. What business is it of his how I feel, anyway?'

'It was just that you wouldn't talk to him. He was worried that something was happening. Is there something wrong, Pam?'

She didn't answer, but I had hardly expected her to.

'If you don't want to see me,' I suggested carefully, 'couldn't you tell me now?'

I thought she was going to hang up, but in the end there was only a kind of paroxysm of silence. I was phoning her from a call box in the middle of Huddersfield. The shopping precinct outside was full of pale bright sunshine, but windy and cold. Sleet was forecast for later in the day. Two or three teenagers went past, talking and laughing. (One of them said, 'What acid rain's got to do with my career I don't know. That's what they asked me.

"What do you know about acid rain?"') When they had gone I could hear Pam breathing raggedly.

'Hello?' I said.

She shouted, 'Are you mad? I'm not talking on the phone. Before you know it, the whole thing's public property!'

Sometimes she was more dependent on medication than usual; you knew when because she tended to use that phrase over and over again: 'Before you know it – '

One of the first things I ever heard her say was, 'It looks so easy, doesn't it? But before you know it, the bloody thing's just slipped straight out of your hands,' as she bent down nervously to pick up the bits of a broken glass. How old were we then? Twenty? Lucas believed she was reflecting in language some experience of either the drugs or the disease itself, but I'm not sure he was right. Another thing she often said was, 'I mean, you have to be careful, don't you?' drawing out both *care* and *don't* in such a way that you saw immediately it was a mannerism learned in adolescence.

'You must be mad if you think I'll say anything on the phone.'

'I'll come over this evening then.'

'No!'

'Pam, I – '

She gave in abruptly.

'Come now and get it over with. I don't feel well.'

Epilepsy since the age of twelve or thirteen, as regular as clockwork; and then, later, a classic migraine to fill the gaps: a complication which, rightly or wrongly, she had always associated with what Yaxley helped the three of us do when we were students. She must never get angry or excited. 'I reserve my adrenaline,' she would explain. It was a physical, not a psychological thing: it was glandular. 'I can't let it go at the time.' Afterwards though the reservoir would burst, and it would all be released at once by some minor stimulus – a lost shoe, a missed bus, rain – to cause her hallucinations, vomiting, loss of bowel control. 'Oh, and then euphoria. It's wonderfully relaxing. Just like sex,' she would say bitterly.

'OK, Pam. I'll be there soon. Don't worry.'

'Piss off,' she said. She was dependent on reassurance, but it made her angry. 'Things are coming to bits here. I can already see the little floating lights.'

As soon as she put the receiver down I telephoned Lucas.

'I'm not doing this again,' I said.

Silence.

'Lucas? She isn't well. I thought she was going to have an attack there and then.'

'She'll see you, though? The thing is, she just kept putting the phone down on me. You've no idea how tiring that can be. She'll see you today?'

'You knew she would.'

'Good.'

I hung up.

'Lucas, you're a bastard,' I told the shopping precinct.

February. Valentine's Day. Snow and sleet all over the country. For thirty minutes or so, the bus from Huddersfield wound its way through exhausted mill villages given over to hairdressing, dog breeding and an under-capitalised tourist trade. I got off it at three o'clock in the afternoon, but it seemed much later. The face of the church clock was already lit, and a mysterious yellow light was slanting across the window of the nave, as if someone was doing something in there with only a forty-watt bulb for illumination. Cars went past endlessly as I waited to cross the road, their exhausts steaming in the dark air. For a village it was quite noisy: tyres hissing on the wet road, the bang and clink of soft-drink bottles being unloaded from a lorry outside the post office, some children I couldn't see, chanting one word over and over again. Quite suddenly, above all this, I heard the pure musical note of a thrush and stepped out into the road.

'You're sure no one got off the bus behind you?'

Pam kept me on the doorstep while she looked anxiously up and down the street, but once I was inside she seemed glad to have someone to talk to.

'You'd better take your coat off. Sit down. I'll make you some coffee. No, here, just push the cat off the chair. He knows he's not supposed to be there.'

It was an old cat, black and white, with dull, dry fur, and when I picked it up it was just a lot of bones and heat that weighed nothing. I set it down carefully on the carpet, but it jumped back on to my knee again immediately and began to dribble on my pullover. Another, younger animal was crouching on the windowsill, shifting its feet uncomfortably among the little intricate baskets of paper flowers as it stared out into the falling sleet, the empty garden.

'Get down off there!' Pam called as she hung my coat up in the tiny hall.

Both cats ignored her. She shrugged.

'They act as if they own the place.' It smelled as if they did. 'They were strays. I don't know why I encouraged them.' Then, as though she were still talking about the cats:

'How's Lucas?'

'He's surprisingly well,' I said. 'You ought to keep in touch with him, you know.'

'I know.'

She smiled briefly.

'And how are you? I never see you.'

'Not bad. Feeling my age.'

'You don't know the half of it yet,' she said. She stood in the kitchen doorway holding a tea towel in one hand and a cup in the other. 'None of us do.' It was a familiar complaint. When she saw I was too preoccupied to listen, she went and banged things about in the sink. I heard water rushing into the kettle. While it filled up, she said something she knew I wouldn't catch: then, turning off the tap:

'Something's going on in the Pleroma. Something new. I can feel it.'

'Pam,' I said, 'all that was over and done with twenty years ago.'

The fact is that even at the time I wasn't at all sure what we had done. This will seem odd to you, I suppose, but all I remember now is a June evening drenched with the half-confectionery, half-corrupt smell of hawthorn blossoms. It was so thick we seemed to swim through it, through that and the hot evening light that poured between the hedgerows like transparent gold. I remember Yaxley because you don't forget him easily. But what the three of us did under his guidance escapes me, as does its significance. There was, undoubtedly, some sort of loss: whether you described what was lost as 'innocence' was very much up to

24

you. Anyway, that was how it appeared to me: to call it 'innocence' would be to beg too many questions.

Lucas and Pam made a lot more of it from the very start. They took it to heart.

And afterwards – perhaps two or three months afterwards, when it was plain that something had gone wrong, when things first started to pull out of shape – it was Pam and Lucas who convinced me to go and talk to Yaxley, whom we had promised never to contact again. They wanted to see if what we had done might somehow be reversed or annulled, what we'd lost bought back again.

'I don't think it works that way,' I warned them, but I could see they weren't listening.

'He'll have to help us,' Lucas said.

'Why did we ever do it?' Pam asked me.

I went down the next day. The train was crowded. Across the table from me in the other window seat, a tall black man looked round smilingly and cracked his knuckles. He had on an expensive brown silk suit. The seats outside us were occupied by two middle-aged women who were going to London for a week's holiday. They chattered constantly about a previous visit: they had walked across Tower Bridge in the teeth of a gale, and afterwards eaten baked potatoes on the north bank, admiring a statue of a dolphin and a girl; they had visited Greenwich. On their last day it had been the zoo in Regent's Park where, gazing diffidently into the little heated compartments of the reptile house, they were surprised by a Thailand water lizard with a skin, one of them said, 'like a canvas bag'.

She relished this description.

'Just like an old green canvas bag,' she repeated. 'Didn't it make you feel funny?' she insisted. But her friend seemed bored.

'What?'

'That skin!'

At this the black man leaned forward and said, 'It only makes me feel sad.'

His voice was low and pleasant. The women ignored him, so he appealed to me, 'I couldn't say why. Except that a lizard's skin seems so shabby and ill-fitting.'

'I don't think I've ever seen one,' I said.

'What if evolution were teleological after all?' he asked us. 'With aesthetic goals?'

The women received this so woodenly that he was forced to look out of the window; and although he smiled at me once or twice in a preparatory way, as if he would have liked to reopen the conversation, he never did.

Later I went down the carriage to the lavatory, and then on to the buffet. While I was there the train stopped at Stevenage; when I returned to my seat I found that the women had moved to an empty table, and the negro had been replaced by a fat, red-faced man who looked like the older H. G. Wells and who slept painedly most of the way to London with his hands clasped across his stomach. He had littered the table with sandwich wrappers, plastic cups, an empty miniature of whisky, the pages of a newspaper. Just before the train pulled in, he woke up, glared at me suspiciously over this mess, and pushed something across to me.

'Last bloke in the seat left this for you,' he said. He had a thick northern accent.

It was a square of folded notepaper, on which had been written in a clear, delightfully even hand, 'I couldn't help noticing how you admired the birch trees. Birchwoods more than any others are meant to be seen by autumn light! It surprises them in a dance, a celebration of something which is, in a tree, akin to the animal. They dance even on cold still days when the air leaves them motionless: limbs like illuminated bone caught moving – or just ceasing to move – in a mauve smoke of twigs.'

This was unsigned. I turned it over but nothing more was written there.

I laughed.

'Was he black?' I asked.

'Aye, kid,' said the fat man: 'He were.' He hauled himself to his feet and began, panting, to wrestle his luggage off the rack. 'Black as fuck.'

As the train crawled the last mile into London, I had seen three sheets of newspaper fluttering round the upper floors of an office block like butterflies courting a flower. The Pleroma demands of us a passion for the world which, however distortedly, reflects it.

I still remember the intelligent eagerness of the negro's smile –
how he always had to talk about the world – the way his sharp-
edged elegant cheekbones seemed, like tribal scars or a silk suit,
to be more designed than organic.

Though he hated the British Museum, Yaxley had always lived
one way or another in its shadow.

I met him at the Tivoli Espresso Bar, where I knew he would be
every afternoon. The weather that day was damp. He wore a
thick, old-fashioned black overcoat; but from the way his wrists
stuck out of the sleeves, long and fragile-looking and dirty,
covered with sore grazes as though he had been fighting with
some small animal, I suspected he had no jacket or shirt on
underneath it. He looked older than he was, the top half of his
body stooped bronchially, his lower jaw stubbled with grey. I
sometimes wonder if this was as much a pretence – although of a
different order – as the *Church Times* he always carried, folded
carefully to display part of a headline, which none of us ever saw
him open.

At the Tivoli in those days they always had the radio on. Their
coffee was watery and, like most espresso, too hot to taste of
anything. Yaxley and I sat on stools by the window, resting our
elbows on a counter littered with dirty cups and half-eaten
sandwiches, and watched the pedestrians in Museum Street.
After ten minutes a woman's voice said clearly from behind us:

'The fact is that the children just won't try.'

Yaxley jumped and looked round haggardly, as if he expected
to have to answer this.

'It's the radio,' I reassured him.

He stared at me the way you would stare at someone who was
mad, and it was some time before he went on with what he had
been saying:

'You knew what you were doing. You got what you wanted,
and you weren't tricked in any way.'

'No,' I admitted.

My eyes had begun to ache: Yaxley soon tired you out.

'I can understand that,' I said. 'That isn't at issue. But I'd like to
be able to reassure them somehow – '

Yaxley wasn't listening.

27

It had come on to rain quite hard, driving the tourists – mainly Germans and Americans in Bloomsbury for the Museum – off the street. They all seemed to be wearing brand-new clothes. The Tivoli filled up quickly, and the air was soon heavy with the smell of wet coats. People trying to find seats constantly brushed our backs.

'Excuse me, please,' they murmured. 'Excuse me.'

Yaxley became irritated almost immediately.

'Dog muck,' he said loudly in a matter-of-fact voice. I think their politeness affected him much more than the disturbance itself. 'Three generations of rabbits,' he jeered, as a whole family were forced to push past him one by one to get to the table in the corner. None of them seemed to take offence, though they must have heard him. A drenched woman in a purple coat came in, looked anxiously for an empty seat, and, when she couldn't see one, hurried out again.

'Mad bitch!' Yaxley called after her. 'Get yourself reamed out.'

He stared challengingly at the other customers.

'I think it would be better if we talked in private,' I said. 'What about your flat?'

For twenty years he had lived in the same single room above the Atlantis Bookshop. He was reluctant to take me there, I could see, though it was only next door and I had been there before. At first he tried to pretend it would be difficult to get in.

'The shop's closed,' he said. 'We'd have to use the other door.'

Then he admitted:

'I can't go back there for an hour or two. I did something last night that means it may not be safe.'

He grinned.

'You know the sort of thing I mean,' he said.

I couldn't get him to explain further. The cuts on his wrists made me remember how panicky Pam and Lucas had been when I last spoke to them. All at once I was determined to see inside the room.

'We could always talk in the Museum,' I suggested.

Researching in the manuscript collection one afternoon a year before, he had turned a page of Jean de Wavrin's *Chroniques d'Angleterre* – that oblique history no complete version of which is known – and come upon a miniature depicting in strange, unreal greens and blues the coronation procession of Richard Coeur de Lion.

Part of it had moved; which part, he would never say.

'Why, if it's a coronation,' he had written almost plaintively to me at the time, 'are these four men carrying a coffin? And who is walking there under the awning – with the bishops yet not a bishop?'

After that he had avoided the building as much as possible, though he could always see its tall iron railings at the end of the street. He had begun, he told me, to doubt the authenticity of some of the items in the medieval collection. In fact he was frightened of them.

'It would be quieter there,' I insisted.

He sat hunched over the *Church Times*, staring into the street with his hands clamped violently together in front of him. I could see him thinking.

'That fucking pile of shit!' he said eventually.

He got to his feet.

'Come on then. It's probably cleared out by now anyway.'

Rain dripped from the blue-and-gold front of the Atlantis. There was a faded notice, CLOSED FOR COMPLETE REFURBISHMENT. The window display had been taken down, but for the look of things they had left a few books on a shelf. I could make out, through the plate glass, W. B. Yeats's *The Trembling of the Veil* – with its lyrical plea for intuited ritual, 'Hodos Chameliontos' – leaning up against Rilke's *The Notebooks of Malte Laurids Brigge*. When I drew Yaxley's attention to this accidental nexus, he only stared at me contemptuously.

Inside, the shop smelled of cut timber, new plaster, paint, but this gave way on the stairs to an odour of cooking. Yaxley fumbled with his key. His bedsitter, which was quite large and on the top floor, had uncurtained sash windows on opposing walls. Nevertheless it didn't seem well lit. From one window you could see the sodden façades of Museum Street, bright green deposits on the ledges, stucco scrolls and garlands grey with pigeon dung; out of the other, part of the blackened clock tower of St George's Bloomsbury, a reproduction of the tomb of Mausoleus lowering up against the racing clouds.

'I once heard that clock strike twenty-one,' said Yaxley.

'I can believe that,' I said, though I didn't. 'Do you think I could have some tea?'

He was silent for a minute. Then he laughed.

'I'm not going to help them,' he said. 'You know that. I wouldn't be allowed to. What you do in the Pleroma is irretrievable.'

'All that was over and done with twenty years ago, Pam.'

'I know. I know that. But – '

She stopped suddenly, and then went on in a muffled voice, 'Will you just come here a minute? Just for a minute?'

The house, like many in the Pennines, had been built right into the side of the valley. A near-vertical bank of earth, cut to accommodate it, was held back by a dry-stone revetment twenty or thirty feet high, black with damp even in the middle of July, dusted with lichen and tufted with ferns like a cliff. Throughout the winter months, water streamed down the revetment day after day and, collecting in a stone trough underneath, made a sound like a tap left running in the night. Along the back of the house ran a passage hardly two feet wide, full of broken roof slates and other rubbish.

'You're all right,' I told Pam, who was staring, puzzled, into the gathering dark, her head on one side and the tea towel held up to her mouth as if she thought she was going to be sick.

'It knows who we are,' she whispered. 'Despite the precautions, it always remembers us.'

She shuddered, pulled herself away from the window, and began pouring water into the coffee filter so clumsily that I put my arm round her shoulders and said, 'Look, you'd better go and sit down before you scald yourself. I'll finish this, and then you can tell me what's the matter.'

She hesitated.

'Come on,' I encouraged her. 'All right?'

'All right.'

She went into the living room and sat down. One of the cats ran into the kitchen and looked up at me expectantly. 'Don't let them have milk,' she called. 'They got some this morning, and anyway it only gives them diarrhoea.'

'How are you feeling?' I asked: 'In yourself, I mean?'

'About how you'd expect.'

30

She had taken some propranolol for the migraine, she said, but it never seemed to help much. 'It shortens the headaches, I suppose.' As a side-effect, though, it made her so tired. 'It slows my heartbeat down. I can feel it slow right down.' She watched the steam rising from her coffee cup, first slowly and then with a rapid plaiting motion as it was caught by some tiny draught. Eddies form and break on the surface of a deep, smooth river. A slow coil, a sudden whirl. What was tranquil is revealed as a mass of complications that can be resolved only as motion.

I remembered when I had first met her:

She was twenty then, a small, excitable, attractive girl who wore moss-coloured jersey dresses to show off her waist and hips. Later, fear coarsened her. With the divorce a few grey streaks appeared in her astonishing red hair, and she chopped it raggedly off and dyed it black. She drew in on herself. Her body broadened into a kind of dogged, muscular heaviness. Even her hands and feet seemed to become bigger.

'You're old before you know it,' she would say. 'Before you know it.'

Separated from Lucas she was easily chafed by her surroundings; moved every six months or so, although never very far, and always to the same sort of dilapidated, drearily furnished cottage, so you suspected she was looking for precisely the things that made her nervous and ill; and tried to keep down to fifty cigarettes a day.

'Why did Yaxley never help us?' she asked me. 'You must know.'

Yaxley fished two cups out of a plastic washing-up bowl and put tea bags in them.

'Don't tell me you're frightened too!' he said. 'I expected more from you.'

I shook my head. I wasn't sure whether I was afraid or not. I'm not sure today. The tea, when it came, had a distinctly greasy aftertaste, as if somehow he had fried it. I made myself drink it while Yaxley watched me cynically.

'You ought to sit down,' he said. 'You're worn out.'

When I refused, he shrugged and went on as if we were still at the Tivoli:

'Nobody tricked them, or tried to pretend it would be easy. If you get anything out of an experiment like that, it's by keeping your head and taking your chance. If you try to move cautiously, you may never be allowed to move at all.'

He looked thoughtful.

'I've seen what happens to people who lose their nerve.'

'I'm sure, ' I said.

'They were hardly recognisable, some of them.'

I put the teacup down.

'I don't want to know,' I said.

'I bet you don't.'

He smiled to himself.

'Oh, they were still alive,' he said softly, 'if that's what you're worried about.'

'You talked us into this,' I reminded him.

'You talked yourselves into it.'

Most of the light from Museum Street was absorbed as soon as it entered the room, by the dull green wallpaper and sticky-looking yellow veneer of the furniture. The rest leaked eventually into the litter on the floor, pages of crumpled and partly burned typescript, hair clippings, broken chalks which had been used the night before to draw something on the flaking lino: among this stuff, it died. Though I knew Yaxley was playing some sort of game with me, I couldn't see what it was. I couldn't make the effort, so in the end he had to make it for me. He waited until I got ready to leave.

'You'll get sick of all this mess one day,' I said from the door of the bedsit.

He grinned and nodded and advised me:

'Have you ever seen Joan of Arc get down to pray in the ticket office at St Pancras? And then a small boy comes in leading something that looks like a goat, and it gets on her there and then and fucks her in a ray of sunlight?

'Come back when you know what you want. Get rid of Lucas Medlar, he's an amateur. Bring the girl if you must.'

'Fuck off, Yaxley.'

He let me find my own way back down to the street.

That night I had to tell Lucas, 'We aren't going to be hearing from Yaxley again.'

'Christ,' he said, and for a second I thought he was going to cry. 'Pam feels so ill,' he whispered. 'What did he say?'

'Forget him. He could never have helped us.'

'Pam and I are getting married,' Lucas said in a rush.

2

N'Aimez Que Moi

What could I have said? I knew as well as they did that they were only doing it out of a need for comfort. Nothing would be gained by making them admit it. Besides, I was so tired by then I could hardly stand. Yaxley had exhausted me. Some kind of visual fault, a neon zigzag like a bright little flight of stairs, kept showing up in my left eye. So I congratulated Lucas and, as soon as I could, began thinking about something else.

'Yaxley's terrified by the British Museum,' I said. 'In a way I sympathise with him.'

As a child, I had hated it too.

Every conversation, every echo of a voice or a footstep or a rustle of clothes, was gathered up into its high ceilings in a kind of undifferentiated rumble and sigh – the blurred and melted remains of meaning – which made you feel as if your parents had abandoned you in a derelict swimming bath. Later, when I was a teenager, it was the vast shapeless heads in Room 25 that frightened me, the vagueness of the inscriptions. I saw clearly what was there – 'Red sandstone head of a king . . .' 'Red granite head from a colossal figure of a king . . .' – but what was I looking at? A description is not an explanation. The faceless wooden figure of Rameses emerged perpetually from an alcove near the lavatory door, a Rameses who had to support himself with a stick: split, syphilitic, worm-eaten by his passage through the world, but still condemned to struggle helplessly on.

'We want to go and live up north,' Lucas said. 'Away from all this.'

As the afternoon wore on, Pam became steadily more disturbed.

'Listen,' she would ask me, 'is that someone in the passage? You can always tell me the truth.'

After she had promised several times in a vague way, 'I can't

34

send you out without anything to eat. I'll cook us something in a minute, if you'll make some more coffee,' I realised she was frightened to go back into the kitchen. She would change the subject immediately, explaining, 'No matter how much coffee I drink, my throat is always dry. It's all that smoking;' or: 'I hate the dark afternoons.'

She returned often to the theme of age. She had always hated to feel old.

'You comb your hair in the mornings and it's just another ten years gone, every loose hair, every bit of dandruff, like a lot of old snapshots showering down. We moved around such a lot,' she went on, as if the connection would be clear to me: 'after university. It wasn't that I couldn't settle, more that I had to leave something behind every so often, as a sort of sacrifice.

'If I liked a job I was in, I would always give it up. Poor old Lucas!'

She laughed.

'Do you ever feel like that?'

She made a face.

'I don't suppose you ever do,' she said. 'I remember that first house we lived in, over near Dunford Bridge. It was so huge, and falling apart inside! And always on the market until Lucas and I bought it. Everyone who had it tried some new way of dividing it to make it livable. People would put in a new staircase or knock two rooms together. They'd abandon parts of it because they couldn't afford to heat it all. Then they'd bugger off before anything was finished and leave it to the next lot – '

She broke off suddenly.

'I could never keep it tidy,' she said.

'Lucas always loved it.'

'Does he say that? You don't want to pay too much attention to him,' she warned me. 'The garden was so full of builders' rubbish we could never grow anything. And the winters!' She shivered. 'Well, you know what it's like out there. The rooms reeked of calor gas. Before we'd been there a week Lucas had every kind of portable heater you could think of. I hated the cold, but never as much as he did.' With an amused tenderness she chided him – 'Lucas, Lucas, Lucas' – as if he were in the room there with us. 'How you hated it and how untidy you were!'

By now it was dark outside, but the younger cat was still staring out into the greyish, sleety well of the garden, beyond which you could just make out – as a swelling line of shadow with low clouds racing over it – the edge of the moor. Pam kept asking the cat what it could see. 'Nothing but old crimes out there,' she told it. 'Children buried all over the moor.'

Eventually she got up with a sigh and pushed it on to the floor. 'That's where cats belong. Cats belong on the floor.'

Some paper flowers were knocked down. Stooping to gather them up she said, 'If there is a God, a real one, He gave up long ago. He isn't so much bitter as apathetic.'

She winced; held her hands up to her eyes.

'You don't mind if I turn the main light off?'

And then:

'He's filtered away into everything, so that now there's only this infinitely thin, stretched thing, presenting itself in every atom, so tired it can't go on, so haggard you can only feel sorry for its mistakes. That's the real God. What we saw is something that's taken its place.'

'What did we see, Pam?'

She stared at me.

'You know, I was never sure what Lucas thought he wanted from me,' she said.

The dull yellow light of a table lamp fell across the side of her face. She was lighting cigarettes almost constantly, stubbing them out half-smoked into the nest of old ends that had accumulated in the saucer of her cup.

'Can you imagine? In all those years I never knew what he wanted from me.'

She seemed to consider this for a moment or two.

She said puzzledly, 'I don't feel he ever loved me.'

She buried her face in her hands.

I got up, with some idea of comforting her. Without warning, she lurched out of her chair and in a groping, desperately confused manner took a few steps towards me. There in the middle of the room she stumbled into a low fretwork table someone had brought back from a visit to Kashmir twenty years before. Two or three paperback books and a vase of anemones went flying. The anemones were blowsy, past their best. Pam looked down at *Love for Lydia* and *The Death of the Heart*, strewn with great blue and red petals like dirty tissue paper; she touched them thoughtfully with her toe. The smell of the foetid flower water made her retch.

'Oh dear,' she murmured. 'Whatever shall we do, Lucas?'

'I'm not Lucas,' I said gently.

While I was gathering up the books and wiping their covers, she must have overcome her fear of the kitchen – or, I thought later, simply forgotten it – because I heard her rummaging about for the dustpan and brush she kept under the sink. By now, I imagined, she could hardly see for the migraine. 'Let me do that, Pam,' I called impatiently. 'Go and sit down.' There was a gasp, a clatter, my name repeated twice.

'Pam, are you all right?'

No one answered.

'Hello? Pam?'

I found her by the sink. She had let go of the brush and pan and was twisting the damp floor cloth so tightly in her hands that the muscles of her short forearms stood out like a carpenter's. Water had dribbled down her skirt.

'Pam?'

She was looking out of the window into the narrow passage where, clearly illuminated by the fluorescent tube in the kitchen, something big and white hung in the air, turning to and fro like a chrysalis in a privet hedge.

'Christ!' I said.

It wriggled and was still, as though whatever it contained was tired of the effort to get out. After a moment it curled up from its tapered base, seemed to split, welded itself together again. All at once I saw that these movements were actually those of two organisms, two human figures hanging in the air, unsupported, quite naked, writhing and embracing and parting and writhing together again, never presenting the same angle twice, so that now you viewed the man from the back, now the woman, now both of them from one side or the other. When I first saw them, the woman's mouth was fastened on the man's. Her eyes were closed; later she rested her head on his shoulder. Later still, they both turned their attention to Pam. They had very pale skin, with

37

the dusty bloom of white chocolate; but that might have been an effect of the light. Sleet blew between us and them in eddies, but never obscured them.

'What are they, Pam?'

'There's no limit to suffering,' she said. Her voice was slurred and thick. 'They follow me wherever I go.'

I found it hard to look away from them.

'What are they?'

They were locked together in something that – had their attention been on each other – might have been described as love. They swung and turned slowly against the black wet wall like fish in a tank. I held Pam's shoulders. 'Get them away,' she said indistinctly. 'Why do they always look at me?' She coughed, wiped her mouth, ran the cold tap. She had begun to shiver, in powerful disconnected spasms. 'Get them away.'

Though I knew quite well they were there, it was my mistake that I never believed them to be real. I thought she might calm down if she couldn't see them. But she wouldn't let me turn the light out or close the curtains; and when I tried to encourage her to let go of the edge of the sink and come into the living room with me, she only shook her head and retched miserably. 'No, leave me,' she said. 'I don't want you now.' Her body had gone rigid, as awkward as a child's. She was very strong. 'Just try to come away, Pam, please.' She looked at me helplessly and said, 'I've got nothing to wipe my nose with.' I pulled at her angrily, and we fell down. My shoulder was on the dustpan, my mouth full of her hair, which smelled of cigarette ash. I felt her hands move over me.

'Pam! Pam!' I shouted.

I dragged myself from under her – she had begun to groan and vomit again – and, staring back over my shoulder at the smiling creatures in the passage, ran out of the kitchen and out of the house. I could hear myself sobbing with panic – 'I'm phoning Lucas, I can't stand this, I'm going to phone Lucas!' – as if I were still talking to her. I blundered about the village until I found the telephone box opposite the church.

I remember someone – perhaps Yaxley, though on reflection it seems too well-put to have been him – once saying, 'It's no triumph to feel you've given life the slip.' We were talking about Lucas Medlar. 'You can't live intensely except at the cost of the self. In the end, Lucas's reluctance to give himself wholeheartedly will make him shabby and unreal. He'll end up walking the streets at night staring into lighted shop windows. He'll always save himself, and always wonder if it was worth it.' At the time I thought this harsh. I still do. With Lucas it was a matter of energy rather than will, of the lows and undependable zones of a cyclic personality than any deliberate reservation of powers.

When I told him, 'Something's gone badly wrong here,' he was silent. After a moment or two I prompted him, 'Lucas?'

I thought I heard him say:

'For God's sake put that down and leave me alone.'

'This line must be bad,' I said. 'You sound a long way off. Is there someone with you?'

He was silent again – 'Lucas? Can you hear me?' – and then he asked, 'How is Pam? I mean in herself?'

'Not well,' I said. 'She's having some sort of attack. You don't know how relieved I am to talk to someone. Lucas, there are two completely hallucinatory figures in that passage outside her kitchen. What they're doing to one another is . . . Look, they're a kind of dead white colour, and they're smiling at her all the time. It's the most appalling thing – '

He said, 'Wait a minute. Do you mean that you can see them too?'

'That's what I'm trying to say. The thing is that I don't know how to help her. Lucas?'

The line had gone dead.

I put the receiver down and dialled his number again. The engaged signal went on and on. Afterwards I would tell Pam, 'Someone else must have called him,' but I knew he had simply taken his phone off the hook. I stood there for some time anyway, shivering in the wind that blustered down off the moor, in the hope that he would change his mind. In the end I got so cold I had to give up and go back. Sleet blew into my face all the way through the village. The church clock said half past six, but everything was dark and untenanted. All I could hear was the wind rustling the black plastic bags of rubbish piled round the dustbins.

Civilisation – if it could be called that – made its bench-mark on the Pennine moors with water and railways, the great civil engineering projects of the nineteenth century. Things have been at ebb since. Over in Longdendale and the Chew Valley, the dams and chains of reservoirs endure, but their architecture is monolithic and not to scale. The human remains of these sites of obsession – handfuls of houses, some quarry workings, a graveyard – are scattered. There is nothing left for people. A few farmers hang on. Myra Hindley and Ian Brady, the 'Moors Murderers' of the 1960s, had buried their victims not far from Pam's cottage. Otherwise the spoil heaps and derelict shooting boxes have nothing to guard but an emptiness. I felt pursued despite that.

'Fuck you, Lucas,' I whispered. 'Fuck you then.'

Pam's house was as silent as the rest.

I went into the front garden and pressed my face up to the window, in case I could see into the kitchen through the open living-room door. But from that angle the only thing visible was a wall calendar with a colour photograph of a Persian cat: October.

I couldn't see Pam.

I stood in the flower bed. The sleet turned to snow. Eventually I made myself go in.

The kitchen was filled less with the smell of vomit than a sourness you felt somewhere in the back of your throat. Outside, the passage lay deserted under the bright suicidal wash of fluorescent light. It was hard to imagine anything had happened out there. At the same time nothing looked comfortable, not the disposition of the old roof slates, or the clumps of fern growing out of the revetment, or even the way the snow was settling in the gaps between the flagstones. I found that I didn't want to turn my back on the window. If I closed my eyes and tried to visualise the white couple, all I could remember was the way they had smiled. A still, cold air seeped in above the sink, and the cats came to rub against my legs and get underfoot; the taps were still running.

In her confusion Pam had opened all the kitchen cupboards and strewn their contents on the floor. Saucepans, cutlery and packets of dried food had been mixed up with a polythene bucket and some yellow J-cloths. She had upset a bottle of household detergent among several tins of cat food, some of which had been half opened, some merely pierced, before she dropped them or forgot where she had put the opener. It was hard to see what she had been trying to do. I picked it all up and put it away. To make them leave me alone, I fed the cats. Once or twice I heard her moving about on the floor above.

She was in the bathroom, slumped on the old-fashioned pink lino by the sink, trying to get her clothes off.

'For God's sake go away,' she said. 'I can do it.'

'Oh, Pam.'

'Put some disinfectant in the blue bucket then.'

'Who are they, Pam?' I asked.

That was later, when I had put her to bed. She answered:

'Once it starts you never get free.'

I was annoyed.

'Free from what, Pam?'

'You know,' she said. 'Lucas said you had hallucinations for weeks afterwards.'

'Lucas had no right to say that!'

This sounded absurd, so I added as lightly as I could, 'It was a long time ago. I'm not sure any more.'

The migraine had left her exhausted, though much more relaxed. She had washed her hair, and between us we had found her a fresh nightdress to wear. Sitting up in the cheerful little bedroom with its cheap ornaments and modern wallpaper, she looked vague and young, free of pain. She kept apologising for the design on her continental quilt, some bold diagrammatic flowers in black and red, the intertwined stems of which she traced with the index finger of her right hand across a clean white background. 'Do you like this? I don't really know why I bought it. Things look so bright and energetic in the shops,' she said wistfully, 'but as soon as you get them home, they just seem crude.' The older cat had jumped up on to the bed; whenever Pam spoke it purred loudly. 'He shouldn't be in here and he knows it.' She wouldn't eat or drink, but I had persuaded her to take some more propranolol, and so far she had kept it down.

'Once it starts you never get free,' she repeated.

Following the pattern of the quilt with one finger, she touched inadvertently the cat's dry, greying fur; stared, as if her own hand had misled her.

'It was some sort of smell that followed you about, Lucas seemed to think.'

'Some sort,' I agreed.

'You won't get rid of it by ignoring it. We both tried that to begin with. A scent of roses, Lucas said.' She laughed and took my hand in both of hers. 'Very romantic! I've no sense of smell – I lost it years ago, luckily!'

This reminded her of something else.

'The first time I had a fit,' she said, 'I kept it from my mother because I saw a vision with it. I was only a child, really. The vision was very clear: a seashore, steep and with no sand, and men and women lying on some rocks in the sunshine like lizards, staring quite blankly at the spray as it exploded up in front of them; huge waves that might have been on a cinema screen for all the notice they took of them.'

She narrowed her eyes, puzzled.

'You wondered why they had so little common sense.'

She tried to push the cat off her bed, but it only bent its body in a rubbery way and avoided her hand. She yawned suddenly.

'At the same time,' she went on, after a pause, 'I could see that some spiders had made their webs between the rocks, just a foot or two above the tideline.' Though they trembled and were sometimes filled with spray like dewdrops so that they glittered in the sun, the webs remained unbroken. She couldn't describe, she said, the sense of frailty and anxiety with which this filled her. 'So close to all that violence. You wondered why they had so little common sense,' she repeated. 'The last thing I heard was someone warning me, "On your own you really can hear voices in the tide – "'

She smiled.

'Will you come in with me?' she said, holding back the top of the continental quilt. 'Just for a moment? After all, Lucas can't mind any more, can he?'

'Pam, you're not – '

'Take your clothes off. Come in and hug me, if nothing else.' She made room. She said, 'You've stayed young while I got old.'

And then: 'There, touch. Yes.' I held her until she fell asleep. All night the old cat moved about uncomplainingly but restlessly on the continental quilt, as if it could no longer be comfortable anywhere. I smoothed the fur on its bony head. Its huge purr filled the room. Once, Pam seemed to wake up suddenly; finding that I had rolled away from her, she murmured:

'I'm glad you got something out of it. Lucas and I never did. Roses! It was worth it for that.'

And, after a moment:

'Hug me. Come inside me again.'

I thought of us as we had been twenty years before. I woke quite early in the morning. I didn't know where I was until I walked in a drugged way to the window and saw the village street full of snow. I fed the cats again. As I left the house Pam was still asleep, with the expression people have on their faces when they can't believe what they remember about themselves. It was the last time I saw her before her illness took hold.

'On your own, you really can hear voices in the tide,' she had said. 'I started to menstruate the same day. For years I was convinced that's why my fits had begun: menstruation.'

For a long time after that inconclusive meeting with Yaxley, I had a recurrent dream of him. His hands were clasped tightly across his chest, the left hand holding the wrist of the right, and he was going quickly from room to room of the British Museum. Whenever he came to a corner or a junction of corridors, he stopped abruptly and stared at the wall in front of him for thirty seconds before turning very precisely to face in the right direction before he moved on. He did this with the air of a man who has for some reason taught himself to walk with his eyes closed through a perfectly familiar building; but there was also, in the way he stared at the walls – and particularly in the way he held himself so upright and rigid – a profoundly hierarchical air, an air of premeditation and ritual. His shoes, and the bottoms of his faded corduroy trousers, were soaking wet, just as they had been the morning after the rite, when the four of us had walked back through the damp fields in the bright sunshine. He wore no socks.

In the dream I was always hurrying to catch up with him. I

was stopping every so often to write something in a notebook, hoping he wouldn't see me. He strode purposefully through the Museum, from cabinet to cabinet of twelfth-century illuminated manuscripts. Suddenly he stopped, looked back at me, and said:

'There are sperms in this picture. You can see them quite plainly. What are sperms doing in a religious picture?'

He smiled, opened his eyes very wide.

Pointing to the side of his own head with one finger, he began to shout and laugh incoherently.

When he had gone, I saw that he had been examining a New Testament miniature from Queen Melisande's Psalter, depicting 'The Women at the Sepulchre'. In it an angel was drawing Mary Magdalene's attention to some strange luminous shapes that hovered in the air in front of her. They did, in fact, look something like the spermatozoa which often border the tormented Paris paintings of Edvard Munch.

I would wake up abruptly from this dream, to find that it was morning and that I had been crying.

'On your own, you really can hear voices in the tide, cries for help or attention.'

A warm front had moved in from the south-west during the night. The snow had already begun to soften and melt, the Pennine stations looked like leaky downspouts, the moors were locked beneath grey clouds. Two little boys sat opposite me on the train until Stalybridge, holding their Day Rover tickets thoughtfully in their laps. They might have been eight or nine years old. They were dressed in tiny, perfect donkey jackets, tight trousers, Dr Marten's boots. Close up, their shaven skulls were bluish and vulnerable, perfectly shaped. They looked like acolytes in a Buddhist temple: grave, wide-eyed, compliant. By the time I got to Manchester, a fine rain was falling. The wind blew it the full length of Market Street and through the doors of the Kardomah Café, where I had arranged to meet Lucas Medlar.

The first thing he said was, 'Look at these pies! They aren't plastic, you know, like a modern pie. These are from the plaster era of café pies, the earthenware era. Terracotta pies, realistic-

44

ally painted, glazed in places to have exactly the cracks and imperfections any real pie would have! Aren't they wonderful? I'm going to eat one.'

I sat down next to him.

'What happened to you last night, Lucas? It was a bloody nightmare.'

He looked away.

'How is Pam?' he asked. I could feel him trembling.

'Fuck off, Lucas.'

He smiled over at a toddler in an appalling yellow suit. The child stared back vacantly, upset, knowing full well they were from competing species.

A woman near us said to the two children with her, 'I hear you're going to your grandmother's for dinner on Sunday. Something special I expect?' Lucas glared at her, as if she had been speaking to him. She added: 'If you're going to buy toys this afternoon, remember to look at them where they are, so that no one can accuse you of stealing. Don't take them off the shelf.'

From somewhere near the kitchens came a noise like a tray of crockery falling down a short flight of stairs.

Lucas seemed to hate this. He shuddered.

'I feel it as badly as Pam,' he said. He accused me: 'You never think of that.' He looked over at the toddler again. 'Spend long enough in places like this and your spirit will heave itself inside out.'

'Come on, Lucas, don't be spoilt. I thought you liked the pies here.'

Eventually he admitted:

'I'm sorry.'

Even so, I got nothing from him. We left the Kardomah in case his spirit heaved itself inside out; but then all he did was walk urgently about the streets, as if he were on his own. The city centre was full of wheelchairs, old women slumped in them with impatient, collapsed faces, partially bald, done up in crisp white raincoats. Lucas had turned up the collar of his grey cashmere jacket against the rain but left the jacket itself hanging open, its sleeves rolled untidily back above his bare wrists. He left me breathless. He was forty years old, but he still had the ravenous face of an adolescent. Halfway through the afternoon the lights went on in the lower floors of the office blocks; neon signs turned and signalled against the sky. Lucas stopped and gazed down at the rain-pocked surface of the old canal, where it appears suddenly from beneath the road near Piccadilly Station. It was dim and oily, scattered with lumps of floating styrofoam like seagulls in the fading light.

'You often see fires on the bank down there,' he said. 'They live a whole life down there, people with nowhere else to go. You can hear them singing and shouting on the towpath.'

He looked at me wonderingly.

'We aren't much different, are we? We never came to anything, either.'

I couldn't think of what to say.

'It's not so much that Yaxley encouraged us to ruin something in ourselves, as that we never got anything in return for it.'

'Look, Lucas,' I explained, 'I don't see it that way. I'm never doing this again. I was frightened last night.'

'I'm sorry.'

'Lucas, you always are.'

'It isn't one of my better days today.'

'For God's sake fasten your coat.'

'I can't seem to get cold.'

He gazed dreamily down at the water – it had darkened into a bottomless opal-coloured trench between the buildings – perhaps seeing goats, fires, people who had nowhere to go. '"We worked but we were not paid,"' he quoted. Something forced him to ask shyly:

'You haven't heard from Yaxley?'

I felt sick with patience. I seemed to be filled up with it.

'I haven't seen Yaxley for twenty years, Lucas. You know that. I haven't seen him for twenty years.'

'I understand. It's just that I can't bear to think of Pam on her own in a place like that. I wouldn't have mentioned it otherwise. We said we'd always stick together, but – '

'Then why didn't you?' I said.

He stared at me.

'Go home, Lucas. Go home now.'

He turned away miserably, walked off, and disappeared into that unredeemed maze between Piccadilly and Victoria – alleys

46

full of wet cardboard boxes, failing pornography and pet shops, weed-grown car parks, everything which lies in the shadow of the yellow-tiled hulk of the Arndale Centre. I meant to leave him there, but in the end I went after him to apologise. The streets were empty and quiet: by now it was almost dark. Although I couldn't see him, I could sense Lucas ahead of me. He would be walking very quickly, head thrust forward, hands in pockets. I had almost caught up with him near the Tib Street fruit market when I heard a terrific clattering noise, like an old zinc dustbin rolling about in the middle of the road.

'Lucas!' I called.

When I rounded the corner, the street was full of smashed fruit boxes and crates. Rotten vegetables were scattered everywhere. A barrow lay as if it had been thrown along the pavement. There was such a sense of violence and disorder and idiocy that I couldn't express it to myself. But Lucas Medlar wasn't there; and though I walked about for an hour afterwards, looking down alleys and into doorways, I saw nobody at all.

I had lied to him about Yaxley, of course. For what motives I wasn't sure, though they had less to do with guilt than a kind of shyness. Even after so many years I had no idea how to proceed. Nothing would have been achieved by telling Pam and Lucas the truth, which was that my dealings with Yaxley began again at their wedding –

3

'Michael Ashman'

Pam's parents insisted on a marquee. They could, they said, afford it.

'And we've a big enough lawn, after all!'

Mr Stuyvesant's family, four generations in the Longdendale Valley, had owned Manchester's favourite department store. Finding themselves, late in middle age, in sole charge of this lumber room – scrolled iron lift gates, revolving doors 'and all' – he and his wife had sold it. Convinced they'd never settle out of England, they bit the tax bullet; and instead of retreating to Marbella let themselves be guided by Mrs Stuyvesant's lively childhood memories to one of the old stone houses in the woods behind Jenny Brown Point, jewel of Morecambe Bay's retirement coast. This they bought. They were a surprise to Silverdale village, with its view of Humphrey Head across the bay, its pretty coves and little limestone cliffs, its gardens full of tranquil yellow laburnum. Restless only a month after she arrived, Mrs Stuyvesant renamed the house 'Castle Rock'. She bought a souvenir shop from which she sold Indian silk scarves. At sixty she still wore an orange leather suit. Pam, her late child, reaching maturity then Cambridge from within a stone's throw of the sea, flowering only to books and epilepsy despite red hair and a Pre-Raphaelite calm, had always puzzled her. 'We're that relieved to have her wed at all,' joked Mr Stuyvesant. Nothing could dispirit him, not even Lucas Medlar, a novice English teacher with a poor degree planning to live near Manchester, refusing first to be married in church at all, then – after Pam had persuaded him it wouldn't matter – coming to the ceremony thin and hostile in a rented morning suit.

My train was late. By the time I arrived, Mr Stuyvesant was on his feet. He wanted to say a few words.

'Ladies and gentlemen, as father of the bride – '

Sitting next to him, Pam was dwarfed by the flounced white satin shoulders of her own dress. She smiled and waved when she saw me, but events seemed to have piled up against her even here, where they were of her own instigation.

The marquee was warm enough, but its floor tilted sharply to the left, so that everyone sitting at that side felt as if they were sliding out of it. The supporting poles, dressed with yellow and white ribbon, creaked uneasily in an offshore wind which that evening had brought mist and rain in from the bay. The air smelt of salt; the canvas bulged and slackened rhythmically; the electric chandeliers swayed. Halfway through the meal, the tennis court had begun to squeeze itself up through the coconut matting. Apart from Lucas and Pam, I didn't know anyone there. I sat on my own with my back against the tent, drank some champagne and stared up into the roof where, far above the central tables on which the ruins of the buffet lay scattered among yellow bows and sprigs of artificial flowers, a bright red helium balloon was trapped. Four or five children were staring up at it too, heads tilted back at an identical angle. Events seemed to have piled up against all of us.

'And so it is that we all wish you well,' Pam's father was repeating. 'To share a life with a young one is a tremendous blessing. Most of all we wish you lasting love.' He pronounced this in such a way as to sound like 'lust and love', sat down suddenly looking surprised, and felt for his handkerchief.

Everyone cheered. The cake was cut. Toasts followed, running into one another:

'Moments like this – '

' – the Reverend, with whom I had the pleasure of sitting a moment ago – '

'It is usual to say a few words – '

' – like to thank my great friends Alec and Katie, the sort of hospitality we've come to expect from them – '

'Brother Simon, for one, had jetted in from Australia "for a couple of days" or so he says, so things aren't very parochial at all!'

Throughout these inane or incompetent speeches – which gave me feelings of nightmare, disorder, the certain failure of every-thing the ceremony was supposed to represent – the children laughed at every pause, as if they were trying to understand less what to laugh at than when, so that in later life they could measure their responses as accurately by the rhythms of an occasion as by its content.

'I can only say,' someone finished, 'that if I had a pound for every time I've found this beautiful girl literally with her head buried in a book . . . Well, Lucas, I hope you know what you've taken on!'

At this Lucas, whose own speech had been inaudible, tentative, full of failed allusions, stared miserably ahead and tried to smile. Pam leaned across to touch his hand. By now the fabric of the marquee was in constant motion, an enormous muscle rippling and tensing over their heads. Pam's father, who lay like a log of wood in his chair between them, stirred. 'Now then!' shouted the young man who had got up to present a cellophane-wrapped bouquet to the bride's mother and aunt – in case, perhaps, they felt left out – 'None of that!' The plumbing, he had to inform us, 'on a more serious note', was broken. 'Could everyone go downstairs until gravity has caused the upstairs to flush.' While they were laughing at this I heard a voice close to me say quietly and very distinctly:

'The Upper World empties itself of everything which has previously choked it.'

It seemed to come from the canvas next to my shoulder; but there was no one there. Eventually, I looked down near my feet. There, I saw Yaxley's face, craning up at me from where the tent fabric met the floor. He must have been lying full length in the mud outside. Visible eye as blue as a bird's egg, stubbled jaw wrenched to one side, his head was at such an odd angle he looked as if he had deliberately dislocated his neck.

'Christ!'

'Something's going on in the Pleroma,' he said.

No one else had seen him. I pushed my way out of the marquee in time to catch sight of his overcoat flapping away across the lawns towards the woods and the sea in the dark. I ran after him.

'Yaxley!'

'It's something big!' he shouted back over his shoulder. 'All the signs point to something on a scale we can't imagine!'

'Yaxley!'

'It's trying to pull me in.'

I caught up with him and grabbed his wrist. Pulpy with new cuts, it twisted under my hand and he was off again into the stinging rain, heading for the beach. 'Yaxley!' I blundered about in the woods, then burst out on to a low headland dark with gorse, from which I could hear the thin rim of the sea breathing tiredly over the sand a hundred yards away. 'Yaxley! Yaxley! Leave them alone!' I called. But this time I had lost him, and my voice went away over the bay without effect. I stood awkwardly on the edge of the headland, certain suddenly that he had wormed his way into the gorse at my feet and would lie there grinning upwards with accumulated lunacy until I went away. Had he been trying to get into the tent? If he had come to warn us, why had he run off? I began to sense that he was as frightened as Pam or Lucas; of what, I couldn't then imagine.

When I got back to the marquee the dancing had begun, and there was only white wine left to drink. Pam and Lucas shuffled round on the muddy coconut matting. Soaked to the skin, I watched them from a table near the back. I had cut my face in the woods, the knees and elbows of my suit were stiff with wet sand. Though they avoided me, no one mentioned this, even obliquely, until I was leaving. By then the party had moved out of the marquee and into 'Castle Rock' itself. Pam's father came up to me in the hall, where I was waiting for a taxi, and asked, 'Have you been in the house before?' It was two or three o'clock in the morning by then, and he was slightly unsteady on his feet, a short man in preposterous clothes who said 'the house' as if this was the only one in the world.

I told him I hadn't.

'I'm one of the bridegroom's friends,' I added. 'Lucas's. One of Lucas's friends.'

He stared at me for a few seconds.

'Ah,' he said. 'It's just that someone rather like you came to the house a few years ago. About seven years ago.'

As far as he was concerned, his probably was the only house in the world. It occurred to me that I must look to him much as Yaxley had looked to me: something forcing its way in from outside, or up from inside, as deranging and unwelcome as his daughter's epilepsy. In his mild, hospitable way he was trying

51

to tell me so. I had drunk so much by then that I rather admired him.

'I think my taxi's here,' I said.

Shortly after the wedding Pam and Lucas moved to West Yorkshire, where they lived in a large square unimaginative place, local stone, with one or two deteriorating outbuildings. Extensive gardens lay behind it, then the moors; at the front, on the other side of a quiet lane, the land dropped abruptly into the narrow valley below the reservoir. The view from its upper windows was gloomy and bare, even in summer when a hot brownish haze spread like a cloudy lacquer over the moors, so that you never knew whether to expect rain, an electric storm, or some property of the atmosphere which had never demonstrated itself before. That winter, though it was so raw and cold, no snow fell, only steady drenching rain. Mist hung above the scrub oaks or clamped down motionless along the sides of the valley. During the school holidays Lucas could be seen at all times of day trying to keep warm by digging over the unproductive garden, clearing undergrowth, lighting rubbish-fires, obsessed with his own thoughts. He was teaching just across the county boundary, in a Thameside comprehensive. He drove there and back along the Woodhead Road in a small Renault he called 'the Tub'.

Pam, though she was uneasy on her own, had soon found how unbearably untidy he could be, and claimed, 'I'm glad he's out all day!'

It gave her a chance to clear up.

'Papers thrown everywhere,' she wrote to me. 'The place always looks as if a bomb has hit it!'

The drugs caused her to sleep late and wake exhausted: loaded with propranolol she would come down at eleven in the morning to find that Lucas, up late the previous night, had thrown everything around in a fit of rage. 'Even the furniture, even his precious bloody books!'

Sometimes at weekends, though she had only left the room for a moment or two, she would return to find him shamefacedly putting records back on the shelves, picking up the sofa cushions, righting a chair. She suspected him of a deep frustration (unable to sound it, grew afraid; unable to absorb or assuage it, blamed herself) but never drew it to his attention. And if in his turn Lucas caught Pam fey and scared, staring with a drowsy helplessness out of the kitchen window into the drizzle at the end of the day, he said nothing either: though he may for all I know have offered comfort. They were twenty-two years old. Already their skills were those of avoidance. They let each encounter slide past them. Off it rumbled, at the last moment, top-heavy with its emotional freight like a train swaying away down a tunnel. As a result, Pam's attacks became more frequent.

'I can't help it,' she would tell herself: 'I can't.'

While Lucas, halfway across the Woodhead Pass in 'the Tub' in the morning, banged the palms of his hands on the steering wheel and repeated savagely, 'I can't help her! I can't!' He hated his heart for lifting when he got out of the house; himself for noticing the way the early sunshine fell across the broad heathery slopes of Longdendale.

To me he wrote, 'It can tire you out, never being allowed to be miserable, or vague, or preoccupied.'

It was in the face of this, I think, that they began constructing between them the fairy-tale of the Pleroma which was to cheer them up in the years when Yaxley and I seemed to have abandoned them. Going through a shoebox of old postcards one lunchtime in an Oxfam shop in Hyde or Stalybridge, Lucas came across a photograph of the Cuxa Cloister in the Metropolitan Museum of Art, New York. 'This cloister contains important architectural elements from Saint-Michel-de-Cuxa,' he read, when he turned it over, 'one of the most important Romanesque abbeys of the XII Century.' No one had ever sent it to anyone. Struck by the enormous tranquillity of the scene, amused at the idea of sending her a card from only ten miles away, he put a stamp on it and posted it to Pam. Half dressed in the hall the next morning, she stared at it. 'Let your heart beat/Over my heart,' he had written on the back. She was so delighted this soon became a habit. He chose only exotic or medieval cards, 'The Creation and the Fall' from the British Library's collection, or Altdorfer's 'Battle on the Issus'; and on the back of them he would always scribble something from one of his favourite writers or painters. 'Every discovery is a rediscovery of something latent,' he informed her owlishly one day, only to advise the next: 'Carnation, Lily, Lily, Rose.'

He often read to her when she felt ill. A few days after he had sent the Cuxa postcard, he read her some chapters from the autobiography of Michael Ashman, a minor travel writer who had walked across Europe in the late Thirties, which began: 'Concrete only yields more concrete. Since the war the cities of the Danube all look like Birmingham.' Ashman, who – as the professional successor of Freya Stark rather than, say, Robert Byron or Christopher Isherwood – had travelled culturally rather than morally, and on behalf of his audience rather than himself, now found he was able to write a more truthful or at any rate a more intimate history of his formative trip –

When I was a boy (he went on) you could still see how they had once been the dark core of Europe. If you travelled south and east, the new Austria went behind you like a Secession cakestand full of the same old stale Viennese Whirls, and you were lost in the steep cobbled streets which smelt of charcoal smoke and paprika, fresh leather from the saddler's. The children were throwing buttons against the walls as you passed, staring intently at them where they lay, as if trying to read the future from a stone. You could hear Magyar and Slovak spoken not just as languages but as incitements. There in the toe of Austria, at that three-way confluence of borders, you could see a dancing bear; and though the dance was rarely more than a kind of sore lumbering, with the feet turned in, to a few slaps on a tambourine, it was still impressive to see one of these big bemused animals appear among the gypsy girls on the pavement. They would take turns to dance in front of it; stare comically into its small eyes to make it notice them; then pirouette away. As performers themselves, they regarded it with grave affection and delight.

I loved sights like this and sought them out. I had some money. Being English gave me a sense of having escaped. I was free to watch, and conceive there and then the Search for the Heart.

By day the girls often told fortunes with cards, favouring a discredited but popular Etteilla. (I don't know how old it was. Among its major arcana it included a symbol I have never seen in any traditional pack, but its langue was that of post-Napoleonic France: 'Within a year your case will come up and you will acquire money'; 'You will suffer an illness which will cost considerable money without efficacy. Finally a faith-healer will restore your health with a cheap remedy'; 'Upside down, this card signifies payment of a debt you thought completely lost'; and so on. It was like having bits of Balzac, or Balzac's letters, read out to you.) They would stand curiously immobile in the street, with its seventy-odd unwieldy cards displayed in a beautiful fan, while the crowds whirled round them head down into the cold wind of early spring. By night many of them were prostitutes. This other duty encouraged them to exchange their earrings and astonishing tiered skirts for an overcoat and a poor satin slip, but they were in no way diminished by it.

To me, anyway, the services seemed complementary, and I saw in the needs they filled a symmetry the excitement of which, though it escapes me now, I could hardly contain. Huts and caravans amid the rubbish at the edge of a town or under the arches of some huge bleak railway viaduct, fires which made the night ambiguous, musical instruments which hardly belonged in Europe at all: increasingly I was drawn to the gypsy encampments, as stations of the Search. It was in one of them I first heard the word 'Coeur'.

Was I more than eighteen years old? It seems unlikely. Nevertheless I could tell, by the way the dim light pooled in the hollow of her collar-bones, that the girl was less. She raised one arm in a quick ungainly motion to slide the curtain shut across the doorway; the satin lifted across her ribby sides. I thought her eyes vague, short-sighted. When she discovered I was English she showed me a newspaper clipping, a photograph of Thomas Maszaryk, pinned to the wall above the bed. 'Good,' she said sadly. She shook her head then nodded it immediately, as if she wasn't sure which gesture was appropriate. We laughed. It was February: you could hear the dogs barking in the night forty miles up and down the river, where the floodwater was frozen in mile-wide lakes. She lay down and opened her legs and they made the same shape as a fan of cards when it first begins to spread in the hand. I shivered and looked away.

'Tell our fortunes first.'

When I drew the heterodox card, she placed the tip of her

right index finger on its picture of a deserted Romanesque cloister and whispered, 'Ici le Coeur.'

Her accent was so thick I thought she had said 'Court'.

Maszaryk had died not long before; the war was rehearsing itself with increasing confidence. Like many European gypsies, I suppose, she ended up in some camp or oven. Birkenau was in the room with us even then. A burial kommando drunk on petrol and formalin was already waiting rowdily outside like the relatives at the door of the bridal suite, as she closed the curtain, spread the cards, then knelt over me thoughtfully to bring me off in the glum light with a quick, limping flick of the pelvis. However often I traced the line of her breastbone with my fingers, however much she smiled, the death camp was in there with us. Any child we might have had would have lived out its time not in Theresienstadt, the family camp, but in Mengele's block. Its number would have been prefaced with a Z.

The Heart!

The war ended. The cold war began. It was clear that Europe would continue to settle elastically for some time, shedding the energy of its new politial shapes as they jostled against one another. Then, not long after the Communist seizure of power in Czechoslovakia, Thomas Maszaryk's son Jan, Czech foreign minister, was found dead in the courtyard beneath an open window in the ministry. I remembered the young prostitute, and the faith she had placed in his father. We don't so much impose our concerns on others as bequeath them, like small heirlooms. They lose one significance then, rediscovered in a drawer years after, suddenly gain another. I saw that the Search grounds itself – that perhaps the Heart itself speaks to us! – in such short-circuits of history. I spent the days in a fever of suppressed excitement: correspondence with European, Mediterranean and near-Eastern exiles had convinced me that their search and mine were the same. Many of us, remembering how the restless, apparently aimless overlapping of boundaries during the early and high Middle Ages had occasionally exposed the Coeur – wavering, equivocal, interstitial, but never less than a kingdom in its own right – felt that in these conditions it might surface again. It never did. And though I may have hoped for this myself in the bitter winters of the late Forties and early Fifties, by then I knew as well as anyone how final had been its downfall: a Czechoslovakian prostitute had shown me how to listen for it along the sounding board of history.

With its low ceiling, panelled walls and red velvet sofa, the lounge at Dunford Bridge was like the lounge of some comfortable 'country' hotel. It was full of indoor plants which Pam had planted in brass jugs, casseroles, bits of terracotta balanced on tall awkward wooden stands, even a coal scuttle made of some orange-blond wood – 'Anything,' Lucas pretended to complain, 'but proper pots.' Every evening Pam's footsteps would go tap-tapping restlessly across the polished wood-block floor, as, increasingly nervous, she looked for something to do. She rustled the newspapers and magazines they kept in a wicker basket by the fireplace; went from picture to picture on the wall – a head in pencil, turned at an odd angle away from the artist; a still life with two lutes more real than the room; a bridge. In the end she would flick the ash off her cigarette and sit down with a copy of *The Swan in the Evening* or *A View of the Harbour*, each of which she had read half a dozen times before.

She could not put away a feeling of dread, even with the doors closed, a life settled.

'Was that a noise in the garden?'

And she was up again, tap-tapping in and out of the shadows among the bulky old furniture she had chosen at some auction in Halifax.

'It's the cat,' Lucas would tell her.

'I must have a cat!' she had said when they were married.

But she showed no interest in the kittens her neighbours offered, or anything Lucas could find in a Manchester pet shop, and in the end adopted an old, blind-looking tom; brindled and slow. In the summer evenings this animal would move thought-fully round the garden, marking each station of its reduced territory with a copious greenish spray. Suddenly it became bored and jumped in through the open French window. All evening it weaved about in the open spaces of the wood-block as if it were pushing its way through a thicket of long entangled grass. It smelled strongly, and its ears were full of mites. Pam put down her book. In a flash the old cat had jumped lightly on to her lap!

'Do you think he's in pain?' she would ask Lucas.

'He's not in pain. He only wants attention.'

'Because I couldn't bear that.'

And to divert her, Lucas would take down Michael Ashman's autobiography, *Beautiful Swimmers*, again. It was a strange book. Every so often you found interrupting the slow powerful stream of his journey from Cuxhaven at the mouth of the Elbe to Constanta on the Black Sea, weirs, rapids, passages so strange and personal they belonged in another kind of book entirely.

'The Expressionists chained to their mirrors – Rilke and Munch, Schiele and Kafka – never able to turn away or look anywhere else. A column of doomed and disintegrating soldiers in the long war against the father and the society he has created to imprison them. The mirror is not a simple weapon. It is their only means of defence, their plan of attack. In it they are allowed to reassure themselves: their nightmare is always of an identity so subsumed under the father's that it becomes invisible to normal light, causing them to vanish as they watch.'

At one moment he was full of the direct human details of the trip – 'I started walking again as soon as the rain eased off, then sat through the next shower in the doorway of an empty church, eating cheese and watching the clouds cross Augsburg' – the next, stimulated by the miraculous westwork of Aachen chapel, 'font of the German Romanesque', he would be speculating again about the nature of the Heart:

'We must sound the historical topboard, then, like someone testing a musical instrument, if we wish to hear the fading resonances of the Coeur – its convulsion, its fall, its disappearance as a kingdom of the World. Less acute researchers allow themselves to be deafened by a catastrophe which, they reason, goes through the fabric like the explosion of a bomb: but we know that by now it is only a whisper, an event implicit in the way other events are organised; less an event, in fact, than what rhetoricians might call a "gap". We can never be sure we have found the Coeur except by its absence!

'Falling into the gap we may glimpse that great light – which, though it takes a million years to fade, would otherwise remain invisible to us even if we knew where to look – in the shape of a ripple in the sand, the position of an empty cardboard box on a building site, the angle of a woman's head as she turns joyfully to listen to three notes of music, a playing-card King seen in a sidelong light.'

'How beautiful,' Pam said. She blinked hard; buried her face in the old cat's fur. 'Do you think it could ever really be like that?'

The point of everything they did was to hide.

Every morning, Lucas drove off into Longdendale. Unnerved by the tight bends and fast local traffic, he would peer anxiously into the sunshine or rain for the spire of Mottram church (known since the fifteenth century as 'the Cathedral of East Cheshire'), which signalled that his journey was almost over. At night the moon's reflection raced him home under the rusty pylons, across the chains of reservoirs. Meanwhile – even if the plans of previous owners had left its walls a confusing patchwork of filled-in doorways, bare stone alcoves, and sections of stripped-pine panelling which didn't quite come down to the floor; even if the connecting doors almost always opened into some odd corner of a room, behind the oak sideboard – Pam waited for him as if theirs was the only house in the world. She would have her own modifications in hand as soon as the builders could be bothered to arrive.

When did it become clear to her that 'Michael Ashman', as Lucas presented him, did not exist?

We can imagine her coming down one morning late. She stares helplessly at the reference books and concertina-files spilled across the living-room carpet, a standard lamp tipped over with its pink silk shade crushed out of shape, the pictures awry on the walls. Before leaving for work, Lucas – who often types on the Lettera portable they keep in a bulky old roll-top desk opposite the french windows – has crumpled up a lot of typing paper and thrown that around too. She smoothes out a sheet of it and finds the draft version of a paragraph from *Beautiful Swimmers*, a version without Michael Ashman's deftness:

'The Expressionists chained to their mirrors – Rilke and Munch, Schiele and Kafka – never able to turn away or look anywhere else. A column of doomed and disintegrating soldiers in the long war against the father and the society he has created. Like the assault rifle or the rocket launcher, the mirror is not a simple burden. It is their only method of defence. It is their only means of attack. In it they are able to reassure themselves of their own continuing existence; their fear is of an identity fragmenting, dissolving, fading to a wisp. The mirror assures them – or seems to – that they are still more than a twist of light at its heart. Those faces ravaged by egotism and insecurity still exist, modified by what is expected of them but not yet quite absorbed or transformed. Rilke and Schiele, glue on to what you can prove! – the bent light, the hard glass. Narcissism was hardly in it for you, your survival was so at stake! (By the same token there is endless despair at the centre of every narcissistic self-portrait.)'

The phone starts to ring, then stops before she can answer it. She stands indecisively in the hallway, barefoot on the cold quarry-tiled floor. The old cat runs up and rubs its smelly head on her ankles. Having seen their furniture moved in, everyone else in the village believes she and Lucas are antique dealers. A rumour is already growing up that they have another house just like this one, in Ireland, piled up with valuable sofas and Japanese firescreens. Staring first at the paper in her hand and then out of the window at the mist on the other side of the valley, Pam tells herself aloud, 'I must make a start.'

Shyly at first, each of them demarcated areas of interest: established a personality. Lucas was the creative one. From the start, his intention had been magical, calming. Pam was the critic. This enabled her to pretend for a long time that her interest in the Heart was archaeological, practical, cynical; she would, had she ever spoken openly, have claimed to be testing the theories of 'Michael Ashman' rather than swallowing them. But they never spoke openly, Pam Stuyvesant and Lucas Medlar. Instead, they sat in that huge front room of theirs, plaiting the quotes on one side of Lucas's postcards into the pictures on the other, until, by degrees, over the next year, perhaps two, they had extended Ashman's researches and woven between them, while pretending it was someone else's, a whole world. By two o'clock each afternoon, whatever time of year, twilight was already in the massive old sideboards and bits of pseudo-medieval art. Her prints of 'Ophelia' and 'The Scapegoat' glowed from the wall. He often looked across at his shelves of books by Alfred Kubin, Rilke and Alain-Fournier. The old cat sat first on his lap, then, yawning and straightening its arthritic legs, stepped cautiously over to hers.

What they believed separately about the Coeur when they began – to what extent, for instance, Lucas saw it as a useful fiction – I can't say. But what they came to agree later, by a sort of sign language, seems to have been this: that somehow, and in special circumstances, the Pleroma breaks into ordinary existence, into political, social and religious life, and becomes a country of its own, a country of the heart.

For a time it blesses us all, then fades away again, corrupted or diluted by its contact with the World. Consequently we can detect its presence as a kind of historical ghost.

The myth of the Coeur was centred on its Fall:

4

Dark Rapture

'In the beginning of course,' Lucas used to say, with a smile across the room at Pam, 'it must still have been perceptible as a catastrophe, the World and the Coeur a great wreck burning in the fabric of the Pleroma like two lovers in the glorious wreck of desire, a funeral done in Byzantine colours on cloth-of-gold – blazing ships, breached walls, smoke towering over everything! If only one had been close enough to hear that huge cry of love and loss, echoing and re-echoing across Europe through the remainder of the fifteenth century (so that, for instance, even the wars of York and Lancaster must be seen as a response – however characteristically cold and sluggish – an unconsciously constructed metaphor not so much of the politics of the Coeur as of its inmost griefs) and well into the sixteenth. We should know much more!'

'We know nothing,' Pam would remind him shortly, opening another packet of cigarettes.

Lucas tried to teach her to be willing to guess instead, taking the whole of the Middle Ages as his resource and ranging in his analogies from the Field of Blackbirds to Duns Scotus and the pursuit of Nominalism; from Courtly Love to the ecstasies of le roi Tafur, that shadowy European knight who relinquished armour and horse to fight on foot in sackcloth, and led the plebs pauperum to the Holy City ('What do I care if I die, since I am doing what I want to do?'). 'On one hand,' he said, 'we have the heresy of the Free Spirit, with its emphasis on the singularity and self-possession of the soul, on the other the beautiful staggered apses *en echelon* of the Romanesque cathedral. Love and order: the very polarity of these visions demands the Coeur as a higher level of appeal, which will reconcile them by containing them as elements of its own structure, just as the Pleroma reconciles the World and the Coeur.'

But this only made Pam laugh.

'What was it like to live there, Lucas? What did they eat? What sort of pottery did they piss in?'

'We don't know.'

'No.' She smiled. 'We don't, do we?'

'For two nights and a day the harbour had been in flames. In any case, there is no escape from inside the meaning of things. The Empress Gallica XII Hierodule, mounted and wearing polished plate armour but – in response some thought to a dream she had had as a child at the court of Charles VII of France – carrying no weapons, waited with her captains, Theodore Lascaris and the twenty-three-year-old English adventurer Michael Neville (later "Michael of Anjou"), for the last assault on the citadel. The outer walls were already weakened by three weeks of bombardment from landward. The labyrinthine powder magazines were exhausted. Smoke from the besieging cannon drifted here and there in the sunlight, sometimes like strips of rag, sometimes like a thick black fog.

'At ten in the morning a force of Serbs and Albanians, on ladders of their own dead, breached the inner defences; by noon they were still only halfway across the citadel, fighting grimly uphill street by street.

'Lascaris was killed there early in the afternoon. Neville, trying wildly to come to his aid with the remains of the small English contingent, seems to have been ambushed and awfully wounded, and it is possible the Empress thought both of them dead. She was last seen on foot at four o'clock, near one of the gates. By then, someone said, she was weeping openly and had picked up a sword. Her armour, though spattered with blood, remained so bright that when the smoke cleared you could not bear to look directly at her. Several people saw her fall. Not content with killing her the Serbs trampled her unrecognisable.

'The invading kings – it seems hardly worth our while at this distance to know who they were – allowed their followers three days in the sacred city before they took possession of it. When at last they rode through the great arch they received into their care a city which seemed to have been in ruins for a thousand years. They wept to see that birds were nesting in the fallen basilicas, weeds growing up between the paving stones.'

Lucas told this story a number of times. At this point he would always pause and look at Pam before finishing.

'What had happened? The Coeur would no longer let itself be known, though it did not perhaps breathe its final breath in the world until they identified Gallica by her beautiful armour, and displayed the mutilated head.'

There was a silence.

Into it Pam said, 'That's all very well. We read "death" where we should read "transformation". But when will it allow itself to be known by us?' And she lit one Churchman's from another, looking steadily at Lucas until he lifted his hands, palms upwards, in a gesture of puzzlement as if she had asked the wrong question.

They were married for a year, then five. During that time Lucas was promoted, but grew no tidier. Pam continued to rise late, take her medication carefully, and stare out of the kitchen window at the trees on the other side of the valley. Lucas replaced his Renault with a more expensive one. The old cat died, and Pam, who had begun to call it 'Michael', buried it quietly in the garden before Lucas came home. Like any childless couple, they seemed a bit aimless, a bit clinging. Neither of them wanted to risk children. 'I wouldn't visit this on anyone,' Pam repeated often, meaning epilepsy. But their real fear was the entrance of some new and uncontrollable factor into a stabilised situation. While the fiction of the Coeur was central to their lives, it wasn't, to begin with at least, their only relief: Pam kept trying to make something of the house, though its size was always to defeat her; and during Lucas's school holidays, they often went to see her parents in Silverdale.

There the tide crept in and out unnoticeably behind 'Castle Rock', while Pam's father stood on his lawn in the moist afternoons, looking out as thoughtfully towards the bay as he had done the morning after her wedding; and her mother sat patiently behind the till of the souvenir shop like a lifesize novelty made of leather, fake fur and red paint. They always seemed glad to see Lucas, and were industrious in making him welcome.

Privately, he thought they drank too much in the evenings. Lucas rarely drank anything. When he did, he became a clinical parody of himself, swinging helplessly between elation and depression.

For Pam, this was a warm coast, full of geological faults which cut down obliquely through her life, where the blackthorn flowered early above the little limestone coves. Winter felt like spring. After her first fits she had stayed for a few weeks at a convalescent home above the thick mixed woods that come down to the sea at Arnside. She still loved to walk the coastal path there. 'It was so different then,' she promised Lucas repeatedly, as they slithered along tracks of blackish earth trodden aimlessly between caravan parks.

'It all seemed more private: the woods were more mysterious, more like woods.'

Lucas had his doubts. The caravans were old, often without wheels. Towed long ago into stamped-down clearings in the woods and painted green, they had quickly surrounded themselves with plastic gnomes which stared implacably out into the undergrowth from railed-off gardens; while inside at night retired couples from Salford wished, 'If only we could have TV.' There were more modern sites at Far Arnside and Gibraltar Farm – great bare strips of dirty grass in the twilight, dogs nosing about the rubbish bins as it got dark. Lucas bought a map – the current OS 1:25000 sheet – only to find parts of the woods marked an empty white. He studied the legend: '"Information not available in uncoloured areas." You don't often see that.'

Pam found him an old snapshot of herself, in the grounds of the home.

'Who took it?'

'One of the other patients I suppose.'

There she sat, squinting into the sun: thin, eyes blackened with convalescence, one leg crossed over the other, smiling out at someone she had never seen since.

'Didn't I look awful?'

One summer weekend she arrived alone, by train. Two o'clock in the afternoon: Silverdale was deserted, awash with sunlight so brilliant it made her hood her eyes and look down, as if modestly, at her own arms. Outside the station, birch trees moved uneasily in a baking wind. That morning Lucas had driven her to Manchester Victoria in the Renault, settled her with a styrofoam cup of coffee in the buffet with its luxurious old tiled walls, and then gone back to Dunford to mark third-year essays, promising, 'I'll come up tomorrow if I get finished.' From Preston onwards, she had entertained herself with the fantasy that he would change his mind, race the train north, and be waiting for her when she arrived. When he wasn't, she began to feel as if she was between lives for a moment – naked to whatever might happen, yet able to have some peace. She shivered with the danger of this, stared out over Leighton Moss, then picked up her suitcase. A crumpled white serviette blew along the up-platform.

Eventually she left the station and walked slowly down the road through the woods towards Jenny Brown Point, where she sat on some rocks in a stupor of delight in the sunshine, looking out over the sea-hardened grass at the distant water of the Kent Channel. Holiday-makers came and went along the shore, laughing and shouting. The tide rose, rearranged the sand and glazed it carefully, and then receded again. All afternoon Pam tried to remember her first fit, the hallucination which had accompanied it, her subsequent appalled dreams of that other seashore, with its rocky platforms shaken by the waves.

The evening was warm, night came: before she knew it the lights of Morecambe hung in the air to the south. She fell asleep, to be woken freezing at 5 a.m. by the astonishing racket of the seabirds on the sand. By then Lucas had arrived and was combing the shore for her; the police were out. 'I didn't remember anything after all,' she told Lucas. 'I only got a very strong sense that I might.' She touched his arm and smiled tiredly up at him. 'I'm sorry.' She seemed happy but dazed for the rest of that day, and kept asking her mother, 'Do you remember someone taking a picture of me, at the convalescent home? What was he like?', to which the old woman could only reply:

'He was a black man. Very interesting to talk to, very educated. You didn't get that much in those days.'

'I knew everyone would be worried about me,' Pam admitted. 'But I felt so lazy.' She laughed. 'Fancy falling asleep on the beach!' Then, in a panic: 'My suitcase! Did anyone get my suitcase?'

*

Pam was certain the woods and sands were benign. But the very nebulosity of the incident had frightened Lucas. Thereafter, he always tried to be at 'Castle Rock' with her.

'Better the devil you know,' he wrote to me: meaning perhaps epilepsy.

Remembering Yaxley's demented face thrust under the edge of the wedding marquee in the mud, I had my own doubts. But as far as Pam and Lucas were concerned, Yaxley had vanished. They seemed to have healed the old wound, and I wasn't anxious to reopen it. Besides, by then I had a life of my own. So I said nothing and, motives aside, this turned out to be a good decision.

As a way of diverting her attention from Park Point and Jack Scout Cove, Lucas organised trips to local towns. There, inevitably, Pam became bad-tempered. Morecambe had good fish and chips, but it was too crowded; Carnforth (though for obvious reasons they were drawn repeatedly to its vast secondhand bookshop) bored her; she was driven to distraction, she complained, by Lancaster's university-town smugness. All of them were needlessly expensive. Oddly enough she liked Grange-over-Sands: she had been there often as a child. It was middle-class, but it seemed to be in the grip of an endless bank holiday, which a real seaside town should be. She was quite happy to sit in the sunshine at the foot of the sea wall with her sandals off, eat ginger biscuits, drink 7-Up and gaze dreamily across the Kent Channel. Lucas was relieved until in September that year he realised she had been staring all summer at the hill above Arnside, where the convalescent home was situated. He shaded his eyes, consulted the now dog-eared OS map. Arnside Knott, 159m. From this distance the woods, wrapped in dusty gold afternoon light and showing no signs of habitation, seemed even more threatening and enigmatic. If he closed his eyes, black, aimless, muddy paths ran back into his memory. (All he could see were plastic gnomes, and then he was finding Pam again, newly awake and shivering on the shore at Jenny Brown Point, her mouth shocked and her soul as visible as a bruise.) When he opened them again and looked sidelong at her, her head was tilted back and she was laughing. Dazzled by her white cotton dress, which he had glimpsed suddenly from the water's edge, a little boy perhaps two years old had screwed up his eyes against the glare, abandoned his parents to the water, and trudged all the way up through the soft dry sand to stand wonderingly in front of her for some moments before he said in a loud voice:

'Shoes.'

Across his bare skin fell sunshine such a thick, sleepy yellow it was almost ochre. Pam opened her arms wide, as if to embrace him, then wider to take in the whole scene behind him: the clear air rippling with heat; the tide, slack and warm; the red setter running in delighted circles over the beach, snapping up at the gulls twenty feet above its head as if they were butterflies.

'Isn't it lovely?' she said.

She smiled.

'Why don't we walk back through the woods?'

Years of hiding had made them adept at manipulating each other's silences. Lucas was unable to refuse so direct a request. Too much else would have to be confronted.

Whatever he expected, the woods turned out to be cool, speckled with sun, smelling of wild garlic. Even the caravan parks seemed transfigured. But when they got home they found that Pam's mother had choked to death on half a Mars Bar, thrashing about like a poisoned chicken behind the counter of the souvenir shop while retired couples from Burnley walked slowly past outside, intent on finding somewhere nice to have lunch, too stupefied by the sunshine to notice anything going on behind the festoons of silk scarves, printed tea-towels and decorated leather handbags which cluttered the display window. Lucas Medlar was less appalled by the death than by its circumstances.

'I can't get that picture of her out of my mind,' he wrote to me.

How Pam felt was less clear. 'She doesn't want to talk about it, and I don't press her. People have their own ways of dealing with things.'

Her father didn't want to talk either. He passed his time between the bar and the big bay window at the side of the house, out of which he stared seawards. Or Lucas would find him on the lawn in the mist and rain. Every blade of grass was covered with drops of water, so that it looked as if a hard frost had clamped down in the night. He would be tilting his head as if listening for something. A few days after the funeral they left him to it. He needed help, you could see: but Lucas wouldn't risk leaving Pam there on her own.

'When we talk about the Fall of the Heart,' Lucas was always careful to point out, 'we are actually using a figure of speech. Further, this "fall" has two opposing trajectories: even as we watch the City recoil from the world and back into the Pleroma – a swooning away from us "into the mirror to die in root and flower" – we interpret this movement as its precise opposite, as a fall into experience of the world, which we read as the loss of ontological purity. It is this aspect which must interest the historian and the genealogist.

'For the Empress there was no escape from "inside the meaning of things"; and by definition we can know nothing of those who survived within the Coeur as it snapped back along that first trajectory, and who were thus withdrawn from the world along with it. But if Neville escaped the revenge of the Albanians, so must others have done, and it is their subsequent history – not as a series of events so much as the clue to a direction of movement – which allows us to plot that second trajectory.

'In this sense, the pedigree of the Heirs of the Coeur is, literally, a fall from Grace.'

The Empress Gallica XII Hierodule, he claimed, had at least three children. Of a shadowy daughter whose name may have been Phoenissa, least is known. 'She was beautiful. She may not have escaped the wreck. You can still hear in the Pleroma a faint fading cry of rage and sadness which may have been hers. The older of the two sons was popularly supposed to have been the son also of Theodore Lascaris, but this seems like a late slander. His name was Alexius and he died in Ragusa in 1460, where, ironically, he had a reputation as one of the secret advisers of George Kastriotis, the national hero of Albania.

'It was his brother, John, who fled to Rome after the Fall, and took with him something described as a "precious relic".'

What this might have been, Lucas was forced to confess, was a matter of speculation. It had been variously referred to as 'the head of Saint Andrew', which when stuffed with chemicals would speak; a rose, perhaps the centifolia brought back to

England from the Low Countries over a century later by John Tradescant the Elder, gardener to the first Earl of Salisbury; 'a magic book of which certain pages open only when a great variety of conditions are fulfilled' (this Lucas saw as a parable of overdetermination); and 'a mirror'.

'One description,' Lucas said, 'has it all or most of these things at once. Whether it was head, mirror or cup, book or flower, it continually "extended its own boundaries through the medium of rays". It was known as the Plan, and was thought also to contain within itself an explanation of the ontological relationships between the Coeur, the World and the Pleroma which continuously gives birth to them both. Whatever it was, it was enough to secure a pension from Pope Pius II; and John remained in Rome until his death, fathering three sons. Yaxley, who believes the Plan is still in the world, would dearly love to get a sight of it, but he's barking up the wrong tree – you could learn more from a pair of little girl's shoes left in a ditch.

'It was stolen some years after John sold it to the Church, in the reign of Clement VII; reappeared briefly in the possession of "an Englishman" during the Sacco di Roma in 1527; and has not been seen since.'

By now the age of religious discord was beginning, and with it the Decline of the Heart. Of John's three sons, two died without issue. Mathaeus married a Roman prostitute whose name he changed to the imperial Eudoxia. He made a secret journey in the late 1470s to try to sell succession rights in the Coeur to Vladimir of Bohemia. (Vladimir is said to have asked, 'Where?'; but clearly he knew.) Nothing is known about Stephen except that he was a follower of Contarini, who in the teeth of the historical wind tried to reconcile the old and new faiths of Europe. Did Stephen see in this conflict of simple minds a parody of the Pleroma's dialectic of love and order?

'We can't know,' Lucas would admit with a smile, while Pam looked away at something in the garden, shaking her head and blowing cigarette smoke out of her mouth.

('He was a child,' she became fond of saying later. 'You couldn't reason with him.' But her own desire was deeply passionate and impatient. She was chafed by the closeness of the

Coeur, and perhaps she was less frustrated by Lucas's rhetoric of the imagination than by the painstaking way he constructed it. 'Phoenissa didn't die,' she interrupted him one day. 'Or if she did, she died into the World, and a bit of her is in all women.' And Lucas could not convince her of anything else.)

The third son, Theodore, had a son of his own when he was fifty. Beyond this his significance is slight. He took the family to Pesara or Pesaro in the provinces and began the Romanisation of it which could be seen over the next two generations until with the birth of Andrew John Hierodule in 1575 the Coeur flared up again like a firework in the genetic material of its heirs. Andrew, Lucas's researches led him to believe, was employed by the House of Orange, 'perhaps as a soldier of fortune, perhaps as diplomat or spy', in 1600. He must have travelled habitually, because he married in Tuscany a year later: the wife died giving birth to a daughter he called, with some irony and an acute sense of his historical position, Eudoxia.

'He disappears quite suddenly after that,' said Lucas, 'but the Coeur is on fire in him, and our next sight of him is at the Hradschin Palace, where the Emperor Rudolph – a solitary and helpless figure more attached to his pet lion Ottokar than any human being – relies in his dealings with Spain on an adviser called "John Cleves" or sometimes "Orange John", who in all respects fits the descriptions we have of Andrew Hierodule. Later he witnessed the Defenestration of Prague. It was Orange John who shouted as Jaroslav Martinez and William Slavata fell fifty feet into the courtyard of the palace, "Let your Mary save you now if she can!" – and then, when Martinez actually began to crawl away: "By God, she has!" Had he gone to Bohemia to hawk the rights of succession in imitation of Mathaeus a hundred and twenty years before? If so, he had been equally unlucky in his choice of Emperor; and he next turns up, still calling himself John Cleves, in England, where he seems to have served the notorious Earl of Lincoln.

'He died in 1638. His sons Leo and Theodore fought on opposite sides during the Civil War. With them – though Theodore, falling among the Royalists at Naseby, was said to have cried out, "Oh, the shiny armour!" – the Coeur withdraws

71

itself again. Leo, less of a lion than his brother, became a pineapple planter in Barbados. Towards the end of his life he was warden of his parish church, and you can see his grave there as Michael Ashman claims to have done. Of his son Constantine we know nothing at all except that he came back to live near Bristol, where he changed his name to St Ives, married twice, and left a daughter to whom he gave the eerie name of Godscall: this little girl, traditionally, is the last of them.

'Whatever happened to her, she carried in her bones the cup, the map, the mirror – the real heritage of the Empress, the real Clue to the Heart.'

PART TWO

The Poor Heart

5

China's in the Heart

Letters arrived from them at irregular intervals. I remembered them guiltily when I was tired or depressed. Though I never had much faith in their solution, which made me think of two monkeys huddled together at the back of a cage on a cold day, I allowed myself to be lulled by it. It was easier to assume they were happy. Of course I knew nothing about the story they had begun to tell one another; it would be nearly twenty years before I found out about 'Michael Ashman' and the Search for the Heart. About a year after the wedding I moved to London, which I'd always wanted to do. Work – in the editorial department of an independent company specialising in reprints from American academic presses – kept me busy. For five or six years after that my life was my own. Then it all came to bits again.

Late May, Westminster Bridge, sudden gusts of wind like bad predictions from the City. A northbound Number 12 stopped briefly at St Thomas's Hospital to let an old man get on. He hesitated at the kerb and looked up briefly, his face a blur. Despite the wind he wore only a pair of dirty white shorts and a singlet. I was on my way back from the London College of Printing, where I had spent most of the morning, I forget why. I was sitting upstairs at the front of the bus. He settled himself next to me, though there were plenty of empty seats, and – as the Number 12 pulled out on to the bridge and began to cross it – put his feet up companionably on the windowsill in front of us. He smelt rank and lively, like a small animal in straw.

'China's in the heart, Jack,' he said, and laughed.

Careful not to answer, in case he was encouraged, I looked out over the river towards Hungerford Bridge. The tide was high. Light came up from the water, filling the space between Westminster Pier and Riverside Walk.

'That's what they say. China's in the heart!'

The bus edged past Parliament in fits and starts, eased itself through an orange light and turned up towards Trafalgar Square. From the corner of my eye I could see the backs of the old man's hands with their prominent ropy veins, his ankles white and dirty above his old suede shoes. Suddenly he put his hand into the pocket of his shorts and brought out a handful of thorns and crumpled leaves. I thought he was going to roll a cigarette with this stuff: instead, palm out flat, he offered it for my inspection. At that moment the bus driver found a clear patch in the traffic and accelerated the length of Whitehall. I heard a familiar voice intone, 'The burnet rose – ' (or perhaps it was 'the burnt rose') ' – five white petals with the light shining through to make a cup for its pale yellow stamens.' I jumped to my feet.

'Yaxley!'

I lurched down the gangway, down the stairs, waited trembling on the platform for the lights to stop the bus at Trafalgar Square.

Yaxley followed me more slowly.

'I'm getting off here too,' he said, showing me his handful of rose leaves again before he crumpled them up with a vague, distributory gesture, as though to scatter them over the stone lions, the dry boarded-up fountains, at the base of Nelson's Column. They were blown under the wheels of a stationary taxi while I waited passively for whatever would happen next. I felt sick. What was I expecting? That he would perform some magical operation, there on the pavement outside the Whitehall Theatre? All he did was study me for a moment. 'Never waste an opportunity!' he advised, then set off rapidly towards the lower end of Charing Cross Road.

I followed him.

'Yaxley,' Pam Stuyvesant pointed out a long time later, 'never did anything to anybody. He always encouraged us to do it to ourselves.'

Up past the National Gallery, left across the toe of Chinatown by Gerrard Place, over Shaftesbury Avenue at the Queen's. He knew I was there. He would step out deliberately in front of a car then stare back at me with a triumphant grimace from the other side of the road; or bump into a woman shopper and shout, 'Fuck me! See that?' Under the tower of St Anne's Soho, with its skeins of dead ivy like a shrivelled venous system, he turned and made pushing motions at me – 'Go back. Go back.' Wardour Street was deserted. He turned left abruptly, to make a curious loop through the gut of the Berwick Street fruit market (where a stallholder's call of 'Twelve for a pahnd. Twelve for a pahnd 'ere!' prompted him to look up and shake his fist at the signboard of the King of Corsica, with its collage of brooding faces), along Broadwick Street, and back on to Wardour Street again. His gait was shambling and agitated. He wavered at the entrance to Flaxman Court. On Meard Street a few blackened pigeons scattered across the cobbles in front of him: he stopped on the corner in front of the old, boarded-up clockmaker's shop – with its faded sign, dusty pillared doorway and stucco rosettes – to stare into a basement area as if he had forgotten something. It was a strange, illogical tour, which ended suddenly when he dodged into the Pizza Express at the corner of Dean Street and Carlisle Street.

I caught up with him as he lurched and shoved his way between the crowded tables to a corner by the window. Disturbed by his smell, people looked up suddenly as he passed, only to look away again when they heard him say quietly but distinctly to himself, 'Cunt!' or 'Who's this nasty little animal then?' He sat down and emptied the plastic flowers out of the little vase in the centre of the table.

The waiters ignored us.

'Yaxley – ' I began, but he had lost interest in me again.

All of a sudden rain began to stream down into the street, and with it a kind of sad, silvery, watery light, which splashed off the front of the pub opposite. Within seconds the road was empty. 'There's a parrot up there,' said Yaxley, in an inturned, empty voice. He was right. I could see it clearly through the upper windows of the pub, running up and down inside its cage like a little mechanical toy. There wasn't much else to look at: another restaurant, the 'TRUSNA' with its pink and purple façade, closed: the rain.

'Yaxley?'

'Just fuck off and leave me alone,' he said.

He seemed to be waiting for something.

77

After a moment two men appeared, pushing a car which wouldn't start. They went round the corner into Dean Street and only one of them came back. He stood in the doorway of the Pizza Express and shook out his umbrella. As he came into the restaurant, his gaze caught mine for a moment. It was absent and empty. I looked away.

Yaxley grinned and leaned over the table. He had torn his paper serviette into several thin strips, one of which he laid across my place mat. Its edges were fibrous and delicate in the washed-out light.

'Look at that!' he said.

I stared at him. I realised that he meant not the torn serviette, but the man who had just come in.

'No, be careful not to let him see you! His name is Lawson.'

The Pizza Express was full of middle management from the advertising and TV industries, lunching each other on the cheap. 'The only reason you go to Germany for two years is to make more money than you do here,' said someone a few tables away. After that I heard only, 'BBC.' There was some laughter. Lawson looked no different to the rest of them. He had furled his umbrella and taken off his raincoat, and was now sitting two or three tables away from us, with people he knew. He wore a gold watch, a striped shirt, one of those pale blue ties with the small white spots you see in the shop next to the men's lavatories at Euston Station. His hair was grey and curly, the curls tiny, tight and wiry: he had on a blue suit.

'Listen to him!' urged Yaxley.

I could see that Lawson was speaking, but in the lunchtime hubbub it was hard to separate his voice from all the others. He talked with his mouth open all the time: the lips moved in a jerky rhythm unrelated to speech, like those of a puppet, so that you imagined left to themselves they would make a constant 'wah wah wah' noise, not loud but penetrating. For a moment I thought I could hear this noise. I was wrong. Then suddenly he said, and I heard him clearly even at that distance:

'Ba-luddy woman. Ba-luddy woman! My God!'

He moved his mouth down to his fork to eat.

Yaxley seemed delighted.

'That man knows four things about the Pleroma,' he said. 'Three of them he learned from me.' He shrugged, and as if to justify himself went on, 'So what. Everyone knows them. But the fourth is important. He is unaware that he knows the fourth, or that he is keeping it from me.'

'I thought you knew everything,' I said.

Yaxley gazed across the junction at the baskets of flowers above the appalling façade of the 'TRUSNA'. The rain had eased off and people were walking past again.

'How are Pam Stuyvesant and Lucas Medlar?' he asked me distantly.

Before I could answer, he went on:

'Let me tell you what Lawson will do this afternoon, when he leaves here. He'll go down to the Thames at Charing Cross Pier, wait in the Victoria Gardens for a very young woman to get off a pleasure boat, and follow her to a house in West Kilburn. She will go inside and shut the door. Then he'll stand outside for an hour, willing her to cross an uncurtained window; while she sits on the bed with her hands in her lap, staring at the wall in front of her. After an hour or two, Lawson will turn away and go home.

'He thinks this girl is his daughter, but she is not. She is a daughter of mine.' He laughed. 'One of my daughters.'

'I don't want to know any of this,' I said.

'Yes you do,' said Yaxley. 'Because if you help me with Lawson I will help you with Pam and Lucas. Would you like me to help them? Things will get worse for them even if I try.'

'What things, Yaxley? What things will get worse?'

He only shrugged.

'If I don't try, they haven't a chance,' he said. 'Look – '

He pushed a Polaroid photograph across the table to me. It showed quite a pretty teenage girl in the white blouse, royal blue V-neck and pleated grey skirt of some private school. Failures of the developing chemicals had drained colour out of her face, so that it had a blank, unformed look. I couldn't see any resemblance to Lawson. She was sitting on a garden bench, leaning forward with her clasped hands resting on her lap. Behind her it was possible to make out a neo-Georgian door; some standard rose bushes in grey, loose, heavily weeded earth; a black BMW. Something about the curve of her back, the clasped hands, the way she seemed to be staring straight ahead into the air, reminded me of a painting. I couldn't think who it was by.

'Lawson wants to fuck his own daughter. Do you understand? He wants to fuck her, but he hasn't the courage or the determination to do it. She lives in Cheshire with his first wife. He says she is fourteen years old, but I imagine she is younger. He is afraid of himself on her behalf. I've explained to him how he can deflect this stroke on to a substitute. I've made him an image of her. When I'm ready I'll allow him to use it in return for what he knows.'

'I won't be involved, Yaxley.'

'Yes you will,' he said.

I stared at him across the table. He pushed his chair back and stood up. 'Keep that,' he said, indicating the Polaroid. 'You'll need it.' He arranged the rest of the torn serviette around my place mat, then as an afterthought added the plastic flowers.

'There,' he said.

For Yaxley, everything had to be clouded, discerned with difficulty, operated at several removes. Even the simplest journey was only the superficial evidence – the diagram – of another, more difficult one. I had seen this clearly, even at Cambridge. It was not so much a 'belief' or a method as a tendency, an intuition about the world. All along he had been trying to pass it on to us. Had he abandoned Pam and Lucas because they learned it too quickly and superficially? I was less in Soho that afternoon, I guessed, than in some scene of instruction, some teaching space of his. Later I would be able to understand the feeling that all of it had been mimed for my benefit. I would recognise St Anne's church, the signboard of the King of Corsica, the front door of 68 Dean Street, a few feathery strips of paper, as the furniture of an initiation. For now I could only sit looking furiously at the torn-up serviette while he left the restaurant, crossed the junction and hid himself in the side doorway of the Nellie Dean. The pub parrot ran nimbly to and fro in its cage above him. The sun broke through.

When Lawson finished his lunch a few minutes later and went off east along Carlisle Street, Yaxley allowed him fifteen yards' start then slipped after him. I followed them in my turn, through

Soho Square and into Sutton Row. It was a useless gesture. They were still ahead of me as I went past the dustbins outside the Society of Our Lady of Lourdes, but by the time I had emerged at the top end of Charing Cross Road they were nowhere to be seen. I wandered about in the shadow of Centrepoint, thinking of Pam and Lucas, and didn't come back to myself until I saw the tower of St Giles-in-the-Fields, with its eight white pillars and white spire, against a very blue spring sky. Four in the afternoon. The clock was a minute or two fast. I had been walking in aimless overlapping loops, like a fly on a television screen. 'Ordinary destinations,' I remembered Yaxley telling us at Cambridge, 'are unearned.' Around me, people were hurrying northwards into the wind, faces set for an hour's commuting home. Even though the traffic was light they still looked suspiciously up and down the street before they crossed.

By then I was married, too.

My wife's name was Katherine. She owned a house which backed on to the canal where it runs between Camden High Street and Regent's Park.

An overgrown garden, with terracotta pots and little figurines, sloped down to the cut: from the upper windows you could look down across it to the surface of the water, green and gold, as solid in some lights as a polished floor, shadowed by trees in the summer, strewn with leaves in the autumn. That was some years before they cleaned up the locks, extended the markets and brought Disneyland to North London in the shape of TV-AM. I had often teased her when I first moved in:

'I can't tell you and your house apart.'

'Touch me here, then.'

Her parents were dead, but remained embedded in the stories she told, like a fossil record in stone. A fortnight after their marriage, her mother had driven a milk float into a ditch. It was a manifesto, or tremor of intent. Later, sleepless in a Cambridge hotel, her father heard knocking late at night behind a bricked-up door. 'That whole family were psychic.' In some way the house still belonged to them. I loved its high, elegantly proportioned windows and polished wooden floors. Every room was full of light, which she encouraged inside – like someone encouraging a shy cat – with white walls, pale eggshell colours.

'Now touch me here.'

She would take my hand, lead me from room to room, and pretend that by touching a cushion, a picture in its frame, the stem of a silk rose woven between the spokes of a dining chair, I was arousing her.

So we exhausted ourselves, dissolving into one another and then further, into a reflection from the bookcases in the lamplight, the smell of a perfume called Anaïs Anaïs. I dreamed of the fold of a velvet curtain, the inside of a cup, the long white curve of her back as she knelt in front of me. A bird sang confusedly in the middle of the night. Everything ran together. On my way downstairs to collect the post the next morning, I would stand still suddenly and say 'Katherine' to myself, just to feel that quick lurch of excitement, like something alive inside, you get when you know that in the next instant you are going to be happy.

6

The Facsimile

'What do you want me to do?' I had asked Yaxley at the Pizza Express.

When his instructions arrived a week later they were scrawled, along with a telephone number, on the back of a postcard. He had sent it from Kensal Rise. Some other project was occupying his time there, but the card, which depicted a street in Meudon in 1928, offered no clue to what it might be.

I rang the number and said: 'I can't drive.'

'Find someone who can then,' Yaxley said, and put the phone down.

I rang him again. 'Be reasonable, Yaxley.'

There was a kind of scraping noise on the line.

'I'll send someone,' he said.

He sent David.

David, a tall lad perhaps twenty-two or twenty-three years old, who wore jeans and a donkey jacket over faded T-shirts and frayed pullovers, lived with his mother in Peckham. He had worked only once or twice since he left school. His face was thin, already muscular about the mouth from the effort of suppressing some internal tension. His eyes, though, remained clear and childish, and he had a habit of staring at you after he had spoken, as if anticipating some response you could never make. He knew you could never make it, never guess what he wanted. Disconcerted, you stared back.

When I asked him what he did with his time, he said,

'Oh, read a lot mostly.'

He enjoyed science fiction, of which he had gathered quite a large collection; or books about concentration camps bought from the non-fiction shelves of W. H. Smith's. He had read Primo Levi, but preferred Wieslaw Kielar. Growing up on this stuff in his mother's one-bedroom flat – the third of four in a gloomy Victorian house with gabled upper storeys – he had failed to notice the gas water-heater above the bath, the loose floorboards, the doorframes which changed shape every summer as the London clay dried out. His mother, who tended to doze off during *News at Ten* or earlier, had the bedroom. This left David to sleep on the convertible sofa in the lounge; more often than not he kept the television buzzing instead and drank Harp lager out of a tin in the wavering half-light.

Two young Asian women lived on the floor below. One of them was a paranoid schizophrenic on community release, who often shouted and screamed deep in the night.

'Get that filth out of here!' David would hear her call suddenly after a long silence.

'The people next door,' he told me, 'had to get rid of their dogs. They used to join in when she started. They'd howl until it got light.' She wasn't too bad at the moment, he believed, because he played his stereo loudly during the day. 'That keeps her awake, so she sleeps more at night.' He was solicitous about her, despite the trouble she caused. 'We keep an eye on her when we can,' he said. 'Her friend has to go out to work.'

The flat above was empty. In that lay much of David's usefulness to Yaxley and Lawson. Sometimes I can still smell the fire that ended all this, and hear the crash of air brakes as the fire-engines sawed back and forth across the street. Eventually they blocked their own access. You could read by the blue lights. David ran aimlessly about until he was exhausted. Because I was careful never to go into his relationship with those two, I have no idea what he owed them. As for his mother, they didn't even know her, although Lawson – who believed in what he called 'family values' – once said:

'God knows what she cooks all day down there. It smells like somebody's bad breath.'

That was typical of the way Lawson spoke. If you rendered his pronunciation of 'car park' as 'caw pawk', you would be close but not quite there. The initials BMW weren't short enough for him – he was always comparing his 'BM' with someone else's 'Jag'. He said 'on the drip' to mean hire-purchase. Sensitised to his voice by half an hour in the Pizza Express, I heard it, or thought I did, every lunchtime thereafter. A glimpse of his shoulders and the back of his neck, two or three places in front of me on the escalators at Tottenham Court Road underground, the sight of a suit I thought was his, in a crowd trying to cross Oxford Street opposite Marks & Spencer's, would be enough to send me hurrying in another direction. He always seemed to be eating something. Once, in the restaurant at Smith's Gallery in Covent Garden, he actually spoke to me.

I came in from Neal Street, hung my coat on the rack by the bar, and realised he was sitting with his back to me at one of the tables near the bottom of the steps, less than ten feet away.

Like David, Lawson was never more than a victim: even so, he had appalling energy. Perhaps in the end this is what attracted Yaxley to him. He was never still. Some barely contained greed caused him to rock about in his seat as he ate, touch his hair and face with his hands, move the chair next to his, move it back to its original position. He called for pepper: let the waiter go: immediately called him back for more.

'Most people want to be pastry,' I heard him say to the woman he was with. 'Don't you think?' Instead of answering, she looked up and saw me standing there helplessly.

'Do I recognise you?' Lawson said loudly, turning to face me.

I shook my head.

'Well then can I do anything for you?'

'I – '

'It's just that when I catch people staring at me like that, I wonder if I can do something for them,' he said. 'But if I can't – '

As I walked away he was leaning across the table to whisper something to his companion – or at any rate to thrust his face into hers – and laugh.

'Because if I can't do anything for you,' he called after me, 'perhaps you could stare at somebody else.'

Smith's was full of people from design agencies, brand new PR firms. I felt them watching amusedly as I followed the waitress between the pillars, through the heat and buzz and the smell of food. I had been expecting to meet a friend of mine who worked in the academic division of Allen & Unwin. I sat down and stared hard at the tablecloth, then the menu; the pictures on the walls.

Lawson's voice was clearly audible from across the room. 'Ba-luddy caw pawk attendants,' I heard him say. 'Ba-luddy little Stalinists!' It was easy to imagine him, still implacable with greed, following his 'daughter' home every afternoon in the rain. How accurate, how sustainable, was the facsimile? Perhaps, when Yaxley's attention was elsewhere, it ran like watercolour, grew blurred and unsatisfying, failed to nourish. And did the real daughter feel any of this, staring out of a stockbroker-Georgian window across the darkening Wirral at the end of the school week? Waiting to hear the low-profile tyres of the BMW crackle up the gravel drive, she would be sticking pictures of ponies and Barbour jackets into a book. 'Term is over. Today the holidays begin.' Did she feel her danger?

When the waitress asked me, 'What would you like with that, sir?' I realised that I couldn't remember what I'd ordered.

That afternoon I rang Yaxley.

'Oughtn't we to move soon?' I suggested. 'He saw me. He may have recognised me from the Pizza Express.'

But although Yaxley had finished his business in Kensal Rise, he still seemed indecisive. The instant he picked up the phone I had received a clear impression of him, sitting in his room above the Atlantis Bookshop, staring straight ahead of himself while the clock of St George's Bloomsbury struck twenty-one and the light fell across his furniture like a kind of yellow varnish that would never set.

'Yaxley?'

I wanted him to succeed with Lawson. By now I was frightened of what might happen if he didn't.

'Don't bother me now,' he said vaguely.

Thirty or forty seconds passed. He still had the phone to his ear.

'Yaxley? Hello?'

David owned an old Hillman Avenger. It was a fawn colour, patched with maroon where he had sanded and primed it for respraying. Inside, it smelled of oil, Halford's air-freshener and foreign food, like a Peckham minicab. His mother, as undeterred by this as by its scabbed chrome and deteriorating wheel-arches, redeemed it every week with a new soft toy. She bought him a sticker which warned, 'You toucha my car, I smasha your face.' On Saturdays in the summer they Blu-Tacked a crocheted blanket to the inside of the glass to keep the sun off the back seat, and David drove her slowly round the Rye into Dulwich Village, so that she could enjoy the posh houses with their oriel windows and hundred-year-old trees. David was her youngest child. He had arrived late and learned slowly. Prone, especially after his father died, to obsessions and enthusiasms – model fighter aircraft, weekly encyclopaedias of military history, anything you could collect or assemble – he had puzzled her by becoming self-contained. 'Very much his own person,' she told people. 'Not like the other three.' That innocent obsessiveness lay curled inside him, waiting until Yaxley – surfacing from dreams of the Pleroma to take a few long ragged breaths – eventually found a use for it. Three days after I had run into Lawson, David arrived at my office, where he undid his coat nervously, gawping like a tourist at the rows of books.

'I'm ready if you are,' he said. 'Where we going?'

Yaxley had told him nothing.

'It's half past three,' I complained. 'I haven't finished work.'

He sat down. 'I can give you another ten minutes or so,' he offered, 'but I'd prefer to be there before it gets dark.' The car had developed an electrical fault: once he turned its headlights on, we wouldn't be able to stop. 'Electrics can be complicated.' Parking had been a problem, too. 'I've left it over in Poland Street.'

He thought for a moment. 'It's probably not what you're used to.'

'We'll go up the M1,' I said.

On the motorway he turned out to be an impatient driver, pushing aggressively through the Friday afternoon traffic with the speedometer up against the stop, where he kept it until near Luton all three lanes began to back up.

'Nice to be out, anyway,' he said.

'Nothing wrong with this engine,' he boasted. 'As long as you stay on top of it.'

Then:

'Look at him. No, him, him over there! Is he a wanker, or what? Three litres, fuel injection, antilock brakes. What's he doing? Fifty miles an hour.

'Fifty fucking miles an hour!'

When there was no one to overtake he became restless, switching the radio on and off, opening and closing the ventilators. He had a trick of swapping his left foot to the accelerator pedal, tucking his right foot up between the seat and the door. He could do this with hardly a blip in the engine revs; although sometimes while his attention was diverted the car itself lurched disconcertingly through the slipstream of a sixteen-wheeler. Spray shattered the light on the windscreen, blowing in all directions through a haze of sunshine and exhaust smoke. We watched two crows flopping heavily away from the hard shoulder, reluctant to leave something they had been eating there.

'I used to drive a van,' he volunteered suddenly. 'Rented van, for a firm of builders. We took it back to the rental place and said, "It's overheating if you do a hundred for any length of time."'

He chuckled.

'The bloke said, "A van like this won't do a hundred." Fuck that, mate!' He looked sideways at me to see if I believed him. 'I had that job a month.'

'Why don't we try the A5 for a few miles, then join the M6 near Rugby?'

'Why not.'

As we turned off the motorway, a Ford Sierra station wagon, logy with children, spare bedding and pushchairs, wallowed past us in the middle lane.

'Can you believe that?'

By the time we got to Cheshire, he had worn himself out. 'I could do with a cup of tea.' He put his feet up on the dashboard, rubbed his eyes, stared emptily out across the Little Chef car park at a strip of bleak grass rising to newly planted trees, where, in the gathering twilight, some children were running around the base of a pink fibreglass dragon fifteen feet high. 'Who would build a thing like that for kids?' he asked me, wriggling about behind the wheel until he could get one arm into his donkey jacket and pull it awkwardly over his shoulders. He looked genuinely puzzled. 'Who would want their kids playing in that?'

'Stay here,' I told him. 'I'll fetch you the tea.'

'Fucking hell.'

The Little Chef franchise includes a carpet with a repeating pattern of swastikas, each arm of the symbol a tiny chef who smiles all day while he holds up a dish. Inside, three sales reps were eating cheeseburgers, fries, a garnish of lettuce shiny with fat. Every so often one of them would read out a paragraph from *Today*; the others would laugh. I found Lawson's daughter waiting quietly in the No Smoking section. 'Be certain it's her,' Yaxley had warned me, as if he expected his substitution to be trumped before he could make it. When she saw me comparing her to the Polaroid, she pretended to be looking out of the window, from which, if she moved her head slightly, she could see the parked cars; the line of the Derbyshire hills a long way in the distance south and east; and against them the fibreglass dragon with its slack, Disney Studio jaw signifying helpless good humour. She had on the identical pleated skirt, with a white blouse; but her hair was in a plait. Close to, she smelled of Wright's soap.

'Your father sent me to fetch you,' I said. Yaxley had schooled me: 'Be certain to say that first. "Your father sent me."' A waitress arrived at the table. I ordered a pot of coffee and sat down while she brought it. Then I added – because what else could I say? –

'He's looking forward to seeing you.'

David came to the door to find out if his tea was ready. 'For God's sake!' I called. 'I'm bringing it!' He ducked away, and I saw him walking quickly back to the car, his shoulders hunched under the leatherette yoke of the donkey jacket. I got Lawson's daughter and her things together and went up to pay.

'Everythink all right for you, sir?' asked the woman at the cash desk.

'Yes thanks,' I said.

'Want anythink else?'

I could see her looking worriedly at the girl.

'No thanks,' I said.

The M6 was deserted. From the moment David launched us down the access ramp into a rushing darkness broken only by the occasional oncoming light, someone else's will clung round us like the smell of the car. Despite our speed we were in a kind of glue. David wouldn't speak to me. If Lawson's daughter had isolated me from him, what I knew about her seemed to detach all three of us from our common humanity. 'The sacrifice,' Yaxley had taught me at Cambridge, 'has its own powers.' She made herself comfortable in the back, and sat so quietly at first that after a few minutes I asked:

'Are you all right?'

'I quite like this grey fur,' she said, touching the seat covers. 'It's soft as a cat.'

Then: 'I'm not often car sick.'

'Are you warm enough?'

'The last time we went on a motorway with Daddy, there were three dead cats,' she said suddenly.

'When we got home we found our own cat had been hurt by a lawnmower and had all the flesh stripped off one front leg. You could see all the lines under the skin. You never know whether it's bones or tendons, or what, do you? He kept pawing us and howling, there was blood all over the kitchen top. Mummy was funny after that. Every time she saw something in the hedge or in the gutter, she made us stop the car.'

She laughed.

'"Is that a dead bird?"' she mimicked.

'"Is that somebody's walking stick, or just a broken umbrella?"'

Unnerved perhaps, David began to talk too –

He had seen the most brilliant film when he was small. '*Flying Tigers*, fucking amazing!'

He was reading a book about the Auschwitz museum.

'In Birkenau,' he said, 'they cut the hair off the women prisoners before they gassed them. It was sold to manufacturers for mattress stuffing. Can you believe that?'

I admitted I could. He added:

'But the worst thing is, tell me if I'm wrong, some of those mattresses could still be on beds. Couldn't they?'

He was worried about his mother.

'She's due to go into the Maudsley for a couple of days soon.' It turned out that she had some kind of bone disease. A broken wrist had failed to heal after two months in plaster, and would have to be pinned. 'It always happens to someone else, doesn't it? Cancer, air crashes, drink-driving, it's never you it happens to.'

He stared ahead for a moment.

'It always happens to someone else.'

He meant to be ironic, but only wound up sounding wistful.

'Look!'

Our shadows had been thrown on to an enormous exit sign by the headlights of the car behind. Briefly we became monumental and cinematic – yet somehow as domestic as the silhouettes of a married couple caught watching TV in their front room – then the journey resumed itself as a series of long, gluey moments lurching disconnectedly one into the next until we reached the outskirts of London, where the traffic, inching along under a thick orange light, filled the steep cuttings with exhaust smoke. Two men fought on the pavement outside the Odeon cinema, Holloway. Lawson's daughter had gone to sleep, her face vacant, her head resting loosely against the window, where every movement of the car made it slide about uncomfortably. She didn't seem to notice when I reached back and tucked a folded pullover under it. Later – or it might have been in the same moment – I looked up and thought I saw roses blooming in a garden on top of the Polytechnic of North London. Between the lawns were broad formal beds of 'ballerinas' grafted on to standard stock, with lilies planted between them. Dog-rose and guelder spilled faint pink and thick cream over old brick walls and paths velvety with bright green moss. White climbing roses weighed down the apple trees. Two or three willows streamed, like yellow hair in strong winter sunshine, over the parapets of the building; briars hung there in a tangle. A white leopard was couched among the roses. It was four times the size it would have been in life, and its tail whipped to and fro like a domestic cat's. Other buildings had put forth great suffocating masses of flowers; other animals were at rest there or pacing cagily about among the service gantries and central heating machinery – baboons, huge birds, a snake turning slowly on itself. 'The Rose of Earth is the Lily of Heaven.' The scent of attar was so strong and heavy it filled the street below: through it like flashes of light through a veil came the piercing human smells of fried food, beer, petrol.

David braked suddenly.

'Jesus!' he said.

The back of a refrigerated truck filled the windscreen, TRASFIGURANTE painted across it in huge white letters. I jumped out of the car in the middle of the road and shouted back through the open door, into the heat and smell and David's surprised white face:

'I'll walk home from here.'

'What?'

I slammed the door.

'I'll walk.'

That night at home I had a nightmare about hiding from people. I was rushing about trying to keep trees, buildings, cars, anything between me and them. I heard a voice say, 'The double paradox. Life is not death, and neither is death,' and woke up to an empty bedroom. It was three o'clock, pitch dark. A rhythmical thudding, with the muffled but determined quality of someone banging nails into a cellar wall or knocking on a heavy door two or three houses further down the street, had carried over from the dream. When it failed to diminish I got up unsteadily. The bedroom door was open, the stairwell dark.

'Katherine?'

Pounding, as distant as before.

'Katherine? Are you there? Are you all right?'

I went from room to room looking for her. All the internal doors were open. Orange street light had established itself everywhere, lodging within the mirrors, slicking along each mantelpiece, discovering something in every room. In the lounge that evening a book, *Painting and the Novel*, had been pulled partly off a shelf – the shadow of its spine fell obliquely across five or six others. In the kitchen, a knife, a breadboard and a loaf of bread lay next to a Braun coffee-grinder like a little white idol. Up in the studio, near the top of the house, something had fallen and broken in the empty grate.

'Katherine?'

She wasn't there. Outside, St Mark's Crescent was full of parked cars; behind the house, the Regent's Canal lay exhausted and motionless. Though I was naked I felt languorous and comfortable, as if I was surrounded by some warm fluid; I had a partial erection which hardened briefly when it touched the fabric of the living-room curtains. At the same time I was filled with anxiety. Its cause was hidden from me, but like that noise it never stopped.

'Katherine?'

Eventually I went back to bed and found her lying there awake in the dark.

'What's the matter?' she whispered.

'I – '

'What is it?'

'I thought you'd got up,' I said. 'That noise – '

'I can't hear anything.'

'Didn't you get up?' I said. And: 'There! Listen!'

'I can't hear anything.'

I had begun to shiver. 'I went all round the house,' I said. 'I can't get warm.'

Katherine put her arms round me.

'What have you been doing to get so upset?'

'Listen!'

Some dreams, I know, detach themselves from you only reluctantly, amid residual flickers of light, sensations of entrapment, effects which disperse quite slowly. Everything is trancelike. You wait to understand the world again and, as you wait, fall back into the dream with no more fear. But there was something awful about that thudding noise, its remoteness, its persistence.

'How do you feel?' Katherine asked next morning.

'Oh fine, fine,' I told her.

But I knew that something had been knocking. Something had come into the house.

'I hope you are,' she said.

She was a painter. We had met one night two or three years before, at an exhibition at Goldsmith's. Somewhat older than me, she had been recovering from an affair I never asked about. At first she was unwilling to commit herself. But soon we couldn't be away from each other for a day, or even pretend to be: so she woke one morning in her perfect house to find me propped on one elbow, staring down at her with a kind of slow delight, and smiled and said, 'I can always feel you near me, even when I'm asleep;' and that was that for both

93

of us. We were married almost immediately. I loved to look at her, in those first few weeks. I would hold her head gently between my hands and stare down into her face and think: She's *in* there.

'I'm fine.'

Later that morning I went up to her studio. There, a ghost of the canal-light, reflective and mobile, lived like a quiver at the edge of vision in the matte white ceiling and walls. I don't know whether she ever noticed it, any more than the smell of the turpentine she kept in a Victorian glass inkwell; but it resides in her paintings too, whatever their subject – the flicker of summer sun off water and green trees.

For Katherine, painting was about space. 'You should always sit,' she had told me the first time I visited her, 'in the middle of a studio, not along the edges of it.' I wandered about now as I had then, leafing through a shoebox in which she kept small sketches on French watercolour paper – wavering pencil lines and little dabs of paint, clues to her inner life; inspecting the brushes – dull orange, blue and brown – laid out on the varnished floorboards beside her on a sheet of corrugated paper to stop them rolling about; or turning over the tubes of oil paint in their wire basket. Vandyke brown, Indian red, crumpled tubes leaden in the dull light. Their names will always delight me. Oxide of Chromium. Monestial green. Speedball oils from America. I still own the picture she was working on that morning. In it a woman stares out at the viewer. Behind her are some other people, and an unfinished, ghostly background of desks in a school or typing pool.

A kind of hypnotic tranquillity always seemed to issue from Katherine as she worked. She had an extraordinary calming effect. You could hear the dab and whisper of the brush on canvas; and behind that, so faint as to be an illusion, the sound of her breathing. It was like watching my mother, ironing in the kitchen on a September evening. I touched the place where the nape of her neck made its soft but powerful transition into the muscles of her freckled upper back. After a moment she turned her face up to me and said, 'Kiss me then.'

We stared companionably at one another. She put her brush down and took my hand.

'Are you sure you feel OK?'

'I'm sure,' I said.

She picked the brush up again.

'I wonder about you,' she said. 'What a lot you keep to yourself!'

7

Number 17, Hill Park

William Blake experienced his first vision during the course of a
family outing to Peckham Rye, which was at that time a village of
quiet, largely agricultural character in the Parish of Camberwell.
Eight or nine years old, his biographers report, William hallucin-
ated (what else can we think?) a tree full of angels, 'bright angelic
wings bespangling every bough like stars'. He escaped a thrashing, though his father wanted to give him one. More importantly,
his foot was on the path. He had his idea. It wasn't yet a burning
spear, but it was never to let him down.

Whether Lawson's daughter saw anything after David in-
stalled her in Peckham, I can't say.

17, Hill Park lay on the left of the Rye as you looked south,
caught between some bleak low-rise flats and two or three point-
blocks built on a hill. A burned-out Vauxhall had sagged on to its
brake drums in the street outside; the basement area was full
of broken furniture – chipboard, Formica, warped and lifted
veneers. If you stood on the doorstep and looked up and down
the road, it was nothing but a line of skips heaped with builders'
rubbish. Inside, I never saw much more than the staircase – grimy
lino, spent matches, missing banisters, a corroded sisal mat
outside each door. At night the stairwell was lit by bare forty-watt
bulbs, one on each landing. By day a kind of grey illumination
leaked in through the skylight, high up in its shaft. You could
hear the sound of rain on the glass. When you walked through
the front door of the upper flat, you were faced with two or three
carpeted steps then a little passage with white plasterboard walls
and chocolate brown woodwork. It was like finding your way to
the toilets of a tea shop in some bleak tourist town at the top of a
cliff.

The morning after Lawson's daughter arrived there, I had a call
from Yaxley.

'I want you to fetch some things for me,' he said. 'A few things.'

Prominent among these was a shoebox of Polaroid photographs he had taken himself, but which he never kept by him, I suspect out of fear. Magic had exhausted him sexually long before Pam, Lucas and I met him. He found it difficult to reach the levels of arousal necessary for a demanding operation. Neither was ordinary pornography of any use. One of the first tasks of my apprenticeship to him – though at the time I didn't think of it in that light – had been to accompany him on a round of the Cambridge public lavatories once a week. He preferred the older ones, seeping and cracked, reeking of piss, which you approached down a dozen greasy stone steps. There would be a soaked uneven floor in the gloom; three stalls with shiny black doors; blue distemper flaking away above the chipped white tiling. Homosexual graffiti covered the walls, done in straight lines and little boxes, in careful expressive designer handwriting. Heterosexual commentary blundered over and around it, in a vigorous but barely legible scrawl. Where Howard had articulately written that he owned his own place and would be happy to try you out any Friday evening – including for your information a hyper-realist illustration of what he claimed to be his penis in an erect state – some drunken boy had added:

YOU POOF.

'These simple endearments,' Yaxley said. He photographed them all. 'See that no one comes in for a moment.'

It was an unnecessary precaution. Places like that are always empty when you go in. A sound in the cubicles turns out to be the trickle of the cistern. Nevertheless, unwilling to be blinded however briefly in such circumstances, I was grateful to establish myself in the doorway and stare across the road – at the rain, the railway station, the woman with the dog – while Polaroid flashbulbs etched at the gloom behind me, and panel by panel Yaxley built his reredos and altarpiece.

'That man,' he had told me the day I first saw Lawson, 'knows four things about the Pleroma. Three of them he learned from me. He is unaware that he knows the fourth, or that he is keeping it from me.' In some sense I couldn't comprehend, Lawson himself was to be made to stand, by metonymy, for that fourth item of knowledge, so that its resources could be drawn upon without it being present in the world. Yaxley called this metaphysical sleight of hand an 'infolding'. I pondered it as I bought or collected objects and artefacts from all over London – books from dealers in Shepherd's Bush and Camden; second-hand garden statuary from Kent; dusty artificial flowers, hanks of hair and a jar of something which looked like preserved ginger from a woman in Golders Green – and delivered them, over the next week, to Peckham.

The upstairs flat at Number 17 could not simply receive these things. First, David must strip it bare. The furniture and carpets came out. The floorboards were scrubbed. In certain places, to erase some stain Yaxley thought might interfere with the operation, they were sanded down to reveal pinkish new wood. All stains, spills, dirty marks, carry an energy of their own. Particular attention was paid to the walls. To ensure success, all the old paper had to be taken off: above the fireplace and near the windows, Yaxley had got down through the old plaster and into the brick. Another kind of magician might have wished to preserve the resonances of Number 17; in other circumstances Yaxley himself would have valued them. But recourse to porno-graphy is by definition a loss of confidence. Where previously he had conceived and assembled the details of such an operation on impulse, holding them together by sheer force of will, he now let caution undercut insight. He made David hire a steamer from a DIY store in Nunhead, and watched thoughtfully as twenty or thirty years of interior decoration bagged and blistered away from the yellowed, sugary plaster in front of his eyes.

'The stuff underneath's not much better,' David told me one evening, when we met on the stairs outside his mother's door. 'These old places are rotten to the core.'

He was sweating. His clothes were covered in dust from the plastic bags of lino, plaster and broken furniture he had been carting down to the bins in the street. Clearly though, it was an effort he enjoyed: something to do. He pushed his hair out of his eyes and had a look at the parcel under my arm.

'What you got there?'

'Gethsemane.'

'You what?'

Gethsemane, in a plastic frame the colour of bone. Painted in greens and golds by someone with no sense of perspective, nevertheless it had in some lights a strange stereoscopic quality. Christ swam out past the picture-plane with his arms spread wide in a gesture of welcome difficult to understand, while the trees and rocks of the Garden, laid on with a palette knife, roiled and eddied behind him like bad weather. It had been much stocked by Catholic outlets a decade before, but after scouring the secondhand shops for two or three days without result, I had taken Yaxley's advice and tried boarded-up premises on the Old Kent Road, under the sign 'ICTURE, Sean Kelly'. Icture, I thought, would resemble ichor, that fluid which runs in the veins of angels as well as kitchen beetles. Or perhaps it was a service, like acupuncture. Anyway, there the picture was, not even dusty, hanging up in a smell of old men and milk bottles, while in the back room an American pit-bull terrier fought with silent determination against its tether to get at me.

'Somethink else for His Nibs, eh?' said David.

He winked.

'Is he mad, or what?'

'Make your own mind up,' I said. 'How's the girl?'

'Hardly a peep out of her. She's with Mum most of the time.' In the day, she stuck pictures in a book, or helped with the housework. 'Watches telly a lot.' It made you wonder what she did at home. You had to give her full marks for quietness, though.

'Mum's teaching her to knit.'

I knew Lawson was in the house with us. I had passed his BMW in the street, black and shiny among the rubbish skips. I could hear his voice, ba-luddy caw-pawking away in the flat upstairs. Somehow this magnified David's good will and made it all the harder to bear. I wanted to shock him out of it. I wanted him to feel the girl's danger. Most of all, perhaps, I wanted him to feel guilty. I pushed him into the corner of the landing and said urgently:

'This is the real daughter.'

He gave me a puzzled look.

'Yaxley's substituting the real daughter,' I said.

'What?'

'He's going to use Lawson's real daughter for the operation! You must have known that!'

'Operation? I don't – '

'Hasn't he told you anything?' I shouted. 'For Christ's sake, David!'

He stared at me.

'I'm just helping him out,' he said eventually.

'Shit.'

The door to the top flat banged open, and down came Lawson. He was in a hurry. He had on a beautifully tailored overcoat in grey wool, which somehow accentuated the breadth of his shoulders, the thickness of his neck, the forward thrust of his head; and he was carrying a bottle of Louis Roederer champagne as shiny and incongruous under the yellow forty-watt light as the car outside at the kerb. 'I can't be bothered with that now,' he called back up to Yaxley. 'Get someone of yours to do it.' There was no answer. When he reached the landing, he inspected David, as if he had never seen him before.

'Just as a matter of interest,' he said, 'what *does* your bloody mother cook all day in there?'

I don't think he once suspected his daughter was behind the same door, watching *Game for a Laugh* and *Celebrity Squares* every evening when he went past.

David, who had never understood Lawson well enough to defend himself, could only laugh and shrug. Lawson laughed too. 'Well, best be off, eh?' he said. I was in his way: he started to shove me aside, then stopped abruptly and, his hand still resting on my arm, eyed me with hatred. Yaxley appeared at the top of the stairs and smiled weakly down on all three of us, his face damp and indescribably vacant in the yellow light. Leaning forward, he looked as if he might launch himself off the top step and float out over us; or else cover us with vomit.

'I'll remember you,' Lawson promised me softly, as if he had only now understood something.

'Oh, I'll remember you.'

The infolding took place two or three evenings later, in the main room of the upper flat, at about nine o'clock. I arrived late and, in the end, saw very little of it.

*

The room was cold. On the wall surrounding the empty fireplace, Yaxley had pinned a dense mass of overlapping Polaroid photographs. From a distance, these tiny, often blurred images seemed to condense into a single sign from some randomly devised but powerful magical alphabet. Above them, like a lock to keep their meanings under control, he had hung the Gethsemane I had found on the Old Kent Road. Its central figure swam out of the cheap frame with motions of despair. In front of the fire had been placed a stripped-pine table with short bulbous legs, which in any other ritual would have taken the part of the altar. Since no actual sacrifice was to occur here, I wondered how Yaxley would use it. For a moment I had a clear vision of Lawson with his trousers down round his ankles, trying to mount his own daughter as she clung pale and goosefleshed to this object, with its cigarette burns and whitish ring-shaped stains. Then I caught a glimpse of the girl, and saw what they had done to her.

She was sprawled legs apart in a corner, naked but for a pair of white briefs designed for someone twice her age, with lace detail and legs cut very high to accentuate the pubic mound. Her ribcage and immature nipples stood out in the forty-watt light. Shadows pooled in the hollow of her collar-bone. A musing, inturned expression was on her face; but every so often she laughed inappropriately at something Yaxley or her father said. They had got her drunk on some kind of cherry liqueur, which I could smell from where I stood in the doorway at the end of the passage.

Yaxley and Lawson were occupied burning something in the grate. Yaxley's wrists were covered in new scabs; Lawson blew on the pale blue flames until his cheeks were red. I could hear them murmuring excitedly, but I couldn't quite see what they had set on fire – glossy paper, I thought, of the sort used for soft pornography: I could see it, wadded, reluctant to catch, curling at the edges. But its thick, stale odour was of something else entirely, wood, hair, kitchen waste. The fourth person in the room was David. David seemed drunk too. He had propped himself up against the wall near Lawson's daughter and was staring at her small white shoulders and arms. Every so often his gaze would fix with a kind of wonder on the place between her unformed thighs where the lips of her sex were quite discernible beneath the thin white fabric.

Apart from the girl they were all fully dressed.

I watched for a minute or two in silence. Lawson was the first to notice me standing there.

'I told you he'd turn up in the end,' he said to Yaxley; and then to me: 'Traffic bad, was it?'

His daughter laughed.

'See any dead cats?' she asked me.

'Christ, Yaxley!' I appealed.

He turned away from whatever he was doing. His eyes were yellow and empty, his face grey. He looked like a cancer patient.

'I'm not going to be involved in this,' I told him.

'Yes you are,' he said.

David laughed suddenly.

'Fucking hell,' he said. 'Eh?'

'Yes you are,' Yaxley repeated.

'Come here, lovey,' Lawson said absently to the girl.

She pulled herself to her feet, then clutched at herself with both hands.

'Daddy, I've wet my knickers.'

I took a pace into the room, said, 'Lawson, this is your *daughter*,' then when I saw the expression on his face, turned round and walked straight out down the stairs and into the street. Rain was falling through the sodium light, pattering on the leaves of the sycamore trees. It would have been easy enough to walk into Peckham and catch a train into London Bridge. I meant to go home to St Mark's Crescent and tell Katherine everything. I knew she would help me. Instead I crossed the road, positioned myself in a doorway with the collar of my coat turned up, and stared numbly at the lighted upper windows of 17, Hill Park.

At about a quarter past ten, the glass blew out of them and tumbled into the basement area beneath. Smoke poured into the air, grey at first then thick black then back to grey again. Shortly afterwards, amid cries of fear and pain, the front door slammed open; Lawson, David and the girl appeared at the top of the steps. Lawson and his daughter were naked, but David still had on his Union Jack underpants. The girl ran off immediately, zigzagging away into the uncertain light of the sodium lamps like some quite new city animal, a vulnerable slip of flesh with a face pale and streamlined to featurelessness – frightened yet touched with all the triumph of the victim. I expected Lawson to follow.

Instead he stared after her; said something incoherent; then, suddenly aware that he was being watched, stormed across the road towards me. The whole left side of his body was scorched and reddened, so that he looked as if he had been dyed. His genitals hung shrivelled and vestigial-looking beneath a belly larded with middle age. He thrust his face very close to mine. Expecting him to hit me, I stepped back into the doorway: but all he did in the end was shake the keys of his car under my nose and shout:

'I've still got these, you bastard!'

And then:

'I remembered you. Don't think I didn't!'

He ripped open the driver's door of the BMW, made one or two hasty attempts to start it, then drove away at high speed.

This left only David, running helplessly about in the street in front of me, trying to say one word over and over again, as if it might describe what had happened in the upper room.

'Ungestalten, Ungestalten, Ungestalten – '

Ungestalten: the shapeless. The pain of being without shape. Some days before, prowling restlessly round the High Street Smith's in search of – as he put it to the assistant – 'Anything about concentration camps,' he had bought the newest Primo Levi. At home, sitting with a can of Harp in the television half-light, he had foundered immediately on this reference to Nietzsche and the suffering of the underclass. It was a strange idea to have encountered between biographies of Myra Hindley and David Niven. I had tried to explain to him the 'price that must be paid for the advent of the reign of the elect'. From the beginning, though, David had understood it all literally and personally. *The pain of being without shape.* It was not the idea that frightened him, so much as the question of who – or what – might suffer this pain.

'Ungestalten, Ungestalten – '

As Lawson turned the BMW out on to the main road at the bottom of Rye Hill, the fire brigade was turning in. They crowded into the narrow street in front of Number 17, the back of one appliance lit up silver by the headlights of the next. The heavy grinding sound of pump engines filled the night. David seemed not to notice them. He ran up and down between the engines, repeating 'Ungestalten, Ungestalten,' in a kind of formless whine; then fell over suddenly. When he got up again, his mouth was slack. Blood and mucus ran out of his nose. Eventually one of the firemen captured him and he was put into an ambulance. His mother was still inside the house.

'Ungestalten.'

Unable to act, I remained in the doorway for some time after he had been taken away. Yaxley's will was like glue: it was all round me still. Brought steadily under control, the fire began to smell like burning rubbish in the distance on a clear day; a human, domestic smell, rather more frightening because of that. They had illuminated the front of Number 17 with a powerful floodlamp, but its white glare revealed nothing. How Yaxley had escaped, I don't know. I hoped at the time he was dead, but I knew it was unlikely. Everyone who lived in the street came out on the pavement to watch the firemen at work – there were frail but cheerful old men and women from the flats, families with children not much younger than Lawson's daughter, a woman who brought her baby with her as if to accustom it early to tragedies and occasions. Someone said:

'They've burnt the dinner again, then.'

Firemen were in and out of the house now. Much of their activity seemed aimless. Blue lights flickered down the hallway, reflected from the pictures on the walls. ('There!' they said in the street: 'Look there!') The smoke abated briefly, the beam of a torch struck out through it: a fireman was in the upper room! Flashes, as the torch moved about. I wondered what he could possibly be seeing, there in that exhausted, sticky zone of Yaxley's will. Finally, a figure in a yellow helmet leaned out of the window and, framed against faint grey smoke, looked down, shrugged. Two hours from the first appearance of the engines, it was all over. People went back to their own houses, a little subdued, whispering, 'Doesn't a woman with kids live there? Ain't that a family with kids?'

'I don't think anyone was in there.'

'There must have been someone.'

I was left in the rain, soaked to the skin, still looking upwards.

What happened that night? It would be naive to think that

Lawson's sexual satisfaction was at issue. A facsimile would have done for that. Yaxley had planned all along that real incest should be committed in the upper room at 17, Hill Park. He had planned all along to reveal this to Lawson as soon as it was too late to withdraw. But though he enjoyed these layers of deception for themselves – it was the mark of his increasing impotence – he must also have had a clear magical purpose, some assumption upon which was predicated the whole ritual of 'infolding'. What this purpose was never really became clear. Neither was any help forthcoming for Pam Stuyvesant or Lucas Medlar. I don't think he had ever meant to keep his word on that. Along with the two Asian women, David's mother died of smoke inhalation. I'm not clear why David had to lose so much.

8

On the White Downs

After the fire nothing seemed to lift me. I was unable to convince myself I had lost nothing by being involved with Yaxley. Each attempt to get him to help Pam and Lucas had only intricated my motives fatally with his. Every night I dreamed of a Pleroma screaming and convulsed by his attempts simultaneously to penetrate it and escape it; meanwhile, Lawson telephoned daily to harangue me, or offer me his daughter, or abuse me incoherently for having taken her already thus reducing her value in any further operation. He didn't seem to understand that Yaxley had abandoned us all again. At first he promised scandal, public exposure, legal action: but he knew quite well the extent of his own involvement. Even now I'm not clear what he thought he wanted, unless it was to retain somehow his links with the magician; to express somehow that dim sense he had of the Pleroma as a power – an immanence, a closeness – he had failed to share.

By then I was bone-tired from morning until night. I wept easily at Japanese films.

At the office I found myself unable to work, staring puzzledly instead at the shelves of paperbacks while my assistant fetched me cups of lukewarm instant coffee the surface of which was always covered with undissolved powder. February came and went. The winter dragged into March and then early April, driving a fine cold penetrative rain across the junctions of Tottenham Court Road. Eventually I caught myself staring at my own deformed reflection in the window of a tube train between Goodge Street, where I worked, and Camden Town, repeating, 'Was that all? Was that all?' Perhaps the agony of the Pleroma was fading. Soon after that Lawson seemed to become less of a nuisance. His threats were replaced increasingly by bursts of uncontrollable weeping, until the calls ceased altogether.

'Why don't you go down to Cornwall for a month?' Katherine suggested. She owned a cottage there, between the road and the sea perhaps two miles north of St Just. Originally she had intended to use it in the winter, rent it out between April and October. 'Have a holiday!'

'I think I might. Everyone in publishing suddenly looks like Anthony Blunt.'

'Have a holiday,' she repeated. 'Recover yourself.'

'I wish I could find a self to recover.'

She stared at me.

'I don't suppose you'd like to come?' I said.

The cottage was one of a neat terrace, built in Penwith granite. While she was waiting for the conversion grants to come through Katherine had filled it with old furniture: a good suite of her mother's with one chair missing, divan beds, one-bar electric fires with perished rubber flexes fitted in 1958, all that detritus which accumulates in houses whose use the middle class have temporarily failed to define, or which they have furnished for the use of others. But you could smell the sea – though you couldn't see it – and hear it, and even at night feel that vast emptying-away of the sky to the west where the headlands fall into the Atlantic like folds in a velours cardigan.

I arrived late and went straight to bed.

There, unused to the silence, I slept fitfully and dreamed I was walking down the coast road towards Zennor Head in the dark:

The air had veiled, brown qualities, draining the colour from the stands of gorse which sometimes appeared at the landward side of the road. Every so often the white finger of an old signpost came into view – not the yellowish white of bone or ivory, but the hard chemical white of typewriter correction fluid: Penzance 5 miles. The figures of Yaxley and Lawson jumped out at me from the gorse, their faces drawn and self-concerned. Lawson's daughter in her white knickers opened her legs – Yaxley mopped his forehead, breathing stertorously. 'Sperms!' he cried. 'Sperms in this picture!' – while Pam and Lucas looked on in sorrow. Something was wrong, clearly, and it seemed important to do what they wanted. But I couldn't make out more than a word or two of what it was. In the dream I was worn out but I couldn't go to sleep: I knew I was too tired to move my limbs, even though I was walking.

This prostration of the will seemed to flow smoothly out of the dream and into the days that followed.

Each morning I would walk into St Just, buy bread at Warren's, milk or groceries from the Co-op in the square, then make my way back exhaustedly to the cottage, where I sprawled in a chair – head thrown back, legs stuck out in front of me – like an old man, so worn out I felt as if I was being pushed firmly down into a hole.

There was no telephone.

I began a letter to Pam and Lucas. 'Katherine Mansfield lived along this coast,' I wrote. Then: 'When I look forward I can only see it getting worse: middle age, apathy, death.' I couldn't post that to them of course. I let it stay on the table while I stood helplessly in the middle of the room wondering what on earth I could say. 'Arthur Symons lived here too.' The next day a cat lay like a splatter of black ink on the concrete path under the window; when I spoke to it, it looked up deliberately, stretched, and walked away. I laughed. I was released. I would probably feel fragile for some time: but the crisis, I believed, had passed. Suddenly I screwed the letter up into a ball, which I squeezed until it was packed and hard.

The downs with their granite outcrops and hut-circles over-shadow everything. They squeeze everything seawards, into narrow bands: the coast road, the linear villages, a little grazing. Long bracken-covered salients fling themselves down between the pasture and the sea, the boggy re-entrants that separate them full of low-lying elder pruned by the wind into a dense, tangled scrub. Old cinder lanes wind over them, linking the abandoned mine workings and empty hamlets from Kenidjack and Pendeen up to Gurnard's Head. Kittiwakes wheel above them in the blustery air and sunshine.

I was grateful for this abrupt falling-away of the coast, the luxurious feeling of light and distance it gave. Half a mile below the cottage, I discovered one morning an unworked quarry, warm and sheltered, from which I could look out at the sea. I sat down and unbuttoned my shirt. Shortly afterwards I took it off altogether. I fell asleep, and woke with a start of surprise in a burning blue space. The curve of the workings drew the skyline away out of my field of vision: above that, nothing but sky, alive and glittering as if it somehow reflected the sea beneath, yet heavy and reverberant with heat. I went back to the house and found a faded woollen blanket; a cold drink.

'After all,' I wrote to Pam and Lucas that evening, 'I'm here to get better, just to lie in the sun and get better – '

The next morning I took a book with me, and by the end of the week I had read *Tristes Tropiques*, *The Gypsy's Baby*, *Mr Beluncle*. In the afternoons I would close my eyes against the glare and let the heat press insistently on their lids. Opening them again suddenly, I saw that my feet were white, blue-veined, delicate-looking. I couldn't remember ever having looked at my feet before.

There at the end of a long sleeve of land, the quarry held its contents gently, miraculously, like a hand opened wrist upwards to face south-west. The leaning walls of dark Killas slate, low at first, with thick green and white masses of vegetation piled up against them in an arrested wave, rose steadily to a height of eighty or ninety feet where they overhung a shallow pool. Here, towards the back of the workings, the rock was always damp and streaked with lichen. Hybrid willow, purple and white foxglove, contorted dwarf oak grew profusely on the collapsing terraces amid colonies of wild roses. A thin perpetual trickle of water ran down through dripping mats of moss and fern to fill the pool. In the oblique gold evening light that wall dominated the quarry: and even during the day, when I lay among the mysterious knolls and reefs of the quarry floor – where the heather was mottled with the bright green of new bilberry, and children had scratched narrow, aimless, sandy paths up and down the blunt salients of old spoil – I sometimes found myself looking up at it in surprise. Then I would smile, bury my face in the aromatic turf, and listen to the sound of the water dripping down behind the foliage. It had become a voice. A gull screamed overhead. The tide poured out of the zawn below the headland, and back again with a muffled thud. With my eyes closed I felt as if I were hanging unsupported in the air – burned, clarified, renewed by the summer light.

I knew that if I stayed there long enough I would be let into a secret.

During the week people used the quarry as a car park, especially at lunchtime. Most seemed content to roll down the driver's window and read the *Western Morning News* with one elbow stuck out into the sunshine; but one or two locked up the car and walked off to look at the sea or wade into the montbretia which, escaping for a hundred years from the village gardens, now roared over the headland like a heath fire. They were gone by one o'clock.

Every afternoon when the quarry was most likely to be deserted, a handicapped couple arrived.

They were shy and strange, easily put off. The woman was blind, the man could not walk. I watched them. This is how, together, they made up a kind of organism:

At three o'clock their little fawn Reliant van, whining in first gear, would bounce down the track from the village; turn into the quarry with exaggerated care; then, chrome winking in the glassy light, roll uncertainly to a stop. The woman expected rain, so she always wore a white raincoat buttoned to the neck. She talked to the driver in a loud, animated voice. He replied in monosyllables. She got out, and a black labrador guide dog jumped out after her and ran about barking. Every afternoon before allowing it to lead her round the quarry she made it stand still for a few moments.

'Can't you behave, you daft old dog?'

Her left leg was twisted so as to point the foot inwards instead of forwards, which gave her a rolling and limited gait. Nevertheless the dog wasn't always quick enough for her. It blinked up at her and sneezed. She laughed with delight, turning her round, perspiring face up to the sun. After a circuit or two like this she let the dog off the lead. While it raised its leg among the nettles, she would feel her way along the side of the van to the rear doors and fetch out a folding wheelchair. This had to be assembled by touch, which took several minutes. By then the driver had got his own door open and was waiting for her to help him out. He was impatient, unhelpful, gesticulatory; she laughed and groaned at his weight. The dog watched them indulgently, hanging out its long red tongue. In the end the driver fell into the chair and lay there breathing hard and staring into the sky.

'Can I help at all?' I asked, the first afternoon I saw them.

The paraplegic, slumped white-faced in his chair, tried to ignore me. He was still in his twenties, with muscular shoulders, black hair and deep-set angry eyes; he had been a swimmer or a cyclist, perhaps: a runner. Suddenly he pulled his mouth into a sweet, extraordinary, practised smile and said,

'We'll manage, thanks.'

'It's easier in the end,' the woman agreed quickly in her loud voice. 'Really.'

They had their own way of doing things, habits long-formed. They had their independence.

'I'm sorry,' I said. 'If there's anything – '

'Thank you anyway,' she said.

She offered me the ghost of her sight: a faint discoloration of the whites of her eyes. She had buttoned her coat unevenly that morning, so that one side was higher than the other.

Every afternoon she hobbled round the quarry then wheeled the man in his turn, while he guided her with curt rights and lefts, his head tilted to one side as if it were too heavy for his neck, his body held with the legs stuck stiffly out in front. Every afternoon he made her stop so he could look across the pool at the tangled roses, the cushions of moss, the waterfall, the tottering ribs of Killas slate. He clutched her arm: pointed here and there: followed with his head the sudden zigzag flight of a bird. Every afternoon she wheeled him back to the van and with a lot of grunting and straining forced him back into the driving seat like someone trying to force a snail back into its shell, whereupon he took charge again, revving the engine on its hand-throttle, calling to her to hurry the dog up.

They were like the parts of the jellyfish, a million years ago, coming together for the sake of convenience and never being able to go back on the arrangement.

At what point do you recover your self?

I wanted to do things, but not the things I had always done.

A barely suppressed excitement drove me out, on to the headlands, into the abandoned tin-streamers' cottages at Nineveh, along sunken lanes, in the mornings before I had time to eat anything.

By eight the tracks were already warm and airless. Bees wavered past on long curving courses. In the grass grew bird's-foot trefoil as yellow as the inside of an egg, tangled up with wild violets and cinquefoil. Great spear-thistles commanded the sagging walls and ruined gardens, thrusting up out of patches of fuchsia. The bramble-covered banks were alive with butterflies like new, complicated kinds of petals. Emerging suddenly on the upland lawn above the cliffs at Porthmoina Cove or Carn Clough, I would stare out at the Atlantic framed violet and silver between blunt brown headlands, and, astonished by the landscape, feel my imagination reach out vainly to touch its essence. The sea! A vigorous wind blew between the white boulders; the cliffs fell away; behind me, waves of gorse and bell-heather broke on the gentle slopes. All around was blue and unrelenting air!

I was elated one minute, tired out again the next.

I felt as if I was listening for something, but that it would never speak.

Subsidiary workings opened off the quarry, two or three interconnected troughs full of dust and flies, used by the local farmers as a rubbish dump. Hanks of last year's fern stuck out of the sandy walls, which nowhere rose higher than ten feet. A dry whirring, the sound of grasshoppers, came and went with the sun.

Crouched listlessly in one of these pits, knees drawn up to chin, arms hanging at my sides, I fell asleep and dreamed of a green woman who led me a dance over the downs:

It was the middle of the day.

All morning a hot enervating wind had scoured the village, bringing with it unidentifiable, tarry smells. Among the quarries it was even hotter. Suddenly there was a movement deep in the shadowy crevice between two walls, and the green woman walked out into the sunlight, relaxed and naked. I watched her carefully, from a distance. While her outline was perfectly sharp, it seemed to have no surfaces, and flowers came and went within it as she turned her head deliberately this way and that. She was like a window opened on to a mass of leafage after rain, branches of blackthorn, aglet and elder interwoven, plaits of grass and fern, all held together with rose briars, over and between which went a constant trickle of water. She knew I was there.

'We are never simply ourselves,' she said.

She stretched her arms, standing with one leg bent and the other stiffened to take her weight.

Now she passed landwards in a stately way, striding between the great rays of light which fell upon Morvah, Rosemergy and the White Downs, to places even beyond that where I stumbled naked after her along the windy edges among the broken stones and earth. Soon she stood in a steep, hidden ashwood, where a stream descended a series of mossy steps and pools. I straddled this and masturbated convulsively, standing up. 'Don't look at her,' I told myself. 'Don't look.' I came again and again until I was exhausted and out of breath. I thought of Pam Stuyvesant, and my wife, and Lawson's daughter, each sprawled and spread open on to the same pink wet rose, and came again. Then the green woman led me back to the quarry, where I felt no fear of the unknown: here she climbed up behind the mat of vegetation on the back wall. She turned and looked at me directly! Her eyes were a pitiless chalky blue, without white or pupil. They were flowers, too. When I knew I could no longer avoid their gaze I ran about waving my arms and shouting, filled with a mixture of terror and happiness.

Hundreds of elder flowers, tiny cream stars with five blunt points, showered down on me in a cold wind. When I woke up it was because clouds had covered the sun and great splatters of rain were falling on my bare arms.

For the rest of that week the weather was bad. Offshore winds packed the clouds down tightly round the cottage, where I sat by myself listening to a length of washing line tap-tapping against its metal pole in the garden, while the foghorn at Pendeen Watch boomed morosely out into the grey Atlantic spaces. The flowerbeds were black with something between mist and rain, and water hung in beads along the power cables. Each evening, just before it got dark, the clouds seemed to lift for a moment: one or two wallflowers, already past their best, glowed in the thin flat light. Inside, a little of this light collected about the spines of the paperbacks; and you could hear a petal fall in the bowl of dog-roses on the bookcase. I had been in the cottage for a month. Neither Pam nor Lucas had answered my letters.

All the telephone boxes on the coast road were damaged. I began catching the ten o'clock bus into St Ives every morning. There I watched people driven into the arcades and surf shacks by the rain; picking over heaps of souvenirs at the indoor market, avid, bored and helpless by turns. 'Esperdrilles,' advertised the handwritten signs on the stalls: 'Plimpsoles.' Plump young couples, their faces as unblemished as their brand new windbreakers, linked hands by the lifeboat station and looked across at the hundreds of houses of Mount Zion, roofs and walls of all colours tumbling up the hill in stacked planes like an amateur post-Impressionist landscape. The tide was out. The moored boats canted in disorder against their weedy strands of rope, a box of sweets tipped out on wet sand the exact colour of the coffee served in the Tudor Rooms; while a hundred yards away the sea lapped like a kitten and the young herring gulls walked awkwardly about trying to eat pieces of paper. I telephoned Pam and Lucas anxiously from a fish and chip café on the front. The phone rang at their end but no one picked it up. All I could hear was the woman behind the counter:

'Yes, love?'

'Coffee, please.'

'Thank you, love. Anything else, love?'

'No thank you.'

'Twenty pence then thank you, love, eighty pence change.'

'Thank you.'

'Next please, yes, love?'

Yes, love (I thought): Love.

I tried the phone again. This time no one could connect me. All the lines were engaged.

Pressing the receiver as tightly to my ear as someone trying to hear the sea in a shell, I stared at the back wall of the café where a few greasy-looking landscapes hung, 'original' but unsold. One or two of them showed the cottages and breakwater of a fishing village in some less well-designed world than ours. There was a sunset of suety ochre bands. The boats with their crude triangular sails, you imagined, would shortly go out and fish for something more amorphous, less evolved, than haddock. Someone there would be looking out of a window, writing in a letter, 'We must not judge God by this. It's just a study that didn't come off.' This

Platonic reversal, the suggestion that ours is not perhaps after all the shadow but the thing – the Pleroma, not its imperfect index – attracted me obscurely. Outside, a black dog ran in circles on the sand in the rain, snapping up at the gulls twenty feet above its head as if they were butterflies.

'Pam?' I said. 'Lucas? Hello?'

I thought about the handicapped couple, who were often to be seen in St Ives, separately and together. They were ill-adapted to it. They were without routine to help them. The blind woman waited at the High Street kerb in the rain, her hair plastered to her scalp, her head directed madly at the traffic. She could not cross; I saw her reach down deliberately and slap the dog. Down by the lifeboat station, the paraplegic lay back blasted in his wheelchair under an afternoon sky so dark it might have been November, ignoring everything that was said to him, his mouth open in boredom or pain. Forced into the same troglodytic existence, I was sympathetic: I stood under a butcher's awning as they blundered along the pavement, their faces showing no anima-tion, thinking, 'How much happier they'd be in the quarry!' I followed them up the steep streets to the car park and watched them drive away.

Eventually the bad weather blew itself out in three spectacular storms. Chocolate brown water raced down the hillsides above the coast road and whirled along the village street. The women ran squealing into one another's houses to borrow buckets. I left the flood to subside and went for long walks across the sodden moorland. I thought I would stay another week, perhaps two. On Carn Down the sun was already boiling the moisture out of the peat. From Boswens Common I went down to the sea. Over everything inland hung a warm haze like watered milk. I could walk all day without tiring myself, along the steep, narrow valleys where streams ran in beds of roseate granite like formal paving; as long as I avoided the White Downs, I could sleep when it got dark. I was well again.

At night, the quarry's pillars and terraces had something of the same soapy, veiled quality as my dreams when I had first arrived at the cottage. Lovers used it then. You would hear them moan or laugh from their car, or see it rock gently on its springs. The waterfall made an uneven spattering sound, like a tap left running all night in a concrete yard. One night I found a car parked in front of it, silent, with the filtered moonlight reflected from its windscreen. I decided it was empty. Just as I got close enough to see inside, its engine started up. The headlights came on full in my face. I flung up my hand. With a roar and a scrape of gears it raced past me. I had the impression of two excited faces staring out: music from a radio. Its rear lights bumped hurriedly up the track. Later a light breeze moved the vegetation on the back wall.

I gave up trying to telephone Pam and Lucas. 'People change,' I told them in a letter. 'You build up opinions like layers of sediment in the bottom of a jam jar. Suddenly someone tips over the jar by accident. Or you get bored and shake it up to see what will happen. Or perhaps you just throw it all away and start again with clean water.' Was I making myself ridiculous? 'You should never assume you're talking to the person you knew five years ago,' I ended lamely. 'All the best.' I looked at the envelope for a moment or two before I put it in the post.

If anyone had come to visit, they would have found me dressed for most of the day in an old pair of shorts. Reading had begun to bore me. Instead I ran about in the lanes below the village, or took the bus to Sennen Cove, where I scrambled down the cliffs to stand grinning on the wave-washed rock plat-form in the glittering spray, dazzled by the sun and rendered speechless by the salt smell and roaring edge of the sea. When I looked in the mirror, I thought of myself as a castaway, with the thin, sunburnt, muscular look by which all castaways can be recognised.

The quarry stood bleached and empty in the sun. Heat clanged soundlessly from its walls until the air began to shiver and dance. I slept with my hands behind my head in a hollow between some boulders, dreaming vaguely. People parked their cars without ever knowing I was there, and went away again without my ever knowing they had been.

One afternoon I woke with a sense of confusion I couldn't attribute directly, to a change in the light, for instance, or the sound from the baling machine which had been chugging to and fro all day in the fields above the headland, leaving a brown stain of exhaust smoke in the clear air. I lifted myself on one elbow and saw the blind woman hobbling round the quarry with her dog; or standing still, rather – as if something had caught her attention in the middle of her walk – and staring up at the spongy green pillows of moss, her head tilted to one side. A light wind animated the willow branches and rustled stealthily along the rose terraces; it stirred the dust round the woman's feet in their square ungainly shoes. She smiled. The man in the car called out to her. Still smiling, she went back to get him into his wheelchair. I watched them for a few minutes then dozed off again, closing my eyes on an image of the wheelchair parked by the pool beneath the wall, so that drops from the waterfall spattered man, woman and dog as they looked up.

When I woke next it was to a coarse and screaming cry like a herring gull's. Filled with panic, surfacing from dreams in which great masses moved against one another in a confused space, I could only imagine that the wheelchair had fallen into the pool. Still half asleep, I went running to see if I could help.

Nothing so simple.

The blind woman and the paraplegic had quarrelled at last.

They were at one another with a frightening muddled ferocity, pushing and shoving and panting while the wheelchair rocked precariously this way and that. Every so often one of them, I couldn't tell which, let out that inarticulate animal cry. Then the woman knocked the chair over, spilling the man out and falling on top of him. He went down slowly and reluctantly, making a noise like a laugh and waving his arms. They struggled there, while the dog first rushed round them in circles then turned yelping and growling to attack me. Fending it off, I shouted:

'Are you all right? Can I do anything?' and 'Stop it. Stop it!'

I was too disgusted and frightened to get close enough to separate them. They were murdering one another. Sick to death of its dependency on the dog, the wheelchair and the van, the violent, miserable half-creature they made had pulled itself apart.

'Stop!'

Neither of them even looked up. Their faces were drawn into snarls of concentration; they were grunting and sobbing frustratedly. Suddenly I saw my mistake. I put my hands up to my face and laughed. Not murder, then. They were fumbling and ripping at each other's clothes. In a moment they would be down to the pale, starved flesh. The dog was only defending their privacy.

I retrieved my things later: two days after that I was back in London.

9

The Place of the Cure of the Soul

We are so quick to look for closure, for the clear termination of
sections of our life, that we often invent it. After the debacle at 17,
Hill Park I had assumed I would never be caught up with Yaxley
again. Indeed, obsessed with the Pleroma, he did leave me alone
for two or three years. But after his failure with the infolding,
everything failed. The fear that he would be absorbed grew daily,
until his whole position was undercut by it. Associated phobias
developed to include a horror of dirt. That, and the residue of one
too many magical operations, drove him out of the rooms above
the Atlantis Bookshop and into a spacious modern block on the
north side of Upper Richmond Road, close to East Putney tube
station. There I found him, on a rainy morning in June. He
needed me again.

   I walked past the building twice. It reminded me less of Yaxley
than Lawson, and perhaps it was in fact some fossil of their brief
partnership, prepayment for a sleight of hand which never came
off. The people who lived there worked in property or invest-
ment banking. Traffic laboured under their windows all day, but
double glazing muted the noise to a comfortable hum. By night
their black European executive saloons lined up outside in rows. I
went through a cold well-kept entrance hall, unrelieved by two
shallow brick structures like small municipal flowerbeds filled
with decorative gravel, and took the stairs to the top floor.
Between landings I wavered; touched for reassurance the white
painted metal handrail. Had I heard someone coming up behind
me?

   'Yaxley?'

Modern flats have a precision, a bleak openness to their angles,
which encourages hygiene. Yaxley's was painted off-white
throughout, with white woodwork. Every wall, every wainscot,
was spotless. There were some rather nice carpets in a kind of

flushed pink. Furnished properly, it might have been comfortable if rather affectless. But all I could find was a telephone on a table and, in the middle of the lounge floor, a state-of-the-art VTR. (When I switched it on, an unlabelled tape began to play. I switched it off again immediately.) The kitchen was fitted expensively enough, with oak units, Creda Solarspeed hob, butcher-striped roller blinds. Under the immaculate stainless-steel double sink I found Flash, Jif, sponge floor-mops, plastic buckets and Marigold rubber gloves – several of everything, all brand new, as if he had cached them against a siege; or agoraphobia.

The night before I had received a telephone call, I don't believe from Yaxley himself. After I picked up the receiver there was a prolonged silence, into which I prompted –

'Hello? Hello?'

Nothing. Then someone said softly:

'Go to this address – '

Other instructions followed, some infantile, some meaningless. I did not recognise the magical operation to which they referred. The voice was hard to hear, let alone to identify. It paused, failed, picked up again. Once or twice it laughed. 'Two fucks and a pig,' it said. It seemed to come from a long way away, and there were other voices behind it. 'Two fine fucks and a pig. Go to this address.'

Yaxley was in the bedroom.

He lay naked on his side in the middle of the uncarpeted floor, knees drawn up slightly. One hand was curled gently under the side of his head to support it. The other cupped his genitals. Death had aged him. With his long deceitful face, grey stubbled jaw, and lips drawn back over blackened or yellowish teeth, he might have been seventy or eighty. He looked like an old untrustworthy dog, shrunk, famished, reduced. Before he died, he had been trying to make something with two sticks. Above him on the wall was pinned a postcard reproduction of the steps of the British Museum. Under this he had scrawled in soft pencil the words 'The Place of the Cure of the Soul', a description reputed to have been carved over the doors of the Library at Alexandria. Otherwise the room was empty. There was no furniture, not even a bed. It stank. Yaxley hadn't washed since I last saw him. The dirt was glazed on, as if he had spent the intervening years living in a doorway off the Charing Cross Road. In addition some sort of fat was smeared all over his emaciated upper body, perhaps as lubrication. He had been frightened the Pleroma would invaginate him. In the event though he seemed to have been not so much sucked in as sucked.

Behind him on the floor I found an envelope; inside that the key to a safety deposit box in the City. In the box, I knew, there would be two thick black notebooks. I had seen them before. I collected them that afternoon, and over the next two days, coming and going under Yaxley's dead ironic eye, fetched his papers, his pictures and other magical paraphernalia from locations to which the notebooks gave access. Some of the larger items – an old-fashioned Dansette record player, a wooden chair with awkwardly curved arms, two crates of books – I was forced to move by taxi. Decaying ring-binders burst and gave forth yellow papers, upon which I read in a scrawled hand:

'The door! The rosy door!'

Or:

'. . . two distinct and irreconcilable worlds, *pleroma* or fullness – which has come down to us as the muddled Christian promise of "Heaven"; and *hysterema* or *kenoma*, pain, illusion, emptiness – the life we must actually live. Between them, it used to be said, lies the paradox or boundary-state *horos*. But the great discovery of this century has been to knock at the door of *horos* and find no one at home. *Horos* is the wish-fulfilment dream, the treachery of the mirror . . .'

Eventually I had assembled it all in the stinking bedroom. The rest of the instructions proved harder to follow. I was required to set certain small objects – including a stoppered bottle half full of rose-water and a Polaroid photograph of someone's left hand – in exact relationships to one another on a small wooden table, about five feet in front of the corpse. The table itself must stand at the apex of a precise triangle, the other two points of which were represented by a burned-out electric kettle from some Tufnell Park bedsitter; and a split PVC bucket. I was to turn on the old Dansette in its peeled grey leatherette case, play a certain record, then to undress and masturbate. That was the difficulty. At that time I rarely needed manual relief. If I did, I would think automatically of Katherine, and one of her favourite ways of making love –

How she would lie on her side with her legs drawn a little way up and encourage me to enter her from behind, then move one leg gently and rhythmically over the other, so that her body rocked while I remained still. How after a minute or so she would moan and stop – the signal for me to begin moving inside her until her breathing became ragged and harsh, she sighed and began to rub one leg against the other again so that her body rocked and rocked on the pivot of the lower hip.

'Is that good? Is that good?' – turning her head to look at me over her shoulder, sometimes reaching round to draw my face down to kiss it.

'Is that good?'

'Yes.'

How, after a few minutes of this, I would reach round to where the base of my penis emerged from her and dabble my hands there until they were wet. Then, with this lubrication, gently insert the middle finger of my right hand into her anus, slipping it in and out in a counter rhythm to hers. How this drove her quickly to orgasm, at the approach of which she would whisper:

'Do you want to fuck me?'

'Yes.'

'Do you want to *fuck* me?'

'Yes.'

'Are you fucking me?'

'Yes.'

'Oh, fuck me then, come inside me. Fuck me, come inside me. Fuck me, *come* inside me. Fuck me, *come* inside me . . .' – until the words lost their meaning and became an intense, moaning, rhythmic incantation. How a deep pink flush spread across her shoulder-blades. How just before her orgasm I would straddle her with my right leg, press her half over on to her front, she would groan in anticipation and push my hand away from her anus. 'Oh God Oh God Oh God. Yes. Oh *yes*. Oh God oh fuck me yes I'm coming I'm coming oh yes oh fuck me.' How, clutching her breast or hip I would drive into her as hard as I could until we both shouted and stiffened and groaned and relaxed, panting and smiling and beginning to laugh –

All men keep to themselves some image like this of love, exciting but at the same time valued, full of sentiment, even if it is only a memory of someone whispering 'Make me wet,' at the beginning of the night. But when in Putney I set out to remember mine, I could see nothing. I took my clothes off and folded them up in the corner of the room. I knelt down before the table, with its burden of futile or malign objects. I pulled bleakly and unhappily at myself for perhaps ten minutes, but every time I felt the drowsy approach of orgasm, I seemed to snap back into self-awareness, and feel upon me the dead magician's amused, dispassionate gaze.

'Fuck me, come inside me –' whispered Katherine.

'Yaxley never did anything to anybody,' Pam Stuyvesant reminded me. 'He encourages you to do it to yourself.'

From the cloth-covered speaker of the Dansette, to a background of crackles and distant music, some chirpy pre-war entertainer sang:

> Who's been polishing the sun,
> Sprucing up the clouds so grey?
> Does she know that's how I like it?
> I hope she's going my way!

Suddenly I felt exhausted and ill. I gave up the attempt and instead was violently sick into the plastic bucket. Yaxley, I suppose, may have allowed for this. It was hard to see whether the act had been designed to free or redeem him; or as a last meaningless sneer. Anyway, nothing seemed to happen, so after a bit I left. I closed and locked the door behind me, and later threw the key and the notebooks off Putney Bridge and into the river.

As far as I know, Yaxley's corpse is still there now.

When I got home that evening I found letters from Pam and Lucas. They had written separately: they were going to get divorced. They were never quite able to say how it had come about.

Lucas claimed they had grown out of one another, and raged with guilt:

123

'I always knew you couldn't cure other people of their character. Now I see you can't even change yourself. Anything in that direction is just thrashing around, a kind of panic. You haul yourself over the wall, you glimpse new country: good! You can never again be what you were! Just as you're patting yourself on the back you see this string of stuff tied to your leg like the tail of a kite, and it's all the fucking Christmas cards you ever sent. All the gas bills you ever paid. All the family snaps which will never, ever allow you to be anybody else: there you are, goggling out, nosing against the glass – your own pet fish.'

He had moved into a flat in Manchester, he said. 'I'm getting a lot of work done.' He asked me to make sure that Pam was all right.

Pam wrote:

'I don't feel as if Lucas knows what he wants.' What had upset her most was that he had left most of his things with her. 'He said he was sick of the clutter, but he must need his books.' She asked me to make sure that Lucas was all right. 'I don't quite know what went wrong,' she added puzzledly.

Neither of them knew, in fact.

'That's why you're being so silly,' I told them. But Lucas would only repeat that he had suddenly felt suffocated under a weight of objects he had never meant to own; while Pam, though desperately miserable, repeated, 'We fell out such a lot,' maintained that Lucas must do what he thought fit, because she only wanted him to be happy; and claimed that she had often wondered what it would be like to try being on your own. And so it all went ahead later that year.

They seemed in such bewilderment, afterwards, to find themselves apart from one another. Lucas kept trying to explain his rage, which was in the end directed less at Pam – or even himself – than at some incurable state of the world. 'A thirty-five-year-old woman,' he wrote to me that winter, 'holds up a doll she has kept in a cardboard box under a bed since she was a child. She touches its clothes, which are falling to pieces, works tenderly its loose arm. The expression which trembles on the verge of realising itself in the slackening muscles of her lips and jaw is indescribably sad. How are you to explain to her that she has lost nothing by living the intervening years of her life? How is she to explain this to you?' Meanwhile Pam fell full length into herself, hour by hour, and was chronically hurt. 'He always used to love the north. That's why we came here.'

They had been not so much divorced, I suspect now, as wrenched apart by some metaphysical event none of us could imagine, precipitated by Yaxley's death. Whatever the meaning of his intrusion into the Pleroma – however he had distorted its shape, however it had vomited itself inside out – one of its effects here had been to cause similar convulsions in all our lives. Pam and Lucas blamed themselves increasingly for living apart. They were bemused. But in the end the very inexplicability of the experience became something they could share. If nothing else, they had been given the fiction of the Coeur, to which they soon returned, developing it by letter.

Yaxley's death, which I believed then would free us all, had filled me with a kind of excitement, to which the divorce only seemed to add. Unable to sleep more than an hour or two at a time, I took to the canal, rowing down to the empty lock basin every morning before anyone else was awake, in an old boat with peeling blue paintwork Katherine had found tied up at the bottom of the garden the day she moved into St Mark's Crescent. An acre of water waited for me, flickering in the cool sunlight. It was very quiet. On the towpath side stood a crescent of Edwardian houses, each with a long thin wedge of overgrown garden. Brambles, willow herb, and some kind of red-leaved ornamental ivy had rioted over the walls to within a few feet of the water. On the other bank wrecked cars glittered in a repair-shop yard; beyond them were the silent arches of a railway bridge.

It was the longest summer, Katherine often said, that anyone could remember.

One morning I lay back in the boat, my eyes half-closed against the reflections from the water, wondering if I could make myself operate the lock. I was never sure of myself with locks. As soon as I looked into one it would bring back some childhood afternoon when, kneeling down to peer at a swarm of fish-fry eight or nine feet below in the narrow cleft, I first suspected the depth of the water. I decided that if I wanted to go any further it would mean dragging the boat out. I let the oars trail. A dog began to bark monotonously from its wired run in the garage yard. A milk-float rattled past on the main road. Tufted ducks were diving in the basin, vanishing unpretentiously under the surface to bob up some seconds later like cork toys, bright of eye and beaded momentarily with drops of water.

A faint breath of air moved the willow herb.

I heard a voice say to me quietly but distinctly: 'The woman that grows, and may be harvested for ever. The grown, not the natural woman.'

When I looked up I saw her watching me from the towpath, her outline filled with the leaves and stems of burnet roses, her eyes blind, intent, and speedwell blue. She raised her arm. Somebody in one of the houses behind her woke up and opened a window. The sun caught it and filled my eyes with light.

PART THREE

The Course

10

It Always Happens to Someone Else

After that my life seemed to settle down again. The publishing industry was expanding greedily to meet the 1980s. Never comfortable with authors, I moved on to the production side of things. Katherine, meanwhile, exhibited pictures in London and then New York. She renewed her membership of the Chelsea Arts Club, and I would find her there sometimes in the evening after work, watching the players nose quietly round the billiard tables like fish in a lighted tank. We had a daughter we called Kit. Kit learned to talk early, then encouraged us to sit her out under the willow in the garden at St Mark's Crescent, where she could whisper at the muted reflections of the water in the foliage. She loved the seaside. At Fowey or Caswell Bay she spent each hot afternoon crouched on the tideline, sorting bits of nacre from the gravel of tiny coloured stones and wave-polished glass. Once she called out in her sleep: 'The lights in the shells. Daddy! The lights in the shells!' Kit turned out to be a dreamy, equable little thing, sensual, patient, pleased with everything she found. As if to compensate for this, Pam and Lucas were as demanding as children. Pam continued to write letters full of vague regrets. Lucas telephoned me in the middle of the night.

'I don't like the sound of her voice,' he would say. 'You try her.'

And I would sigh and shrug and in the morning catch the Huddersfield train and visit whatever bleak village she had removed herself to this time.

'You try her. See what she says.'

What she said was always the same. She was lonely and ill. The Pleroma was aware of us, even after all those years. Lucas Medlar didn't love her any more. I would hug her – though I got into bed with her only that once – and telephone him. 'You should see more of one another,' I would tell them. 'We never see enough of you,' they always replied; and I would promise to write more often. Each time, some kind of balance of anxieties would have to reassert itself before I could go home again. Nevertheless it was a relationship which suited us, until I saw the White Couple in the snow outside Pam's kitchen window on the third anniversary of Yaxley's death. Even then, something might have been salvaged. I admit that the White Couple frightened me. How could they not, after everything else that had happened? I had hated the look on their faces as they hung in the air in front of Pam's kitchen window. I was angry with Lucas, and disappointed by his feeble attempt to avoid the issue. But whatever I told him the day after, in the Manchester Kardomah with the rain streaming into the crowded shopping streets outside, I would still have been happy to help (less out of guilt than he assumed, or at any rate, less out of the guilt he knew about); and things would have gone on in the same way for ever if, in the following spring, Pam's illness hadn't flared up suddenly.

No one knew what was wrong. Migraines paralysed her. Epileptic incidents increased in frequency and scale. She fell asleep, sometimes for a day, two days, at a time; then ranged restlessly about the cottage for a week, reading, smoking and shouting at the cats late into the night, unable to sleep at all. Her weight fluctuated violently over quite short periods. To these metabolic disturbances were added outbreaks of ulcers, ringworm, colitis, abscessed teeth. She became allergic to increasingly exotic forms of penicillin. Finally her skin flared up bright red with erysipelas – St Anthony's Fire, often called simply 'the Rose'. (Afterwards, it would be easy to see this portfolio of symptoms as a secondary stage; a transition. It was as if the illness was searching for its own best expression. Her original symptoms, you will say, were so clearly hysterical – fits, headaches, a hallucination in a kitchen – that this must be a form of speech, the language of some quite common psychic disorder. I wouldn't deny that, even now.)

Then, in April, Lucas telephoned me from Manchester. He was panicky and fey, he didn't know what to do. Pam had been taken into Huddersfield General Hospital.

'She needs a heart bypass,' he said.

'Lucas, a week ago her heart was sounder than mine. It must be a mistake. What are they saying?'

'They don't know what's wrong with her!'

'Try and stay calm,' I advised.

'It's easy for you. She isn't just breaking to pieces in front of you.'

'I'll come when I can.'

But spring is a difficult season. We were publishing as many books as we could print. It took time to extricate myself, and by then Pam was already recovering. I found her propped up in bed in the front room of her cottage, wearing a Marks & Spencer's cotton nightdress and a blue woollen bedjacket with short puffy sleeves. Her hair was longer; she had tied it back with a piece of ribbon. Her face and arms were very white. Around mouth and eyes the skin had a soft, powdery, inflated look; the flesh was yielding, deeply cut with crowsfeet and lines of strain. She seemed to have gained weight in the hospital rather than lost it; despite this you could feel the presence of the bones beneath.

'How are you?'

'Sore!'

Lucas had manhandled the bed downstairs and arranged it by the window so she could look out at the great bars of sun and shadow chasing each other all day across the moors towards Holme. There was more light in the room than I remembered from my last visit, falling on the lively red and black design of the quilt-cover, where it found scattered an invalid's things: Kleenex, the *Guardian* folded tightly to display yesterday's half-completed crossword puzzle, a spectacle case, two or three paperbacks with predominantly pink-and-lavender covers and titles like *Sweet Dawn of Desire*.

'You can't be serious about this,' I complained. Knowing her taste, I had brought her Willa Cather's *A Lost Lady*.

'They belong to the woman next door,' she said. 'It was very kind of her to think of me. And look at all these flowers! You never know how nice people are until you're ill.' Everyone had been kinder than she had a right to expect: they fed the cats, they did the housework even though a home help came in twice a week; they went shopping for her. 'The old man two doors along offered to lend me his television.' She laughed. 'And it's cleaner in here than I ever managed to get it. So keep your literary pretensions to yourself! Here. Let me hug you. Oh, it's so nice to see you!'

She blinked, blew her nose.

'I cry very easily now. Make us some coffee, eh?'

'I'm not sure I want to be in that kitchen,' I said, trying to make a joke of it. 'Remembering the last time.'

There was a silence. To occupy herself, she moved her books about; smoothed the quilt with quick deft movements of her hands.

'Do you still see them, Pam?'

'The cats?'

'The White Couple.'

She lay back on the pillows and turned her head away from me.

'What do you think? What did you expect? That it would all go away like magic once you became involved?'

I couldn't think of an answer to this.

'Don't worry,' she reassured me tiredly. 'They're not out there now. I'd know.' Silence drew out again. She asked it, as if I wasn't there, 'Do you remember the Moors Murders? All those dead children buried up behind Saddleworth? They weren't the only ones.'

'A moor is only a moor,' I said.

She wiped her eyes again – 'I know. I know.' – then sat up suddenly and took both my hands in hers. 'Go into the kitchen and make some coffee,' she said. 'All that's changed is that we've admitted something to ourselves.'

'I hope you're right.'

In the event, there was a yellow roller-blind to pull down over the window.

'I haven't seen this before,' I called.

'No.'

Pam's neighbours, Yorkshirewomen with determined views, had scrubbed down the Formica surfaces and pine shelves. They liked order and optimism; they liked to see a place clean. New coffee-mugs, with cheap and cheerful artwork and optimistic slogans, had replaced her old chipped favourites. When I needed a tea towel, I found them all freshly laundered. Even the stainless steel cat-bowls had been polished until they shone. The kitchen was a kitchen. I filled the kettle. Nothing happened to me.

'You see?'

We drank the coffee. We talked about this and that. We tried to finish the crossword. The afternoon darkened towards evening. Eventually I asked her: 'Do you see Lucas much?' I meant something like: Does Lucas fulfil his responsibilities to you? Instead of answering directly, she showed me a pendant he had bought her nearly twenty years before. It was a teardrop of Iranian mother-of-pearl, about an inch by one and a half, mounted in a silver filigree of tiny roses and decorated with peacocks and flowers, in blues, oranges and greens which glowed in the darkening room like paint from Byzantium. God knows where Lucas had found it, or what he had paid.

'It's beautiful, Pam.'

'Isn't it? He bought me that when he was in London the first time.'

'Lucas?'

'Oh yes. He often went down during those first few years, to see if he could find Yaxley and make him help us. Poor Lucas! He was frightened; he didn't know where to look. He wandered about, I expect, and then just came home again.'

'I had no idea.'

She smiled drowsily at me. 'Lucas does his best.' Then: 'It wasn't that we didn't trust you. Our own feelings let us down.'

I could see that she was tired. I got up to leave.

'Take care of yourself, Pam,' I said. 'I'll come again soon.'

'Do you know what I'd like?'

'What?'

But she was asleep.

I talked to Lucas a day or two later.

'She's much better,' we reassured each other: 'Isn't she? So much better.'

Within weeks she was back in Huddersfield General. A nagging discomfort in her left hip had migrated to her chest on that side, where it settled in the ribs previously broken for cardiac surgery. A consultant described this condition as 'arthritis', but kept her on hand anyway, for observation.

Lucas was frantic.

'They aren't being honest. She knows there's something else wrong with her.'

Pam drifted, ill in some unacknowledged way, assuaging her anxieties with *Love's Stormy Heights* and *Dark Music of Delight*: suddenly, breast cancer was confirmed, and the mastectomy carried out in early July.

'We've caught it in plenty of time,' the consultant assured her. But when Lucas went to see her the day after, all she could do was shake her head and say:

'Something's still not right.'

He was at the hospital as often as his work allowed, which was perhaps more often than he could cope with. I still have his letters of the time, addressed less to me than to himself, crammed foolscap pages typed out furiously at night on the old Lettera portable he had brought to his marriage like a statement of intent. Yellow with age, they break apart at the folds when you try to open them; but there inside are Pam and Lucas, as easily visible – and just as distant – as figures in a glass paperweight. He wavers between the appalled and the self-pitying. She is a woman already deeply ill, bemused by morphine (though as yet in quite light doses), uncertain of the future. Every time he sees her, she has grown thinner. The visiting hour breaks into her isolation; his appearance is always a relief. She clutches his hand so hard it hurts, but woe betide him if he should give her the wrong drink from the bedside table! Or if her back-rest needs adjusting, and Lucas, shy of seeing the amputation scar when she leans forward, makes a muddle of it –

'For God's sake leave me alone, Lucas. You were always so useless!'

She has become more demanding, he tells himself, 'only as a way of saying "We don't have time for this any more." Not just because she's in pain, but because these things are now the measure of our love for one another, our humanity.'

If he infuriates her, the doctors infuriate him.

'None of them will admit how ill she is,' he writes, after one of the endless courses of chemotherapy has come to nothing: 'It's always, "try this, try that". With these people there's always "hope" and never any progress!'

No one will tell Pam anything. No one will tell him anything. 'Worse,' he alleges, 'she isn't even given proper care. This morning she had a fall trying to use the lavatory on her own. At

134

visiting time all she said to me was, "My knee's gone red. The doctor's going to come and paint it." Sometimes she has no idea what she's saying. But this time she was wide awake. She wouldn't let go of my hand. "Don't go yet, Lucas. Don't go." Those bastards had really allowed her to fall down and hurt herself!

'Why are they letting this happen?' he asks, and concludes wildly:

'Doctors need disease. It's the source of their power.'

The hospital was a maze, with every exit marked 'Oncology'. They were both trapped there. As a result they found themselves closer together than they had ever been. Whatever its source, Pam's distress upset Lucas too. Her pain hurt him. The letters go on, shocked, bitter, uncertain, more and more underscored for emphasis. But what they don't explain is how Lucas was trying to staunch the wound. Every evening after work in Manchester, he started up the Renault and edged it carefully into the dense eastbound traffic of the M62, leaning forward anxiously over the steering wheel to peer through the streaming rain for Junction 23: Outlane. An hour later Pam's hands would be held tightly between his, and he would be reminding her, in a low, persuasive voice –

'Always remember: what we mean when we talk about the Heart is that it is a real place.'

He knew he mustn't stop.

It was harder to catch her attention than it had been in Dunford Bridge, with the light going slowly out of the heavy old furniture and the brindled cat weaving about the woodblock floor. There he had only ever to ask 'What would you like tonight?' to be answered: *'Beautiful Swimmers!'* Here, nervous and agitated, unable to concentrate, she would look away from him restlessly at first, up at the clock or the other visitors trooping in and out, or the ward television where *Emmerdale Farm* or *All Creatures Great and Small* unwound episodically and in silence the stories of shrewd but likeable locals, faces skewed by poor colour-balance to a purplish red. Eventually, struck by a phrase – 'disillusioned with the actual'; 'bound in wood and velvet' – she would stare at Lucas as if he had only just begun to speak. From that moment the haunted look would gradually leave her face; and by the time

135

the ward sister called cheerfully, 'Come on now. Nine o'clock. Throwing-out time,' she would be smiling drowsily and ready to sleep on the complex promises he had begun to make her –

'At the end of his life, Michael Ashman seems to have lost his way. It's hard to understand why. His own best explanation leaves us frustrated, wondering if he has quite deliberately left something out: "As a child I had often spent Christmas with my grandmother, who lived near Catesby in a biggish Victorian house of warm orange brick, to which fake Queen Anne chimneys and an overgrown garden lent an air of history I loved – "'

In that part of Northamptonshire (Lucas read on) the winter copses seem to hang for ever in the moment of darkening against a pale blue sky – as if it will take for ever for night to fall – in a gesture so perfect there will never need to be another day. Medieval strip-fields, Tudor gateposts; narrow lanes and banks choked with ivy awash in horizontal light; yew berries, waxy and tubular, somehow lit up from within so that they look like fairy lights in the gathering dusk: even without snow this is a landscape continually composing itself as a Christmas card. Even now, a chance configuration of cottages and bare elm trees will remind me how I trudged home across the cold ploughed fields at the close of an afternoon in late December: a boy thirteen or fourteen, composed only of the things he wanted at that moment – the warmth of a front room with its Christmas lights and strings of tinsel, the smell of toast.

I loved the holly that grew by my grandmother's door. Every spring, among its new leaves, you found clusters of small flowers as complicated as cyphers, four petals and four white stamens arranged to make up a sort of eight-pointed star. The petals had an almost hallucinatory touch of purple near the tips. Male and female holly flowers grow on separate trees; only the females bear berries. In winter, my grandmother's holly bore 'a berry as bright as any wound'.

The holly and the ivy! Every time you hear that carol, whatever its provenance, you take the full weight of the medieval experience, which was itself just like a childhood. To them, words seemed mysterious and valuable in their own right; the berries so bright against the dark foliage of the tree! But rowan and yew berries are just as bright. So are hawthorn berries, especially when they are new. Hips and haws are as bright. All are instrumental and have their magical and symbolic associations, but none as dark and childlike as this myth of conscious sacrifice, organised, performed, expressed, as the matrix of a culture!

When I came back to that house to live, I was forty-five years old. 'You can't understand the Middle Ages,' I had just written to a friend, 'until you begin to feel death treading on your own heels.' As for that 'elasticity of boundaries' I had once recognised as the necessary prelude to the return of the Coeur: it had quickly exhausted itself. Kennedy was in Berlin. Europe was frozen into the postures of the Cold War. '*Ich bin ein Berliner*'! I told myself that I had been born into a world which, despite its horrors, had always promised more than this.

'That poor man!'

Caught up despite herself, Pam began to look forward to Lucas's visits.

'Can't you come in the afternoons too?' she asked him.

He didn't see how he could.

'Because I get so bored here.'

Correctly reading 'middle age' for 'Middle Ages', she had identified in Ashman's despair the footprint of her own condition. But where Pam saw melancholia, fear, bewilderment (in some archaic sense of that word which implied lost bearings, night, tangled woods), Lucas saw only a failure of imagination.

'By this time Ashman could read the fifteenth century out of a damp cardboard box on a building site. He had built one of the most powerful metaphysical instruments in the history of European thought but he didn't know what to do with it next.'

'Read me some more anyway,' said Pam.

'Listen, then –'

The ward staff, a rich mixture of SENs, trainees, and unqualified 'helpers' in green overalls – heavy women with big feet and grown-up families, who came in by bus from as far away as Bradford and for whom lifting and carrying had been a life's work – were soon intrigued. Seven o'clock in the evening: Lucas would enter the ward carrying a plastic briefcase and a

Sainsbury's carrier bag; sit on the side of the bed; and take out the round, steel-rimmed reading glasses he now affected. These made him seem vulnerable; or, as one of the women put it, 'too young for his age'. They liked him anyway. Pam wasn't much more now than a lot of bones and heat: they were impressed by the care with which he embraced her. And they grew used to his low, even reading voice. 'You two and your stories!' they would call. 'Whenever we come through here, you're telling her some story! Has it got any rude bits?'

Lucas could only give a shy smile.

'I'm afraid not.'

'Shame!'

He stared after them. Then he said:

'Ashman continued the research with a kind of wan intensity. After all, it represented the years of his life since that formative European journey; and sometimes brought back to him – with a shiver of delight now only the memory of a memory – images of a dancing bear, the frozen floodwater of the Danube, the legs of the Czechoslovakian girls as they spread their tiered skirts like a fan of Tarot cards. But he had begun to believe that the historical past of the Coeur was only a kind of involution of his own life, a way of twisting or folding the outside of his experience to imply an inside, a meaning.'

Lucas thought for a moment.

'It's not entirely clear what changed this,' he said. He took his spectacles off and rubbed his eyes.

'Don't tease me,' Pam warned him.

'Early one April morning, Ashman caught a train from Birmingham Central station and made his way first to Bath, then Weston-super-Mare on the Bristol Channel. From there he went ten or fifteen miles inland, to a small village near Burrington, on the northern edge of the Mendip Hills. What he found in the parish church there is important to us, and easy to understand. The rest is more difficult – '

'Lucas!'

Lucas took the point, and read on –

I left the church quickly.

There were two churchyards, the inner one well-kept and

intimate, with trimmed squares of box hedge, little curving lawns and paths. Yew and elm surrounded it; lesser celandines edged each path; daisies and dandelions were already out in the grass. There I sat down for a few minutes, listening to the song of a thrush as it shaped and defended its spring territory among the ornamental shrubs. The church itself was Norman, small but massy: nave, choir and sanctuary quarried block by block, with all the enormous energy of that time, out of a rosy limestone which reminded me of Tintern and the Wye Valley. Faint shadows of the surrounding trees, cast by the light falling across its south flank, were like the shadows traced on a white cliff by a warm winter day. All this filled me with delight. When I got up to go, much of the excitement of my discovery had drained away into the thrush's song, the pale but warm sunshine on the grass: but it was replaced by an extraordinary happiness.

The outer churchyard was less secluded. In an acre of obscure untended sites among colonies of rhododendrons, masses of bramble, and thickets of sapling trees, it served a less favoured clientele. I looked for them as I made my way towards the gate. Some lay completely hidden under the coarse, tangled grass. Headstones were rare. Instead the graves had rusty ornamental chains, and over them a kind of iron cage, as if something were needed to hold in the dead. From the three or four stones I was able to find – all greenish, and with shoulders carved to represent a scroll – I read messages incomplete, ordinary, strange:

'. . . also his Beloved Wife.'

A little way in from the gates, attempts had been made to clear the vegetation. Here for some reason the graves were simply heaps of earth with unpainted wooden crosses at the head of them: an unaccustomed sight, shocking and yet somehow exciting in that it bared a process usually so well hidden under marble chippings, urns, angels standing on great pillars. Across this raw ground, you had a view into a long bleak sloping field, where not far from the churchyard wall some men were tending a fire, staring at it aimlessly but with a certain satisfaction as one of them turned it over with a rake. Going through the gate and out into the road, I wondered what they could be burning, on a Saturday afternoon in April.

The village smelled of furniture polish. A fat woman with red arms sat in her garden eating an apple. From inside the house behind her came the sound of a vacuum cleaner.

They were used to visitors. Someone had converted the old toll house into a bookshop. In the square, with its chestnut trees and limestone cross, I found three whitewashed cottages knocked together to make a café called the Naked Man, a popular starting place for parish outings to Burrington Combe, where, caught in the rain nearly two hundred years earlier, Augustus Toplady had taken shelter in the famous cave and been inspired to write 'Rock of Ages, cleft for me'. That morning a lot of old people had come down from Bristol: frail but lively men in braces, flannel trousers and straw hats with a black ribbon, who trooped in and out of the public lavatories; women with faces like buns, sailing along in their cotton print frocks only to stop and exclaim over a baby as if they had just found it. Now they were waiting for the bus to take them home. It would be another hour. Meanwhile they packed the Naked Man, where under the low ceiling beams and in front of a fireplace decorated with paper flowers and ears of corn dyed transparent green, they examined a sepia photograph entitled 'Washday *c.* 1900' (three or four sullen-looking women outside a stone building) and asked one another:

'Now do you like seafood, because they do a really nice seafood platter here, dear – '

'Seafood platter? Seafood platter?'

'Oh no, not for me, dear!'

When the food came they shovelled it down themselves vigorously, then chewed with inturned expressions as if they weren't quite sure what they were eating. Forty-five minutes passed. The sky darkened and a few spots of rain dashed against the windows. At this the men consulted their watches, while their wives smiled indulgently at a toddler. (It ate for them a cream cake, then banged its blue plastic cup repeatedly on the table.) They were less certain about the mother. She was chain-smoking Players Number Six and kept saying, 'I'm never satisfied with anything.' To this her companion, a woman of about forty with a deep, measured voice and pulled-back hair which made her face look like a bone on the shore, only replied:

'You should wait until you see something you really like, then buy it. You can always throw away something you don't like as much. You can pass on something you've grown tired of.'

She sniffed suddenly and added:

'Can you smell that?'

The child stopped banging its cup and stared at them both.

Suddenly, everyone was getting up agitatedly.

'That smell!'

'Is it the bus already? It's the bus!'

'I can't smell anything.'

'What is it?'

The old men gathered round the war memorial in the square, staring up at a huge plume of dark grey smoke which rose, out of proportion to any possible cause, from behind the houses. Rain streamed down their tilted faces, darkened the shoulders of their jackets. 'Oh dear, oh dear, what is it?' called the women anxiously from the café door, their expressions vague, loose, expectant.

We all ran down towards the church. Intense heat met us at the gate. The graveyard had caught fire.

A rake lay abandoned in the empty field next door, and two or three figures were running in and out of the edge of the smoke. I could hear them calling to one another, their voices distant and panicky beneath the roar and crackle of the fire. One of them toppled over; confused, the others took hold of his feet and pulled him inwards, towards the church. 'This way!' shouted the old men. They began to take off their coats, but nothing could be done. 'Over here!' Too late. However it had started, the blaze seemed to have seated itself everywhere at once, crackling and hissing in the saplings, racing through the grass between the railed and caged graves. (Through the heat mirage they seemed to bob like small boats on a burning sea, their ironwork glowing a dull plum colour. They remained unexpectedly afloat.) Tangle by tangle, the brambles quivered like red hot barbed wire and fell into ash. The elms nearest the church went up like bunches of straw: from where I stood, thirty or forty yards away, I could feel the heat on my skin.

The woman with the toddler held it up to see the flames. 'Look,' she urged. 'Timmy, look!' Her friend, who was occupied lighting a cigarette, said neutrally:

'It'll be the church next.'

This stopped the old men short. While they were considering it, the wind shifted a point or two and blew the flames towards us. Smoke roiled and eddied, alive with sparks. Eyes watering, I stepped back, expecting the acrid, powdery but reassuring smell you get from a garden bonfire on a wet day. Instead it stank of chlorine and putrefying bodies, then the crematorium chimney; and I heard a voice speaking as if from a great distance, in a middle-European accent so thick I could understand only a phrase or a sentence here and there. 'Ice,' it whispered. Then something that might have been, 'Our clothes.' And then, quite clear: 'They took us from Theresienstadt without warning at night.' I was in Birkenau. It was October. I could hear dogs barking somewhere a long way off across the river Sola, which had frozen early. The huts were dark, filled with the smell of exhausted women. 'All killed. Killed by injection.' Birkenau! How can I explain? History, not smoke, had enveloped me. Racked and nauseated, I stumbled across the road away from the church gate, knelt down, and vomited copiously into the grass verge. By the time I felt like standing up again, the fire in the churchyard had consumed itself. I thought: 'You're nearly fifty years old.'

It was the year of the Prague Spring. Dubček had yet to be defeated; Jan Palach had yet to make his appallingly confused gesture of hope and desolation in Wenceslas Square.

Were the borders beginning to move again?

The dead remain with us, passed down as the things that concerned them while they were alive. I recalled, suddenly and in succession: the prostitute in her booth above the Danube, light pooling in the hollow of a collar-bone; the orgasm of an eighteen-year-old boy, sad as an exhaled breath; the yellowed photograph of some old statesman who had meant so much to her. Had she died in Birkenau?

'I know you're here!' I shouted.

I knew she wasn't.

I wiped my mouth, raised my eyes, and found the toddler staring at me in bewilderment from his mother's arms. The rain poured down on us both.

Lucas closed his briefcase. The ward was quiet.

'What happened to Ashman that afternoon? He can only answer: "I'm not sure." It's almost as if he wants us to decide for him –'

Pam touched Lucas's arm tiredly.

'Lucas, what had he found in the church?'

'A cup, a map, a mirror. A rose. The real heritage of the Empress. The real clue to the Heart.'

'Lucas . . .'

'He had found the record of a marriage.'

'Will you come and see me in the afternoons?'

'I'll try.'

11

The Slave of God

However Pam had described Lucas to herself, however she had thought of him during their life together – as a demanding but perfect child; as the mirror of her own supernatural guilt; as the author 'Michael Ashman' – he had always been able to comfort and convince her. What he now achieved in this direction was as extraordinary as his original success with the Coeur. Folding her pain across itself repeatedly until it was so small she had no sensation of it, he placed it exactly at the heart of the Heart (that Romanesque cloister, he said, where whatever our anxiety we are always able to listen to the fountain playing in silence). There, though she could feel it once more, it was very distant; perhaps even a blessing.

'The first great echoes had died away,' he began. 'Yet visions and revelations were still possible. Put your ear to the cavity of history and you can still detect them – sighs, confused harmonies, ripples of ripples intersecting across the whole surface of a lake after some great significant object has submerged!

'1683:

'William Penn was founding Philadelphia. In Britain, Christopher Wren had abandoned astronomy for urban renewal. A bracing pragmatism seemed to rule. But while the modern world had its back turned, the Ottoman Empire besieged Vienna with scimitars, polished brass culverins, horsetail banners in gorgeous reds and yellows, and camels whose tulipwood saddles glowed in the sun less like earthly wood than some perfect Platonic material. And in the Low Countries, Christiaan Huygens was intuiting his way towards a wave theory of light! As an approach to the day-by-day meaning of the world, the dream might have fallen into disfavour; but that great European bestseller *The Judgement of Dreams* had entered its fifteenth edition since 1518.

Nicholas Coleman of Norwich experienced visions of "an army of men" whose beggar's rags disguised finery beneath, "burning the market towns of England at night". A tailor from Stamford was encouraged by dreams to try "the miraculous healing of the deaf and blind". And then, suddenly hallucinating a rose which opened "not in but somewhere behind" her sleep, a Bristol woman, christened in the year of the Great Fire with the extraordinary name Godscall St Ives, renounced her faith to marry a gardener named Joseph Winthrop.

'Winthrop was a man of his time. Commercial and scientific botany delighted him equally. He had corresponded with the younger Tradescant, and worked with Philip Miller on what they hoped would be a new centifolia rose. His Dutch connections balanced a distant relationship to the governor of Massachusetts: he was able to exploit both.

'Three of their children chose the New World. We know nothing of them. The fourth, Liselotte, prone to chlorosis, melancholy from an early age, married a Leiden pump-engineer called Boerhaave. At this, saddened perhaps by the whole charade of Enlightenment, Godscall fell prey quite suddenly to a quartan ague – of which Winthrop, plant-collecting in the Netherlands, learned only on his return – and died. "Something burns within me," she had written in her diary in 1695, "but I am never consumed."'

Pam loved this.

Lucas was delighted by her delight. It would be over-simplifying, whatever my opinion, to claim he had been disappointed by his life since the divorce. Nevertheless, an unfamiliar excitement now filled him whenever he thought about her. At first, surprised to find himself daydreaming in the school staff-room after lunch, he would shake his head and go back to marking books. Soon, though, the work itself began to bore him. The children seemed wilfully slow and uncooperative, the things he was trying to teach them rang with meaninglessness. Clearly, he was approaching the crux of things. He and Pam had been telling themselves the story of the Coeur for twenty years: its worth as an invention – never mind as solace – now depended as much on his ability to convince as on her desire to be convinced. This was the moment of greatest danger. Despite that, he wanted to be at the hospital as often as possible. He wanted to be next to her. Stuck in the classroom, he yawned; heard himself tell some twelve-year-old boy, 'For God's sake go, then. But don't ask me again this afternoon;' and stared out of the window.

He could see Pam, sitting up in bed reading a book!

Four in the afternoon. Time to be off. It was a momentary relief to throw his stuff into the back of the Renault, slam the door, start the engine: but predicating his whole day on this gesture solved nothing. An hour later he was as impatient as ever.

He loathed the drive out through Rochdale, with its debilitated public buildings and small businesses. 'The Pine Brunch Bar & Coffee Lounge' replaced 'Carol's Wools', to be replaced in its turn by 'A Maze of Pine & Roses'. These fantasias of transformation and escape – pursued with increasing anguish as they approached the depressed outskirts – chafed him into misreading familiar traffic signs, so that he missed a turning he always took. Or he would brake suddenly for an imaginary dog or child. Further east there was only moorland, successive arcs of water-logged peat, elegant concrete bridges connecting nothing to nothing across the motorway. It was dark even in the afternoon, and the traffic was always bad. The aggression of the other drivers as they jostled nose to tail at eighty or ninety miles an hour through this desolate landscape made him nervous and contemptuous at once.

'They look so stupidly greedy,' he wrote to me, 'you wonder how they ever managed to learn to drive at all. I suppose none of us do more than the minimum necessary to get what we want.'

He would arrive at Huddersfield General in a mood impossible, he said, to describe; though he tried hard enough, and in fact it wasn't hard to recognise – 'Impatience, anger, elation, all at once: sometimes so intense I can feel myself draining away out of my own body, like water.' It made him look through the nurses as though they weren't there; and advise the hospital florist, always slow to calculate change from a five-pound note, 'Keep it!' The lifts had been full so often he no longer bothered with them but took the stairs instead, three at a time. Every evening there seemed to be more people in his way. New patients with sheafs of documents en route for Haematology, new visitors on timid quests for husbands in Cardiac or daughters in Maternity, they were easily snared in the web of primary-coloured lines painted on the corridor floors, which is where Lucas came upon them.

'Excuse me. We're looking for . . .'

He stared at them as if they were deranged.

'. . . X-rays.'

'I can't help. Sorry.'

He pushed open the door of Primrose Ward at last. 'Lucas,' Pam called: 'Here.' They had moved her bed again! For a moment he stood confused in the middle of the polished floor; then she waved and suddenly he could relax. She took the flowers from him. His heart was pounding. He had been walking so quickly, he found, that he was out of breath.

'Lucas, they're beautiful!'

'Listen,' he said –

'"Something burns within me, but I am never consumed!" But whatever it was, it clearly failed to kindle in Godscall's daughter. Boerhaave settled in East Anglia, where – encouraged by the success of the Haddenham Level project in 1727 – he planned to drain and farm. But his capital proved insufficient, Liselotte soon died of smallpox, and, its income fallen radically, its only issue daughters, the family followed her into oblivion.

'We have only glimpses of them after that.'

Liselotte's children, Lucas maintained, were to marry into the hand-looming industry which had grown up around Norwich. As for their descendants:

'For nearly a hundred years, they drift north. Norwich to Nottingham and then Manchester; flying shuttle to spinning jenny; figured cloth to stockings and lace. Their names have not survived the famines, wage cuts and migrations, the long slow tragedy of the eighteenth-century cottage industries. When they re-emerge, it is with the invention of the power loom, and the death of Paul Sturtevant, a middle-aged artisan from Horrocks' Stockport factory who walked all the way to Manchester one day in August 1819, because he wanted to hear the radical Henry Hunt speak in St Peter's Fields.'

Sturtevant fell under the hoofs of the cavalry as they swept across Peterloo to break up the meeting. He survived hideous injuries to his head, only to die of an infection twelve days later. 'In his delirium,' Lucas told Pam, 'he dreamed of "the perfect time which will come to us all". He was able to describe it: but it was nothing like the life we have now. Six daughters huddled round the deathbed. The youngest, Alice, only seven years old, records:

'"Before he died he cried out, 'What does it matter that I'm dying, since I am doing what I want?'"

'Anything we make of this glimpse depends on the quality of our intuition. Was the Heart waiting for something? (Nothing, surely, that could ever happen in Manchester!) We can only say that we feel it beating again before silence sets in. By the last quarter of the century, its heirs have passed through the Industrial Revolution as if through a fire. They will never retrieve Godscall's sense of something beyond and yet within herself. They will never prophesy like Sturtevant. They no longer allow themselves rage. They repress their fear, their sex, their dreams. The skills of the affect have been burned away from them. All they can do is seek advancement.

'They become shopkeepers.'

Outside in the corridor after each visit, Lucas took off his spectacles and rubbed his eyes.

'I'm tired out,' he told the ward staff.

'You're doing her the world of good,' they reassured him.

It was, he knew, too simple a diagram of the relationship.

One weekday afternoon had turned into two. By then, Rochdale no longer seemed such a labyrinth to him. He would stop off there at 'A Maze of Pine & Roses' to buy her a figured silver bracelet from Nepal, or a photograph of someone else's Victorian ancestors slipped naively into a small art deco frame because, the woman behind the counter said, they looked so nice together.

Pam responded with physical improvements like shy gifts of her own. She woke early and, with the blue bedjacket round her shoulders, sat up more often during the day. As a result she slept better at night. Though her skin was still very white, it lost the floury look which had so frightened Lucas at the outset of the illness. The pain was still there, of course, but easier to ignore. She entered into the life of the ward around her. Some days this was hardly more ambitious than a discussion of the events at Emmerdale Farm, but even that helped: where previously she had stared clueless and owlish at the TV, allowing the soaps to wash her as smooth as a stone in a stream, she now followed them with a kind of amused greed. The opposite of innocence is not irony but emptiness. Halfway through *Love's Gold Dream* she lent it to one of the nurses, who forgot to give it back.

'What do I look like with my hair like this?' she asked the other women tentatively.

She put on weight. She put on make-up.

It is easy to see that Lucas, who would have done or said anything to preserve the delight he saw on her face when he entered the ward, had rediscovered the excitement of being pivotal to someone else's happiness, a condition which promised to alleviate all his own wounds. But what Pam had rediscovered could only be inferred from her clear intention to get well. The ward staff thought they knew. Mistaking her smile, her intensity, the attentiveness that came back into her face when she looked up at Lucas, they often conspired to leave him there for half an hour after the rest of the afternoon visitors had gone. They knew, anyway, that left to his own devices he would only make his way back to the waiting area and write furiously with a cheap red ballpoint pen until visiting began again at seven o'clock.

'You've just got to look at her,' trainee nurses told one another delightedly, 'to see.'

'I can't fancy him myself.'

'Get on!'

It was too early to talk about remission, and they were careful never to use the word near her. Would Pam have heard them if they had? With Lucas constantly at her side offering the life-jacket, part of her at least was free to abandon Huddersfield General the way you abandon a ship. This she did with relief. At night, lapped in the faint fake radiance of morphine, she could remember herself as a little girl dancing on a low wall (though she couldn't remember whose hands caught her again and again when she jumped). Falling for ever, always being saved, she heard Lucas say –

'Alice Sturtevant grew up frail-looking and pretty, but more obstinate than she seemed. A photograph taken in middle life shows her in an amazing black bombazine dress. If her eyes are dark-ringed like all that family's, it is less from anxiety than determination. In 1835, she had married a milkman named John Duck. His surname amused her; but they wanted the same things, and he promised a life without visions.

'He came from Mottram, a village east of Manchester in the gape of the Longdendale Valley, and at the time of their marriage was poised to convert his milk profits into a small shop on the old saltway, close to the Packhorse Inn. There, in the shadow of the fifteenth-century church, 'the Cathedral of East Cheshire', Alice helped him sell groceries by weight (a piece of bacon was stuck with its own fat to the base of the scales to 'adjust' them); cough mixtures full of opium which went down like warm pitch; and boot laces from a card.

'Alice had seven children. Of five girls, one died at birth; another, three years old, from diphtheria. The boys survived, which was a blessing. She was happy enough; and if she never liked the dark gape of Longdendale, she could always look back at the Altdorfer sunsets burning away above the chimneys of the city.

'John Duck, meanwhile, looked eastward. Under construction ten miles up the valley were railway lines, tunnels, a chain of dams and reservoirs intended to water the industries of Manchester. From 1838 until the end of the century, these obsessional works drew a massive labour force to the shanty villages of Rhodeswood, Woodhouse and Dunford Bridge. Conditions were bad. Men, women and children died in subsidences and premature explosions, of privation, overwork, bad housing, puzzlement, or grief; and were often buried on the moor with less ceremony than the victims of Ian Brady and Myra Hindley a hundred years later. Pictures of the time show them grouped outside their 'homes' in New Yarmouth – blurred faces in the foreground, bleak oak woods behind, then the high black edge of the moor.

'John supplied groceries to the survivors. It was a good business, and – apart from the younger son, who seems to have registered as a quarryman at the age of thirteen – all the Duck children went into it.

'By 1880, the oldest boy William was ready to branch out on his own. John bought him a milk round in Salford, and taught him to keep the product fresh by adding formalin. With the death of his parents within two months of one another in 1900, William brought his sisters to Manchester and liquidated all three enterprises, along with a Salford public house – the Junction – he had acquired in the meantime. This enabled him to buy a share in a modest but successful department store on Victoria Street.

'He began with three partners. Buying out the last of them twenty years later, he determined to give the store his own name. But by then it was the biggest in Manchester, and his wife – a publican's daughter from Burnley – persuaded him that "Duck's" had no ring to it. Looking back through the family history, they chose his mother's maiden name, modifying it after some thought from Sturtevant to Stuyvesant. Stuyvesant! It was European yet transatlantic; it was American yet aristocratic. William loved it. He changed his name by deed poll.'

'St Ives to Sturtevant. Sturtevant to Stuyvesant. Godscall's descendants have found their way down to us. The Heart has its Heir.'

Thursday afternoon, Primrose Ward.

Patients and visitors exchange desultory talk.

'We got toast this morning.'

'Move, Nina, move and let your grandma sit down. She's not been very well.'

'Thanks, flower: 'as your 'eadache gone?'

'In Ashton they were all dreaming of toast. It was all they ever thought of.'

'It's not time yet is it? It's not time. Do they come and check if the visitors have gone?'

'You had to have an operation to get toast. Or else be in the Maternity Unit – '

Laughter.

'Nina, love, it's not time yet.'

Only Pam and Lucas are silent. Lucas, having told his story, turns away for a minute or two as if out of shyness. Given this time to herself, Pam regards him thoughtfully. The afternoon, swinging round on its pivot, isolates in a kind of flat light one flower vase after another: tulips, asters, lilies, 'like a tart's boudoir'. On the TV a dog is running through rubbish by some docks, under the stern of a ship. An old woman's voice sings a few quavering notes. 'That's nice, isn't it?' And, to a passing nurse: 'I'm singing. Ha ha.' Rain scratches at the windows.

Eventually Pam says:

'Somehow that makes it even sadder.'

'Oh, Pam!'

Lucas laughs. They hug.

'Pam, Pam, remember Valentinus: "Do not be afraid. In death you shall not die." You were in the Pleroma all along without knowing it!'

'Less of that, you two,' orders the ward sister, coming in briskly to fuss with an empty bed. 'Throwing-out time now. Come on, it's four o'clock, you've had a good innings.'

Over the years Lucas too had wrung from the myth what comfort he could. By allowing him to experience the Coeur as if it came from outside himself, 'Michael Ashman' had relieved him of responsibility and salved his intellectual guilts. More importantly, 'Ashman' hid – or at least disguised – Lucas's own intuition, of which he had an almost comical fear. Pam understood much of this. It was, after all, a shared dream. But while she could accept Lucas's needs, they had always chafed her. As soon as he confirmed what she had somehow sensed all along – that the whole of this history aimed itself through her – she lost interest. Her sense of urgency prevailed. She laid the Search aside like a crossword puzzle faintly pencilled in with guesses and instead focused her attention on the dream itself.

Increasingly, it centred on the Empress's shadowy daughter Phoenissa, of whom Lucas had said, 'She may not have escaped the wreck. You can still hear in the Pleroma a faint fading cry of rage and sadness which may have been hers.'

The crux, Pam claimed, the absolute meaning of Phoenissa's 'death into the world', lay in its counter-trajectory to the Empress's.

'From the start Phoenissa was fucking her mother's general, Lascaris; he only had to be near her to drive her into a kind of delighted paralysis – she could feel herself tremble and moisten if he walked past fifty yards away not even looking in her direction.

'Things had begun to slide long before the siege began.

Everyone knew that. The court was split, the Empress already fatally inattentive. Weeds sprang up between the stones. The wells faltered. In the afternoons the City baked silently in the heat. Lascaris and Phoenissa met in the little deserted courtyards beneath the inner walls. At first he was brutal with her. He would bend her over a dry fountain, enter her, come suddenly with a groan. The sunlight illuminated them mercilessly in this moment: both helpless, half out of their fine clothes, weak with sex. Towards the end, when smoke from the besieging cannon hung above the City like strips of black rag, he seemed to relax. In some cool empty room with broken earthenware scattered over the tiled floor, he would cup the back of her head in his hands, and whisper "Don't be afraid," a kindness which disappointed her inexplicably.

'Then suddenly it was all over. For two nights and a day the harbour had been in flames. The outer walls, weakened by twenty days of bombardment from landward, went down. Lascaris was killed early in the afternoon, the Empress two hours later near one of the gates. She was weeping openly, they say, and had picked up a sword: but they never say why. No one could bear to look directly at her.

'In the moment of her mother's agony, as the Coeur snapped back away from the world and into the Pleroma, Phoenissa was given a choice. Alone all day in a deserted cloister, she had watched the air suffuse with a dusty glow the colour of rose petals. The sounds of battle faded. She could hear the nearby fountain; and behind that a thread of music, one phrase repeated over and over again on some stringed instrument. Eventually Lascaris, dressed in his beautiful armour, walked slowly across the courtyard in front of her. 'Theodore!' she wept. The air smelled of attar, called the heart of the rose. 'Theodore!' He turned back to face her and she saw his wound; she remembered the wounds he had given her. He was, of course, already dead. She had mistaken the tawdry glitter of the world for the light of the Pleroma! She fled towards it: her very desire for fullness led her to choose the world.'

Pam laughed.

'She's been whoring through it ever since, under the impression that it's Heaven.'

153

Lucas was rather shocked.

'We can't know that,' he said.

'The Empress knew. Oh, Lucas, Lucas! It's easy to talk about the World and the Coeur as "burning in the fabric of the Pleroma like two lovers in the glorious wreck of desire". But we can mean only one thing by that. All those years ago, you talked about "a huge cry of love and loss, echoing and re-echoing across Europe."

'But who lost the most?

'If the Coeur would no longer let itself be known, we mustn't blame the invading kings and their conspiracies. It had breathed its final breath long before they identified Gallica by her beautiful armour, and displayed the mutilated head.'

There was a silence.

Into it Lucas said, 'We can't know that, either.'

Pam smiled.

'We can't, can we?' she said.

And looking steadily at him she lifted her hands, palms upwards, in a gesture of weighing: as if he had asked the wrong question. But if he remained a bit unnerved by the energy and sensuality of her vision, Lucas was always willing to contribute what he could. There were days, too, when she seemed to falter. 'I'm tired, Lucas,' she would whisper, blinking back tears and staring at the bed opposite hers: 'I can't remember things which happened so long ago.'

To help, he told her a story of Richard Coeur de Lion which went like this:

'Traditionally, of course, Richard, returning to England incognito from the Third Crusade, is captured by Leopold of Austria who imprisons him at Durnstein. He is found and freed by the troubadour Blondel, who sings the first verse of a popular ballad outside every keep in Europe until Richard replies with the second. In fact by 1193 Richard's place had already been taken by a hostage called Hugo de Morville. Hugo, who had helped murder Thomas à Becket on behalf of Richard's father, is supposed to have died of guilt on a pilgrimage to the Holy Land. But a poet called Ulrich von Zatzikhoven saw and talked to him, there in the Durnstein keep. So there was no Richard. Was there ever a Blondel? Who knows. But there was certainly an exchange of songs. Hugo de Morville gave von Zatzikhoven a copy of the Anglo-Norman Legend of Lancelot, Zatzikhoven's translation of which – though authorities regard it as both banal and dilute – must be seen as one of the late flowers of German chivalric poetry.

'The insoluble conflict between ideal and reality! Richard vanishes from his own story for a year. Where does he go while de Morville is impersonating him in Durnstein? Only the codes embedded in his name enable us to guess.

'Gallica carried the blood of the Lion.'

'Really, Lucas,' Pam interrupted suddenly, 'I don't care what fucking colour she bled.'

Soon she was laughing at him again.

'"Ideal and reality"!' she said.

In this way, turn and turn about, losing their confidence one day only to regain it the next, they steered the Course of the Heart. Pam's compass was hidden, glandular, difficult to read: less romantic than Lucas's. But she was equally determined; and perhaps in the end she had the truer sense of direction. Her health continued to improve, while Lucas watched in awe and Huddersfield General held its breath. The disease went into remission. Within a month – though she was a little too frail to fend for herself and would still need treatment as an out-patient – they had allowed her to go home.

From then on Lucas spent his free time at the cottage, although he always drove back to Manchester at night. No cook, he bought what he called 'middle-class convenience food' – filled pasta and tins of ratatouille – after school at Sainsbury's; and in the evenings did the housework (rarely to the standard of Pam's neighbours, who came in and did it again during the day). Pam slept a lot; Lucas sat by the bed and wrote letters to me, in red ball-point on lined paper. 'We try and get as much fresh air as we can.' At weekends he carried her out to the Renault and drove to one local beauty spot or another – anywhere she could look out over a reservoir and some woods without having to leave the car – or pushed her round the Huddersfield shopping arcades in a wheelchair. When he picked her up, he told me, she was just a lot of bones and heat that weighed nothing.

One Saturday in late August they drove through Dunford Bridge, past their old house.

'Look, Lucas!'

Lucas parked the car on the grass verge, where the road dipped northward into a valley with beech and dwarf oak. The valley was full of haze, the haze full of sun. A strange bronze light fell on the tangled grass in front of the house. From behind rose a plume of smoke so thick and perfectly detailed that it looked like a solid object.

'Wind your window down,' Lucas said.

He studied the house.

'Good God.'

Builders were at work on it again. They had opened one gable end, then sealed it temporarily with heavy-gauge polythene. The front windows were out, the stonework above them jacked into place until the lintels could be replaced. A yellow JCB lay hull-down among the muddy hawthorn stumps it had grubbed out of the gardens at the back, where two men were burning a dozen or so metal chairs. Only the frames remained, tangled together inextricably and outlined with fire.

Lucas wheeled Pam across the road and through the gates.

'Let's have a look round.'

'Your poor old garden!' Pam said. She studied the empty windows. 'I think I'll stay here.'

'What a warren!'

It had always been too large and complex for them; perhaps for anyone. The Local Authority had bought the building when they left, converting it into a home for disturbed children, a kind of halfway house for those bemused before they reached the age of consent. Now cutbacks had returned it to the private sector, where according to the builder's signboard it would become a small exclusive 'estate' of five or six houses round a courtyard. Lucas looked in through one of the windows and tried to imagine this. All he saw was an empty room, flowered wallpaper, dusty air across which slanted a bar of light. He mooched round for a bit among the demolished outbuildings, picking up pieces of broken lath, stooping over a pile of brand new yellow drainage pipes, then made his way back to the front garden, where he had left Pam. He found her trying to smile and cry at the same time. To cheer her up he said:

'I loved this view.'

'You didn't like the house much.'

'It was never very lucky for us,' he admitted.

She touched his hand.

'I'm glad they're doing something with it at last,' she said. 'Aren't you?'

He began to push the wheelchair back to the car.

'Do you know what I miss most, Lucas?'

'What?'

'A cigarette.'

'Wipe your nose now.'

All along they had known that the one word neither of them must ever pronounce was 'metastasis'. But in September, cancer was diagnosed in the remaining breast. From there it seemed to rage across her like a fire. As he said bitterly, there wasn't much left of her to burn. In case anything could be done, the consultant had her admitted to Christie's, the Manchester cancer-hospital, where she underwent state-of-the-art scanning, exploratory operations and then a second amputation; radiation treatment followed. It was too late. By November she was very ill indeed, and in December we knew she would die.

Lucas telephoned me a few days before Christmas.

'You'd better come up here,' he said.

He sobbed suddenly and put the phone down.

12

Trasfigurante

My train rolled slowly into Manchester Piccadilly the next morning just before twelve. I had an overnight bag with me, and a copy of *Roman Tales*. While I was waiting for the train to stop, I pushed the window down and had a look along the platform: there was Lucas, reading the travel posters outside the buffet while he warmed his hands round a styrofoam cup. His cashmere jacket hung open over a thin grey cotton T-shirt with the word 'Technique' printed on it in fluent red script like lipstick on a mirror. He had wrapped a long black scarf twice round his neck. The way he hunched his shoulders made him seem vulnerable as well as cold. I wondered how long he had been standing there. The train lurched twice and drew to a halt at last. I opened the door and got down, wincing in the raw air. Sleet had begun to fall as we crossed the south Staffordshire plain, only to turn to wet snow at Stockport. Piccadilly smelled of gas turbines, acetylene, diesel.

'Lucas!'

We shook hands.

'How are you?' I asked.

'I can't seem to get warm nowadays,' he said. 'Especially in the mornings.' He offered me the cup. 'Want some? It's hot chocolate. No? The cold seems brutal to me. I'm getting old, I suppose.' We were forty that year, I reminded him: if he was old, so was I. He had the grace to laugh. It wasn't far to the Christie Hospital, he told me: though at this time of day traffic would be heavy. 'Let's go straight there,' he said. 'I've got the car out the back.' He touched my upper arm shyly.

'Pam will be so glad to see you!'

'You don't wear enough,' I said. 'That's why you're always cold.' As we trudged across the car park through the snow I warned him, 'Lucas, I haven't got long.' It was important he didn't expect too much. 'A week at most. Kit and Katherine want me home at Christmas.'

For a moment I wondered if he understood.

Then he said: 'Oh, I see. You mean she'd better get it over with in the next couple of days.'

'It wouldn't be fair to them, Lucas.'

His face white and miserable, he unlocked the front passenger door of the Renault for me, then went round the other side to get in. 'I'm sorry,' he said, as soon as he had the bulk of the car between us. 'I shouldn't have said that. Of course you must go back.' He started the engine, put the heater on. The windscreen misted up. The windscreen wipers batted back and forth, making a soft thudding noise as they piled the melting snow against the glass. 'What's the weather like in London?'

'Bad,' I said. 'It's bad all over the country.' I felt emptied out by his distress. 'Lucas, why don't you come down to us, just for Christmas Day?'

He put the car into gear.

'Because she'd be alone,' he said.

Ward Three was long and narrow, with tall sash windows, a dozen beds along either side and a red sign at one end which said ZONE 3 WASHROOM. Later I would remember it as having a ghoulish air of fancy dress, like a concentration camp Christmas. Radiation and chemotherapy implants had slowed the women down. Their hair had fallen out. Despite this, morale was high, and morphine often left them as cheerful and vague as toddlers. White plastic strips fastened to each emaciated wrist – as a precaution against the wrong medication – reduced their responsibilities. Haggard yet childlike, they had a name, an age, an admission number. They needed no more unless it was to vomit: for that they were given a thing that looked like a papier-mâché bowler hat.

Pam's face was all bones, yellowy-white skin, eyes in deep black hollows not much larger than the eyeballs themselves. She hardly seemed to recognise us. Perhaps as a way of protecting herself from her memories, she had begun to keep the outside world at a distance. If she had to live, she would live inside her condition. Consequently, most of her talk was about the ward or the other patients. 'Mrs Eddy goes home tomorrow,' she told us. We had no idea which one Mrs Eddy was. 'We call her "Mary Baker". Everyone gets a name. That's her husband just come in.' She added, with a certain professional scorn: 'How they expect him to manage her on his own – !' Then something else caught her attention.

'See the old dear over there? No, there. Just going off to Radiology.

'We used to call her "Steve Ovett".'

To all intents and purposes cured, but needing exercise to build her up before they could discharge her, this old woman had dutifully pushed a walking frame round the ward for fifteen minutes twice a day, scraping it along the worn polished floor in front of her and telling everyone:

'I'm joining a marathon when I get out.'

'You'll win!'

Without warning, circulatory complications had made it necessary to amputate her left leg just beneath the knee, and after that, as Pam said, 'Steve Ovett' seemed a bit close to the bone. The old people were typically cheerful, 'But a thing like that would give anyone a shock.'

'So what do they call her now?'

'"Long John Silver".'

We watched as, with some care, two nurses knotted the old woman's stocking below the stump; helped her put on a dressing gown decorated like a running strip in different shades of blue; and finally manoeuvred her into a wheelchair. 'I must have a fag before I go!' she shouted. 'I must have a smoke.' The nurses tutted her. Amused by the baldness of the irony, the rest of the patients were prompted to call out 'Tarra, duck!' as she was wheeled away.

'Tarra!'

Suddenly Pam said:

'There are only two paces in this place, slow and dead stop.'

After that she seemed to go to sleep; but then as we were leaving she touched my arm and smiled. 'I'm glad you came,' she said –

'Look after Lucas.'

*

160

Stuck in traffic on Oxford Road, Lucas stared out of the Renault at slushy pavements, hurrying shoppers, the remains of a late December afternoon.

'This will be gone tomorrow,' he said. 'It's not the kind of snow that lasts.'

He lived in a large flat at the top of a Victorian house.

'An entire generation disappeared into places like this,' he had written to me just after the divorce, as if it was inevitable he finish up in some bedsitter with a shared bath and lino on the stairs. 'What have they got now? A bookcase full of outdated sociology texts and some old records. They always wanted to go to Budapest, but somehow it couldn't be done.' As usual he had seen only what he wanted to see.

It was nearly dark as we made our way up the stairs. A curious thing happened at the top. While Lucas stood on the little landing outside his front door, fumbling with the keys in the cobwebby grey light, I heard a quiet, indistinct noise from inside the flat.

'Lucas! There's someone in there!'

Lucas seemed unnerved for a moment. Then he laughed and explained, 'You get that every time they run the water next door. These walls might as well be made of plasterboard.' He opened the door. 'Let me go first. The light switches are difficult to find.'

The flat was two-bedroomed, with high moulded ceilings and central heating. He had furnished its massive living room – which doubled as a study – with a kind of absent-minded energy, buying from junk shops one day and Habitat the next. As a result some gold brocade cushions hobnobbed with a black-and-chrome chair, while the tiny bulb of a very modern anglepoise lamp cast its light on a sofa covered with chintz. The fitted carpets were pale and neutral, the rugs old-fashioned and figured. The shelves bore a characteristic mix of books – Bruno Schultz next to Henry Miller; Cawte's *Ritual Animal Masks*; works of European history and modern literary criticism. The front windows had once looked out over gardens reminiscent of a London square, of which a few trees and some of the original railings remained. Lucas closed the curtains, switched on the gas fire, rubbed his hands.

'I'm sorry about the mess,' he apologised. 'I never get time to tidy up.'

Dark, peaty earth, studded with the remains of an earthenware plant pot, was scattered all over the floor. The plant itself, quite a large streptocarpus, lay in a corner where it had shed its thick white petals like a bag of prawn crackers. 'I knocked it off the mantelpiece last night,' Lucas said off-handedly. But I suspected that rage or misery had made him throw it across the room. Either way, the carpet was ruined, 'He was always so untidy!' I remembered Pam saying. This pretence – that Lucas was a child – had never entirely relieved her fear that he had some core of anger she could neither understand nor assuage. 'So untidy and so easily hurt.'

Lucas had been her life. Now she often forgot him altogether. Freed by her condition to be the centre of attention, she would talk for hours then fall asleep in the middle of a sentence; or refuse to talk at all, withholding herself almost as if she were blaming us for the illness. Riding an hourly see-saw of pain and morphine, she revised her memories, acted out her childhood in Cheshire and Silverdale, spoke in tongues: the coy whisper of the little girl, the boom of the father's laughter, the cooing of the mother. This eerie archaeological theatre was never fully performed. She needed help we couldn't give; asked questions we couldn't answer; wept distraughtly when we couldn't supply details she had forgotten.

She was three years old, escaping towards the sea with some other child's toy. It was an inflatable horse. It was blue. But what colour of blue was it? Lucas didn't remember. How could he?

'Go away then!' she told him. 'Go away.'

Her other relationships were equally confused.

'They've been so wonderful, whatever happens,' she would say suddenly of the doctors or nurses; only to beg a few minutes later, 'You've got to get me out of here! They won't tell me anything!'

We shared the visits. Since Lucas could rarely get away until four, I went to see her in the afternoons. Lucas took over when he had finished work. In the evenings I left them together as often as I could. I would go to the cinema, eat at McDonald's, call Katherine from a vandalised box on Oxford Road – 'Hello. I love you.' 'Hello?' – then go home and try to tidy up Lucas's flat. Afternoons were Pam's best time. On the cusp between one dose and the next, she sometimes salvaged half an hour of the Pam Stuyvesant I remembered. 'Aren't these gladioli beautiful?' she would insist: or, 'Have you seen the view from my window? I never get tired of it!' Looking out through the wavy Victorian glass you found the snow had melted to reveal a few trees and tilting board fences touched at that time of year with deep green lichen. Some sunlight, bright but dilute, slanted across the street, making you wish for frost, holly berries, one vigorous figure, one event which might give it the effect of a Christmas card. This didn't matter to Pam. 'It cheers me up, it really does.'

But the recapture of lucidity had dangers of its own. Two or three nights before Christmas Lucas came home early and complained: 'The whole time I was there, she just stared at the TV. *Celebrity Squares*. The whole fucking time! Can you understand that?'

Later, when he had calmed down, he added:

'She looked horrified. I don't suppose we'll ever know what she was actually seeing.'

I knew.

'How are you?'

Three thirty: Christie's. Two beds along from Pam on the other side of the ward, a fat woman stood up, retrieved her handbag, sat down again abruptly. She wore an angora wool skirt with a matching scarf; pinned to her head was a kind of trilby hat apparently made out of carpet material. She had been trying to leave for half an hour. 'Well, goodbye dear,' she said cheerfully each time she got up. 'I expect I'll see you this time tomorrow.' The air in Ward Three was brown and gloomy. Every so often, coloured light from the television flickered through it like sunshine through moving branches; discovered Pam's white face; and pulled the cheekbones this way and that in shifting relief. Her eyes were wide yet uninterested, her voice filled with a faint disgust.

'About the same.'

She seemed to be about to add something, but in the end only gestured tiredly at the screen. 'That about sums it up today.'

'What's the programme?'

'What do you think?' she said.

It was hard to say. Faces and limbs in some sort of crisis, filmed at odd angles by hand-held camera and lost in interference, had been intercut with pictures of sheep and goats running to and fro in an empty stone building. Gradually these images were allowed to leak into one another until there emerged something like a damp watercolour landscape – mud and rocks in umber colours: indistinct animals: another face staring anxiously out. This in its turn flared and darkened into soft ungeometric shapes which pulsed gently like the organs of the body. After a moment or two the colour faded entirely, as though the set had gone out of adjustment. Patches of whiteness began to merge and separate rhythmically against a uniform grey background. 'There!' said Pam. The picture had resolved again. I caught a single glimpse of white limbs intertwined, and looked away as quickly as I could. At the same time the sound-track came up. 'In the afternoons,' I heard a faint dull voice say, 'it was too hot to sit still. She lay on her back on the sofa with her skirt pulled up and her hand between her legs. Her knickers were always damp. At night she would crouch down over him, push his cock into her, and move strongly up and down on it grunting and panting until she came.'

'Christ!'

'Ask everyone else what they're watching,' said Pam. 'It won't be this.'

'. . . this,' echoed the sound-track: 'His cock detumesced and fell out. Mixed sperm and juices ran out to cool and dry between his pubic hair and hers.'

Poor Pam! She was shaking. When I tried to put my arm round her shoulders, she moved away.

'No. No.'

'It's the morphine, Lucas.'

'I suppose so,' he conceded. 'I suppose it is.'

Morphine, heart's ease, hinge of truth. He had hauntings of his own, for which he had hardly begun to find comfort. It would only have distressed him further to know that she could see right through *Celebrity Squares* or *Take the High Road* to where the white couple hung just inside every TV set, smiling out at her while they clasped and pushed and panted and turned to and fro like a chrysalis in a hedge. To divert him I asked:

'What shall I do with this?'

We had decided we would clean the kitchen. A baking tray, earthenware casseroles of different sizes, the scorched oven glove shaped like a fish: Lucas had a way of handling each object as if he hoped to recognise something he had mislaid when he moved house years before. He took hours to cook anything and longer to wash up.

'I don't know.'

That evening it started snowing again. Wintry weather was moving across the north-west on a broad front. Falls would be quite heavy, the television predicted; winds light. I went to bed early, and woke surprised not long after. Midnight. Laughter amplified by the cold air. Couples were still floundering past outside with linked arms, feet turned out, heads wrapped up dark and globular against the cold. People love snow. I lay there listening to them for a moment or two, wondering what had woken me. Then I heard a thud and a low cry from Lucas's room, followed immediately by an extraordinary outbreak of banging and crashing, as if someone was breaking up the front-room chairs and then throwing pieces of them about. 'Lucas!' I called. 'Are you all right?' Never a good sleeper, he was up and down all night, disturbed by his nightmares or making his way to the lavatory to pee noisily into the silence. Despite this, he would never switch on the lights. I assumed he had fallen over something at last. 'Lucas?' He said something indistinct but reassuring, then cried out suddenly in such an appalled voice I got straight out of bed and went to the door. Nothing sounds worse than a raised voice in someone else's house at night. Bad dreams, illness, self-pity in the small hours: you have no idea how to respond. Both bedrooms opened on to a short narrow passage painted white, an uncurtained window at one end of which admitted snow-light reflected up from the street. In this cold but buoyant illumination I could easily make out the pictures on the walls either side of Lucas's door, clip-framed photographs of a visit to some exotic country, Turkey perhaps, or Afghanistan, where very bright sunshine flooded through a deeply recessed window on to broad-striped orange and ochre rugs. I stood there in my underpants, shivering, and knocked. The noise redoubled. Something was flung heavily against the door itself, which flexed under the impact. I pushed. It resisted. Everything went quiet again.

'Lucas?'

Nothing.

'Lucas!'

I was about to turn away when the door jerked open and Lucas stuck his head out so suddenly that I backed into the wall of the passage. It was hard to see what was wrong with him – the bedside lamp in the room behind him was flickering like a damaged fluorescent tube – but his face seemed both white and dirty, and there was blood running down one side of it from a cut above his eye.

'What do you want?' he said irritably, as if it was me who had called for help in the middle of the night.

'Lucas – '

'There's no need to come in,' he said. 'I had a bit of an accident. Go back to sleep now.' He closed the door until all I could see was his left eye and the cut above it, swollen, blue with bruised tissue. He was trembling. 'Go back to sleep,' he repeated. 'It's all right.'

'Lucas – '

The door closed suddenly.

'Lucas!'

Silence.

I went back to the spare room and stood at the window for some time with the duvet wrapped round my shoulders, staring down into the street. The snow directly beneath each sodium lamp was orange: a little further away it became a fragile tremulous pink, a colour on the edge of tenure, unassuming, shy, threatened. Though Pam was still alive, Lucas already felt bereaved. The bereft, we say, are less dismayed than in a rage; and I was afraid Lucas's rage would damage him. How can you protect someone from a grief which causes him to throw his furniture about in the middle of the night? This may have been the wrong question to ask. By now the street was empty. Parked for the night, the cars had grown strange and shapeless. In the morning, I knew, they would look as if they had been moulded from styrofoam – blind, blunt models in some early, uninteresting stage of design.

*

166

The next day Pam was moved into a small side-ward. Her bouts of pain and delirium had been upsetting other patients, the ward sister told us; it would be easier to manage her there.

'Easier to manage her death,' Lucas said bitterly.

Pam put a brave face on it. 'How nice to have a room of your own.' In the end though I think she would have preferred to stay where she was. 'They were real characters in Ward Three,' she said to me, as if I had been there too: 'Weren't they?'

She laughed.

'Oh, Lucas, aren't people funny?'

'I'm not Lucas,' I said.

She took my hand.

'I know that, really. Tell him I love him.'

That was one of the last lucid things she said to me.

When I got back to Lucas's flat late that afternoon, I found that he had been in at lunchtime and wrecked it. All the internal doors were propped open. The plates had been taken out of the kitchen and smashed in the bath; fragments of the bedside table from the spare room were scattered round the kitchen. Though he had chosen the hall outside his bedroom as the best place in which to wrench the house plants out of their pots, the earth they had been potted in now formed a thin careful layer over every carpet in the house. The bathroom wash-basin was cracked where it had been hit repeatedly with a ballpein hammer. Some of the kitchen cupboards had been emptied and their contents thrown around under the intense bleak light of the fluorescent strip – packets of dried soup, pasta, and tortilla chips, Marks & Spencer's coffee beans, bottles of vegetable oil and Hungarian red wine, in a congealing slick on the tiled floor. But the front room was the preferred site of destruction. The shades were off the lamps. The chairs were on their backs. Awed, I gazed round at Lucas's pictures, broken in half as if they had been snapped across someone's knee; the bookcases which lay on their faces in the centre of the room, volumes spilling out from under them like talus; the shattered plastic moulding and sheaf of coloured threadlike wires which was all that remained of the telephone. Lucas's grief had led him to tear up his own shirts. Finally, he had pulled all the papers out of the filing cabinet in his bedroom and thrown them in on top of the pile. It looked as if he had planned to make a bonfire in his lounge.

I stood there trying to take in the scale of it. The flat was so quiet you could almost hear him dragging the bulkier items from room to room, panting with effort, sobbing perhaps, repeating over and over again, 'Easier to manage her death. Easier to manage her death.'

'Lucas, for Christ's sake.'

An hour later I had righted the bookcases, vacuumed the carpets and cleaned the kitchen floor, thrown the pictures in the dustbin. Most of the books were undamaged, but it took another hour to pack them back on to the shelves. By eight o'clock I had gathered all his papers into a pile, made myself a cup of coffee, and come back to start sorting them out. I was pushing crumpled sheets of A4 into an old blue concertina file, when my eye caught the first sentence of the following paragraph:

'For two nights and a day the harbour had been in flames. In any case, there is no escape from inside the meaning of things. The Empress Gallica XII Hierodule, mounted and wearing polished plate armour but – in response some thought to a dream she had had as a child at the court of Charles VII of France – carrying no weapons, waited with her captains, Theodore Lascaris and the twenty-three-year-old English adventurer Michael Neville (later "Michael of Anjou"), for the last assault on the citadel. The outer walls were already weakened by three weeks of bombardment from landward. The labyrinthine powder magazines were exhausted. Smoke from the besieging cannon drifted here and there in the sunlight, sometimes like strips of rag, sometimes like a thick black fog.'

I looked for the title at the top of the page.

Beautiful Swimmers.

'What are you up to Lucas?'

I was fascinated. I put the sheets in order, made another cup of coffee, and began at the beginning –

'Concrete only yields more concrete. Since the war the cities of the Danube all look like Birmingham. When I was a boy you could still see how they had once been the dark core of Europe. If you travelled south and east, the new Austria went behind you – like a Secession cakestand full of the same old Austro-Hungarian cakes – and you were lost in the steep cobbled streets which smelt of charcoal smoke and paprika, fresh leather from the saddler's.'

The manuscript, though it amounted to sixty or seventy thousand words, was incomplete: the life of 'Michael Ashman' between 1947 and 1968 being sketched in with annotated cuttings from the *News Chronicle* and other newspapers of the time, a faded snapshot or two labelled 'Ashman in the Garden at Catesby' or 'Ashman's aunt', and a few thousand words of notes. Ashman's creative revision of history was documented at length, along with the conclusions he had drawn from it, in footnotes which referred to writers as far apart as Gilbert Murray (*Five Stages of Greek Religion*, 1933) and Norman Cohn (*The Pursuit of the Millennium*, 1957). One or two elements were preserved on the original postcards Lucas had sent to Pam in the early years of their marriage. Most of the text was typed, single-spaced and with very small margins, on the old Olivetti; much, though, had been handwritten at high speed in ball-point pen on the kind of ruled, punched paper students use. After the events at Burrington Combe, all pretence of an autobiography or memoir was abandoned. Instead, Ashman embarked on a dense, disconnected meditation around the theme of self-sacrifice (which he had originally described as 'the narcissism at the centre of Christianity'). He was trying to convince himself of something, though it was difficult to see what. 'Every sacrifice is a "sending on before", an attempt to prophesy or bring about the conditions of prophecy. All art, all religion, all "history", is only this pained clue dispatched to the future.'

Beautiful Swimmers took two hours to read, perhaps a little more. The final chapter began with such a barely coherent outpouring of delight I could hardly tell whether Ashman was describing 'the Coeur', or the world we already know –

'A rainbow like fire pouring down from heaven. Bare trees glimpsed through the violet end of the rainbow, transfigured, delicate, fragile and complex as a sea-creature in a bowl of water. Gold light on everything. Every object or event in this moment has idealised itself, every hawthorn hedge or gate in the twilight, every fold of a hill, every peach and silver line of cloud above an orange sun, every conifer in a suburban garden black against the house with its strings of fairy lights round each yellow window.'

Later, though, he passed into doubt and anger – 'We were all mad people, who heard voices and misinterpreted dreams' – to end with this strange and bitter cry:

'Willows bending over the roads, their leaves silver in the wind: comprehend the Heart, and you will never experience it.'

The flat was chilly, and I had eaten nothing since two o'clock that afternoon. Nevertheless, I sat for a long time with the manuscript on my knee, amused and thoughtful.

Remember, I knew nothing about this. In all those letters, miserable or elated, written to me over the years since their marriage, Pam and Lucas had been careful never to give anything away. I had never seen the word 'Coeur' written on paper, or heard it spoken down a telephone line. I was a publisher. It was easy for me to assume that Lucas – that dark horse! – had almost completed rather a clever novel. So I was quite unprepared for what happened next.

He got back from Manchester just after midnight and parked the Renault exhaustedly, sawing it up and down for several minutes in the snow. Then he came slowly up the stairs and stood in the centre of the room the way you stand in someone else's house waiting for them to make you feel comfortable. Last night's cut, inflamed and sore, embedded in its yellowing bruise, made his face look paler than it was. He had arrived at Christie's just after I left, he told me. He had been there ever since. 'That ward's bloody noisy in the evenings,' he said. 'You can't hear yourself think.' Then: 'She's not good today.' To make things worse, there was fresh snow on that side of town. 'I had a lousy drive back.' He blinked and rubbed the inside corners of his eyes with the tips of his fingers. I caught him staring in a vague way at the faded patches on the wall. Perhaps he was trying to remember where the pictures had gone.

'Lousy,' he repeated.

He took his coat off and sat down.

'Turn the fire on if you're cold,' I said, 'and I'll make you some coffee.'

I held out the manuscript of *Beautiful Swimmers*.

'What have you been hiding from me here?'

He took it, stared down at it in a shocked way, then up at me. Tears began to run down his face.

'Lucas! What's wrong?'

'I'm sorry.'

'What for? Lucas, it was a joke!'

'After Cambridge,' Lucas said, 'we couldn't believe that was the end.'

I stood over him. I touched his shoulder.

'Come on, Lucas. I only meant I didn't know you'd written a book.'

He didn't seem to hear.

'We'd done everything Yaxley suggested and nothing had come of it. Nothing could come of it. Pam was ill. Yaxley had vanished. You had lost interest in us.'

'All that was over years ago, Lucas.'

'Listen!' he said. He had to turn his head up at an odd angle to look at me. 'Just listen, for once! –

'The Pleroma isn't what the Gnostics thought it was. It's terrifying. Impossible to understand. Without something like the Coeur to buffer it, Heaven is harder to bear than – ' he made a helpless gesture ' – all this. The world. Do you see? We had nowhere to turn. We had to believe something.'

I let him sob.

'What have you promised her, Lucas?'

'At least try to understand. It isn't just a book. She's the Heir. She's the Empress.'

'Jesus Christ.'

'She *is* the Coeur. She won't die. I've told her she won't die.'

13

Fatalité Intérieure

I hadn't slept properly all week. Tomorrow I would have to get up early, catch the train home, buy Christmas presents, put an ordinary face on it for Kit and Katherine. And now this again. I went over to the window. If I looked into the street I wouldn't have to look at Lucas. There was a clear moon through the trees. A few clouds high up redistributed its light, which had lent them the colour of a fish's skin. 'Lucas . . .' I began, but I couldn't think of anything I hadn't said a hundred times before, and I got no further. Lucas wasn't listening anyway. He had turned the gas fire up full and huddled close to it, his face lax and tear-streaked.

'You're always waking up at the exact moment your life goes away from you,' he said.

He added:

'That's what Pam thought.'

Hot and tired and a bit nauseated, I stood as close to the window as I could and gently touched my forehead to it. My breath bloomed on the glass, but I could still see moonlight glittering in the long thin discoloured icicles hanging from the sash windows on each side of the street, where condensation had run down the inside of the window panes to seep out yellow with tobacco smoke and cooking fumes.

'Life's aware of itself,' Lucas proceeded, 'even as you piss it down the drain. You're forever catching its last signal: the urge to laugh or fuck or give your money away which you've just ignored.'

'Lucas, we're free to change our minds.'

'Too late. As soon as you stop acting spontaneously, your life becomes a fiction.'

I could only laugh.

'That's a simple philosophy,' I pointed out, 'for a couple who invented their own Middle Europe.'

But he was already too confused to notice this.

'I won't live a lie – ' he said.

An old Bengali woman came out of the house across the road and stood looking up and down the street. In the lighted passage behind her I could see a child's bicycle, a pair of stepladders. She wore cheap wellington boots, and over her traditional dress a council worker's coat. To her, snow was an alien, Sisyphean substance. Every day since the first fall she had been busy trying to clear her front steps, using a small red plastic dustpan. Morning, afternoon, quite late at night, you could see her shuffling to and fro across the pavement, the dustpan held stiffly out in front of her. It was too small for the job. Much of its contents remained compacted inside each time she emptied it. She had an air of inexpendable patience. As I watched, the wind got up and blew a cloud of spindrift round her. She bent down. I heard the distinct scrape of the dustpan.

Live a lie: it was one of Pam's phrases. You're living a lie. They're living a lie. I won't live a lie. Like all the others, it had signalled only a need for medication.

' – and Pam never would, either.'

'That was her trouble, Lucas,' I said bitterly.

The Bengali woman stopped work for a moment and went inside. When she reappeared, she had wound a coloured woollen scarf round her slack brown neck. Her breath puffed out white in the freezing air.

'Look, Lucas: the world's ours. We make it, minute to minute. Pam would never admit that. It frightened her to have responsibility for her own needs. She wanted the universe personalised. A father who would look out for her. Happy accidents. Gifts. Things that came demonstrably from outside, so she felt special. That's the biggest lie of all.'

'Why are you talking as if she's already dead?' he shouted.

'Grow up, Lucas.'

I waited for a moment then added deliberately:

'Kicking this place apart every day isn't going to help you, either.'

There was a brief awful silence.

'You don't know anything!' he said. 'What do you fucking know?'

'Lucas. Don't. I'm sorry. I – '

He got up with such violence his chair fell over, and ran out of the room. 'Lucas!' I heard his footsteps all the way down the stairs and into the hall. The front door slammed. From the window I could see him floundering across the square, trying to run against the resistance offered by the snow. The Bengali woman watched him too. She remained there for a moment, her breath visible in the sharp air, then emptied her dustpan for the last time, drew her clothes tightly round her and went up the steps into her house.

'Lucas,' I said. My head felt like an empty cinema.

He was back some time in the small hours. He had forgotten his keys. He stood there on the doorstep, frail, tense, resigned, incapable of organising his own resources. It was his favourite act, and just for once I wanted to tell him so: all that came out was, 'You look utterly buggered.' Inside, he crouched down over the gas fire, coughing and rubbing his hands together.

'Look,' he said. 'You should go home tomorrow. Come back when you can. I really don't mind.'

He did: but he was losing ground against himself.

'You do mind, Lucas.'

He nodded. He narrowed his eyes. I could feel him measuring something. It turned out to be me. 'I do,' he admitted. 'And so do you. You know you do.'

'You're a bastard, Lucas.'

'You love her as much as I do.'

I made him have a bath while I got him something to eat. Then I went to bed and left him to it, and in the morning caught an InterCity 125 to Euston so I could spend Christmas at home with my family. If they found me miserable and withdrawn they didn't say so, for which I was grateful. 'How are things up there?' Katherine asked me on Boxing Day. 'Not good,' I answered. She put her arms round me. 'It will soon be over.' Kit had given me some marker pens and a new shirt. 'I wrapped them myself!' After some thought she had also given me her favourite postcard, featuring a Botticelli Venus with whom at that time she strongly identified. Lucas didn't telephone. I returned to Manchester, as I had promised, on the morning of the 27th. From the train, everything looked astonishingly beautiful: factory chimneys dissolving in a blaze of sunshine you couldn't bear to look at, smoke wreathing in the clear blue sky. Some children were playing with a tyre in a snowy field, enveloped in transparent, bitter air. The sun reflected pink and gold on the icy surface between them.

Lucas was at Piccadilly to meet me.

'I'm sorry,' we said to each other in unison.

As if she had been waiting for us to be reconciled, Pam hung on another day or so and then died.

'Make the most of your life,' she often repeated. 'It doesn't matter how.' She clutched Lucas's hands. 'Promise me you'll make the most of it.' In her brief moments of lucidity she could still be optimistic. She would look out of the window and say, 'Do you know, I don't regret a day that I was sent. Isn't that odd? Not a day!' Much of the time, though, she was in despair. You would have a job to recognise her in the games this caused her to play with us.

'Sit here. By me. I want to watch you commit suicide.'

She would open her eyes drowsily and smile.

A moment later, terror forced her back to the safety of childhood, from which she recited nursery-rhymes, hymns, the nominies for skipping or ball-games, some of which had a deadly irony: 'Touch your head, touch your toes,' Manchester children recite when they see an ambulance, 'Never go in one of those.' Lucas was distressed. She eluded him increasingly in this surreal half-world of pain and morphine addiction. That is a bad way to put it, I know. It was Lucas and I who found it 'surreal', because of the contrast between the catheterised woman with the amputated breasts – nightdress riding up round her white body, emaciated, bed-sored and perpetually trembling – and the childish voice. God knows how she experienced it.

Somewhere down inside herself, you sensed, she was holding on with both hands when all she wanted to do was let go. She wouldn't relinquish the promises she and Lucas had made to each other. The Coeur, and through it the Pleroma, was all to be hers; and through her, his. She was the Heir. She could not die. She was determined to dispatch the 'pained clue' of herself into

175

the future, accomplish on Lucas's behalf that extraordinary act of prophecy and sacrifice Michael Ashman had talked of in *Beautiful Swimmers*. Her glazed, taut expression was as much the result of determination as it was of fear, pain, the animal need to endure. Whatever Lucas had intended – and I'm sure it was comfort – he had ensured that her death would be as much of a struggle as her life. I couldn't forgive him that, despite what happened later.

'As children none of the women in that family would ever go to sleep,' he had once written to me.

'You see them in photographs at three years old, almost blind with tiredness, puffy-eyed, heavy-lidded as vamps from a silent film, white, thin, with expressions as old and vulnerable as baby mice. They won't let go. They won't give in. In later life, rather than sleep, they smoke another cigarette, make another cup of instant coffee, read another page of *Lost Horizon*.'

At the very end, she wasn't anything at all. Whatever they had promised each other was a rag in the wind, the disease took it all away. Lucas stayed with her and held her hand, but I couldn't bear to look at her. I wanted to remember her ill but still human, saying something like, 'I never get tired of the view from this window.' Out in the corridor the afternoon she died, a little nurse with frizzy orange hair offered me a cup of tea and said,

'You can't imagine how we all admire her. We've never had a patient who sent her relatives away so happy.'

I stared numbly at the vases of flowers.

'I'm not a relative.'

Pam shrieked.

'The white couple! The white couple!'

Lucas wouldn't be comforted. His eyes vague with an undischargeable energy, he abandoned the Renault in Christie's car park and set out to walk through the snow into central Manchester. I followed him along Oxford Road trying to persuade him to take a taxi. 'Or at least get on a bus. Lucas!' I could hardly keep up with him. Every so often he turned back and said something unforgivable; but I could see that his hatred was for himself as much as me.

'Lucas.'

'Fuck off. You killed her.'

'Lucas!'

As the day began to fade, he made for the pedestrianised streets and softly lit malls where, preyed upon by greeds aroused but unassuaged by Christmas, shoppers clogged the replicated space, drifting slowly from window to window – past the ethnic knits and Barbourwear, the soft toys and 'collector' ceramics – looking for some way of relieving the emptiness between Boxing Day and New Year. Sensing this, wounded long ago in his own optimism, Lucas had no way of controlling his rage and misery.

'Look at these fucking bastards!' he said loudly. 'Haven't they got anything better to do?'

Women stared at him angrily.

He sneered.

'The middle classes are always on watch!'

I edged him along Market Street towards the monolithic tiled shed of the bus station. I still hoped to get him on a bus. Lucas gazed up into the dim ceiling structures, full of dust and diesel smoke from revving engines, then down at a Mars Bar wrapper blowing along near his feet. Against the grey concrete it looked like a small dun bird. He nodded judiciously.

'See that?' he said.

Without waiting for me to answer he continued, 'It was very important to her to buy me a birthday present. Maltesers. I had to eat some of them in front of her.'

He said: 'I loved her, you know.'

A bus arrived, bouncing on its suspension with the weight of children inside. Lucas watched them nervily, but allowed me to buy him a ticket. We would be home in ten minutes: less. I felt able to relax. Two stops later he was on his feet. 'Let me off! I'm going to be sick!' This amused the children, who got down at the same stop to watch. I asked the driver if he could wait. It was snowing again, and I had no idea where we were. The illuminated signs of bed-and-breakfast hotels, electrical dealers and Chinese chippies receded along a wide street brown with slush, seamed and sagging with old repairs: halfway down I could see the trees at the corner of a park, traffic lights green and steady at an empty junction. Lucas leaned over a low brick wall and groaned his vomit out into the car park of the Floral Hotel. The bus driver grinned and shrugged as if to say 'Well that's that then,' and drove away before we could get back on. For a moment the children tried to push one another under his wheels then lost interest and dispersed without warning into the shops and narrow side streets. Five minutes later I could still hear them howling and shrieking motivelessly in the distance. They seemed to be speaking another language, African or Asian. Echoing away between the dark walls of the houses, their voices conveyed only excitement inflated out of all proportion, cries of fear and panic, urgent, insistent, penetrating.

'Christ,' said Lucas, wiping his mouth.

I knelt down facing him and held his head between the palms of my hands. His cheeks were damp from the falling snow. I had the feeling that if I couldn't get him to listen, things would slip away from us for good.

'It was never your fault, Lucas.'

I made him look at me.

'None of it was your fault, Cambridge or any of it. All three of us chose to do it, whatever it was.'

He shook me off, stood up, and tried to turn away. 'What do you know?' he accused. Suddenly, the thin, intelligent lines of his face went flabby, his eyes wide and appalled.

'Lucas!'

He wasn't looking at me at all, but over my shoulder. He whispered something I couldn't catch, then: 'Not here. Please.' A small dark object came turning over and over out of the gloom behind me, landed on the snow at Lucas's feet with a soft wet thud, and burst, spraying his trousers with sticky, fizzing liquid. Someone had thrown an open soft-drink can at us. I stared up and down the road. It was still empty. 'Christ!' Lucas repeated. 'Not now!' He walked off quickly. Ten or fifteen yards on the left was the lighted doorway of a pub, the Golden Crown, and beyond that a dimly lit sign in yellow day-glo: IDEO CLUB. As Lucas passed beneath it, two motorcycles parked at the kerb fell down with a clatter. Lucas, who was nowhere near them, whimpered and brushed at his trouser legs. 'Go away!' he shouted, and ran off into the residential maze behind the pub. These old crescents of glazed red brick seemed deserted despite their renovated windows, figured glass doors, gardens full of clipped laurel and shiny-leaved holly. Snow whirled and eddied in the lamplight; snow lay thick in the open gateways.

Lucas hadn't got far when a small figure slipped out from between two parked cars and began to follow him closely along the pavement, imitating his typical walk, head thrust forward, hands in pockets. When he stopped to button his jacket, it stopped too. I thought at first it was a boy or girl about six or seven years old, in an adult coat which trailed around its feet. But when I called 'Lucas!' and started running to catch up, it paused under a street lamp to look back at me. In the sodium light I found myself looking at neither a child nor a dwarf but something of both, with the eyes, gait and pink face of a large monkey. Its gaze was quite blank, stupid and implacable: warning me off, but frightened of me too. Lucas became aware of it suddenly and jumped with surprise; he ran a few aimless steps, shouting, then dodged round a corner, but it only followed him hurriedly. I thought I heard him pleading, 'Why don't you leave me alone?' and in answer came a voice at once tinny and muffled, barely audible yet strained as if shouting. Then there was a terrific clatter and I saw some large object like an old zinc dustbin fly out and go rolling about in the middle of the road.

'Lucas!' I called.

When I rounded the corner I found that he was alone. He had fallen – or been knocked over – on his back in the slush at the side of the road, then turned half over and, like a dead insect contracting, curled up into the foetal position. His clothes were sodden. He was clutching his left wrist or forearm with his right hand. As I approached him, he tried to sit up.

'Christ,' he said thickly. 'Not again. Give me a chance. Oh, it's you.'

'What was that thing, Lucas?'

He laughed bitterly. 'That's my little gift from the Pleroma,' he said. 'That's what I got for wrecking my life all those years ago.' He winced, and sat down again in the half-melted snow. 'Once it starts, you never get free. I think the fucker's broken something this time.'

'Where does it hurt most, Lucas?'

After a moment he laughed wildly and pointed at his own head.

'Here,' he said. 'In here.'

He ignored the arm I was offering, struggled on to his knees, looked down at himself. 'It's hurt in here for forty fucking years,' he said. 'Ever since I was born.' He brushed disgustedly at the mess. 'What can you, a mere priest, do about that?'

'Lucas,' I warned him.

He shrugged and held out the heel of his hand.

'I scraped that when I fell.'

'You'll live.'

'I'm buggered if I will,' he said. 'Not this time.'

He staggered off into the sodium light.

'Lucas!'

Suddenly he stopped and turned back to face me.

'So much for the fucking Pleroma!' he shouted. 'Eh? So much for fucking magic! I got the dwarf. Pam got the white couple. What did you get? I'll tell you. You fell in the shit and came up smelling of flowers. No wonder you can afford to be so fucking patronising!'

'I'm going home, Lucas,' I said.

But I didn't. Sooner or later someone would have to spend time at Pam Stuyvesant's last cottage and there sort out her life – order it, if only in the sense of finding a home for the cats; ask, 'Is the father still alive?' and try to get in touch if he was; bring things to a close. It might as well be me, if only because it was always me. Lucas would never face up to it. I left him to his despair and his vile little familiar, walked back to the city centre, and then, after an hour's wait in the raw cold at Victoria Station, boarded a train to Huddersfield.

14

Burnt Rose

It was raining on the other side of the Pennines. Outside Huddersfield station I got into a taxi which smelt warm and sweaty, as if it had been used all day to transport dogs. The driver was wearing two or three unravelling cardigans; as I opened the door he reached out and turned the heater up. We went slowly through the town centre – it had a varnished appearance in the rain and orange light – while he carried on an interminable argument with his dispatcher. 'Well if you can't find it there,' he kept repeating, 'get Addie to try downstairs.' Once he said, 'Get her off her arse then.' Outside the town, he drove boredly, treating intersections and traffic signs with a kind of indolent irony as if he was too clever for whoever had put them there, occasionally looking sideways at the stone walls and farmhouses with no show of interest. 'Don't bother,' he told the radio eventually, his eyes focused somewhere off past the windscreen. 'I'm coming in. I'm getting nothing but rubbish tonight anyway.'

'This will do,' I said, although I knew I would have to walk another four hundred yards to Pam's house: 'I'll get out here.'

He looked round at the empty village.

'Please yourself.'

He drove off slowly. I could see him staring at me over his shoulder, one arm stretched along the back of the passenger seat. I swapped my bag from my left hand to my right and wondered what he was saying to the dispatcher. The rain was still coming down. If I had wanted to look I could have seen my face in the gleaming pavement.

I found Pam's gate hanging open and a woman in a pale-coloured raincoat knocking at her front door. She seemed to have been waiting there in the shadows for some time.

'Can I help?' I called from the pavement. 'No one's here now.'

She stood away from the door with a sudden apologetic movement.

'Pam?' I said.

But it wasn't her. The face was that of a much younger woman, about my own height, with heavy dark hair which she pushed patiently out of her eyes, revealing them to be grey, rather large and childlike. They gave you the odd idea that at some time they had seen something she had not. I had no conception of what it might be, but later I was unable to stop thinking about it. Her smile had a kind of warmth and sensuousness. If her face lacked animation, the broad, full-lipped mouth warmed it; and the eyes, which knew something she didn't – or at least something I didn't – illumined it: together they rescued it from blankness and lack of affect and made it deeply attractive.

'I'm sorry,' I said. 'It's the light. I mistook you for someone else.'

'Are you the owner?'

'A friend of mine lives here,' I caught myself saying.

'I see.'

I wondered if she did. As far as I could understand, she was collecting for some charity, Oxfam or Christian Aid; or at least conducting on its behalf a preliminary survey.

'We don't reach as many people as we'd like to.'

'I'm not very religious,' I said.

She would have a Volvo parked further along the road; two children at a local school; she would live in a converted cottage on the road to Manchester, where her husband worked during the day in the personnel office of an insurance company. I could imagine her drying her hair with a white towel in front of the mirror when she got home, repeating, 'Not as many as we'd like,' to someone in another room. She had a very faint accent I couldn't identify.

Suddenly she said:

'Isn't this beautiful?'

Almost filling the little garden at the front of the house was a blackcurrant bush which Pam Stuyvesant had allowed to grow tall and woody because, she said, it obscured part of the lounge window and made net curtains unnecessary. Now the night was full of its pleasant musty odour.

'Isn't it?' I agreed.

The flowers, which I knew would be pink in the daylight, looked like yellow wax. I pulled some of them towards me – drops of water showered down – and broke them off. I was glad to have something to talk to her about.

'This smell always reminds me of my childhood – '

But when I turned back to offer her the flowers I found that she had walked off without a word. Her pale figure moved rapidly up the street into the rain, shoulders hunched as if she had lost interest.

'I can't think why, though,' I finished. 'Still, you often can't.'

Pam's house was exactly as I remembered it, a little colder, a little dustier from disuse. Her neighbours had been feeding the cats, which ran up purring, tails high, as soon as I switched the lights on inside, and began to weave about in front of me, rubbing their heads against the furniture. I went straight through to the kitchen and put the kettle on. Staring out at the passage where in another life Pam had been compelled to witness the mating of the white couple, I shuddered; I closed the blind. I gave the cats a tin of meat and liver dinner.

Then I remembered how late in the year it was.

'Christ!'

I rushed back out into the front garden, where the damp air was still haunted by the breath of flowers. I stood there in a kind of fury of understanding, staring first at the blackcurrant with its freight of delicate yellow candles, then along the empty street. I had been in the house for no more than a minute or two. I listened, and thought I could hear, a long way off, the tap of high heels.

'Hello?' I shouted. 'Come back!'

The door slammed behind me and I was filled with panic. I couldn't get my key into the lock. For a moment I thought I had the wrong one, but when I held it up to the stuporous orange light I saw that embossed on it was the logo 'Mr Minnit'. Soon after Pam became ill, Lucas had had two or three of these duplicates cut somewhere in Manchester, and they never seemed to fit as well as the original. Eventually it turned.

As I let myself back in the smell of the blackcurrant grew acrid and overpowering, and the sense I had of understanding something faded. I knew that if I looked back there would no longer be any blossom on the bush, only drops of water like tears on every stem.

By then, the conversation on the doorstep seemed distant and confused. At one point, I believed, I had heard her say, 'I wanted to die.' (Her eyes had closed, as if she were testing the idea briefly, then opened again.) I thought about this in Pam's front room while Pam's cats sat licking themselves companionably on the carpet. Rain blew against the window behind me; I turned up the gas fire and drank my tea. If she had been collecting for charity why had she talked of dying, and let so many silences fall between us?

I fell asleep in the chair and dreamed about her:

In the dream she came to me as Phoenissa, the muse who has 'whored with many'. This enabled me to understand clearly, though it would become meaningless to me once I woke up again, the paradox of the mouth that warmed, the eyes which knew. What I failed to understand then, though it would become plain within weeks and has stayed plainly with me ever since, was the origin – or simplicity – of the message she had brought when she asked me to fetch her some roses,

'Like those on the graves over there.'

I looked in the direction indicated and saw instead of graves, as if through the wrong end of a telescope, groups of sad, exhausted boys in a wood, digging wide pits amid the fallen trees and uprooted secondary growth. It was spring. The woodland rides were muddy and poached, filled with lines of emaciated women dragging the dead up from the burned and fallen City by the cartload, and the cold air smelled of rain, raw timber, excrement.

Phoenissa giggled and whispered,

'Did you see the way that boy smiled when he saw me? The one with the mark like a rust stain down his cheek? Another girl said to me, "He was brave in the fighting around the Basilica, but he has such a disfigurement, running down from the corner of one eye, exactly like the stain on the side of a building under a rusty bolt. As if he had been crying rust!" But did you see how he smiled at me?'

She touched my hand affectionately and then pushed me away with a laugh.

She drew me back. She said:

'Later he wrote me a note. Look!'

I woke up confused but still able to remember some of what the boy had written. 'Attar, the secret heart of the rose: one ounce of this colourless fluid may be extracted from the petals of two hundred and fifty pounds of Gallica roses by means of a suitable solvent.' It didn't occur to me to think of this as nonsense – dreams often speak, Yaxley had once been careful to teach me, in the very inappropriateness of their elements. It was two o'clock in the morning and so quiet I could hear a car change gear off towards Huddersfield. I yawned, stretched, switched off the fire and then the kitchen light. Pam Stuyvesant's cats purred; rain pattered in the garden outside the lavatory window. I went upstairs and opened the door of the bedroom and found Phoenissa waiting for me there.

She was sitting in the dark on the very edge of the bed, gazing fixedly into the reflector of a cheap electric fire, her hands clasped on her knees and her body curled forward over them. A deep orange light lay across her face, which was turned very slightly away from me, elucidating the line of the jaw, the long tendons of the neck, but leaving her eyes in shadow. How long she had been there I couldn't guess. She hadn't taken her coat off, and while the air in the room was warm it smelled strongly of scorched dust, as if the single bar of the fire had only recently heated up. She had made some attempt to dry her hair on a towel which now lay like a small animal on the carpet near her feet. It seemed to take her a long time to see me. Eventually she murmured, almost to herself,

'Sometimes I think I'll never get warm again!'

I stood in the doorway, filled with an extraordinary excitement and tension. I could feel myself rocking a little with every heartbeat, as though I were being tapped politely but repeatedly between the shoulder-blades. The muscles of my arms and upper back were rigid. Phoenissa looked up from the fire, at the same time unclasping her hands so she could draw my attention to it.

'Isn't this lovely?' she said, like someone who had never seen one before.

'Pam and Lucas used to have dozens of them,' I heard myself answer. 'They could never get warm, either. Look,' I went on quickly, so as not to give myself time to think, 'I don't understand how you got in here.'

I switched the light on.

She jumped to her feet.

'I'm sorry,' she said. 'You were fast asleep. I just came up here, I suppose.'

'Did you have a key, then?'

'It was so wet. I had waited for a long time.'

'I thought you were collecting for charity,' I explained. I laughed. 'You should have said you knew Pam.'

At Pam's name a further wave of immobility – this is the only way I can describe an emptiness the warmth of her mouth simply could not redeem – crossed her face. She stared at me. The unkind wash of electric light revealed her large eyes surrounded by smudges of make-up like bruises. She looked as awkward and impermanent as she had done when I first saw her, on the doorstep, in the rain. It was the raincoat, a brisk tailored design meant for a much older woman, which had made me think of Christian Aid. By now it had lost much of its crispness. Her hair hung damp and tangled over its sodden collar. Nevertheless in Pam Stuyvesant's bedroom under the unforgiving light it only increased her sexual attraction.

Quite suddenly I imagined her turning away from me, pulling it up over her behind to show underwear made of oyster satin, white skin a little reddened in the creases below the buttocks so that she seemed at once inviting and ordinary (or perhaps I mean real), and made vulnerable as some women are by their own sensuality. I entered her at once and with miraculous ease. She groaned, and I heard myself whisper, 'Christ, Christ.' The rain spattered against the window. 'I died in Birkenau,' she said. She did not know how she came to be here with me, even in a dream. The electric fire was burning my bare calf – I paid no attention.

To visualise this took only a moment. I had no control over it. At the same time I was asking her:

'Would you like another towel? For your hair?' and she was blinking as if a sheet of glass separated us and then saying with a quick smile like someone waking up,

'Yes.'

Outside on the landing I shivered convulsively.

By the time I came back from the bathroom carrying the towel across my arm, she had switched off the ceiling light and arranged the bedside lamp to face the wall. It was hardly brighter than the firelight. She had taken off the raincoat and hung it up. Under it she had been wearing only a shiny grey slip which bared her thin shoulders and clung to the sides of her body, accentuating every rib.

From the doorway I had a clear view of her.

She was kneeling over me where I lay naked on Pam Stuyvesant's bed, talking in a low, persuasive voice while she fanned out in front of my drawn, surprised face a handful of dusty picture postcards she had taken off a shelf at the head of the bed.

I didn't see how I could be in the open door with a towel in my hand, and at the same time on the bed, breathing heavily with my clenched fists at my sides and the blood pumping and aching in my sex: but there she was, astride me. The slip had ridden up round her waist. I could see the soles of my own feet, yellow like the soles of the feet in some painting by Munch or Schiele. An instant later I was inside myself there, looking only at her, past the offered cards, seeing only her mouth and eyes while I struggled to drag the satin slip up further, perhaps pull it over her head altogether, and she laughed and urged,

"Pick a card. First pick a card!"

so that in the end I had no option but to take one. While I was looking help- lessly at it she reached down between her legs, adjusted herself slightly, then lowered herself deftly on to me. 'Oh!' I cried: and came, immediately and despairingly, as you often do in dreams. The rest of the cards showered down, spilled in an alluvial fan across the black and red motifs of Pam Stuyvesant's continental quilt and pattered on to the bare lino. Phoenissa's eyes were open but she could not see me; her lips were parted but she did not speak. I remember her smiling, moving on me for a few minutes in a slow, self-hypnotised parabola, raising herself in a long-drawn-out motion then sliding down with a quick limping flick, a rhythm with a strange lacuna at its heart, like a comet passing close to the sun. Then in complete silence her head seemed to transform itself into the head of a huge red rose, blind and perfect, and I shouted 'Phoenissa!' and fainted from pleasure or fear, to wake in the dawn with the bedroom empty and the fire unplugged, my semen drying stiffly on the sheets, and still clutching in one hand the postcard she had made me choose.

It was a colour print, mystified by the faint milky light coming through the window, of a Romanesque cloister or courtyard: perhaps the exact one from which Lucas Medlar had constructed, to pacify the young Pam Stuyvesant, the first myths and anecdotes of the Coeur – though when I sent it to him later he didn't seem to recognise it and, interested only in its curiosity value, described its architecture in a letter as 'less calm than dispassionate, less tranquil than detached'.

In the middle and foreground of the shot, neat flowerbeds, in which I could identify only the hyacinths – 'Lord, the hyacinths are blooming in the Roman garden' – surrounded a font built of pale rosy marble. Behind them was the low wall of the cloister, topped with serenely curved arches of the same stone as the font. In its dim recesses you could just make out a window, though whether it was glassed and modern was difficult to see. Growing across much of this part of the view were the blossom-laden branches of an old hawthorn tree. It was that type which flowers pink. You could imagine its heavy equivocal scent, half confection half corruption, filling the court; while a tiny jet of water sprang perpetually from the font, falling whitely back on itself in perfect order, so that you saw how passion and clarity need never be divorced again as long as they became aspects of some thing which is neither.

I got out of bed. I had a wash. I got myself something to eat. I was in love – as Lucas had often complained – with contradictions. The postcard I carried about with me from room to room the way you carry a paperback you are reading, propping it up by the soap dish, the kettle, and finally next to my plate. I stared into it, like someone staring into a shaving mirror, but found there neither myself nor the answer to the riddle which may be loosely stated:

'The house is empty but two damp towels lie on the bedroom floor.'

If I looked past the card and out of the window I could see the blackcurrant bush, its branches dark and wet, a few yellowed leaves still clinging to it out of terror at what their new lives might bring. In the north and the midlands, the weathermen were saying, more snow had fallen overnight. Though it was melting, the month would continue cold. Pam's cats ran in and out making sudden little noises of encouragement to one another: fights broke out between them, raced up and down the stairs like a burning fuse, then fizzled out. I thought I would go home that afternoon. At around eleven o'clock I had a telephone call from Lucas Medlar, who told me without preamble: 'Pam's come back.'

'You've seen her?'

Lucas said something that sounded like, 'No, of course not!' (although it might equally have been, 'The Course of the Heart!'), adding after a pause a sentence which made no sense whatsoever:

'None of us ever die,' and then 'Scars,' or perhaps it was 'Wounds.'

'Lucas?'

Unintelligibility was to mark this whole exchange.

The line was full of rushing noises which built up, saturated then discharged, in steady tidal patterns; distant voices were audible in them, like people calling to one another from boats; and sometimes voices not so distant, so that at times I wasn't even sure I was talking to Lucas. When I was, he was clearly distraught, often unable to finish one sentence before starting another, so that I was never sure if he was telling me about something which had actually happened, or about a dream of his own.

In an attempt to be sure I repeated again and again, as clearly as

I could, the questions, 'You've seen her?' and 'Have you actually seen Pam Stuyvesant?'

'I can't hear you!'

'Did you see her last night?'

'Thank God for that.'

'Lucas? I said, did you see Pam last night?'

I tried to get him to put the phone down and try another line, but he ignored me.

'Like a lunatic!' he went on. 'Early this morning. Wandering about babbling and soaked to the skin on the moors – ' I couldn't tell whether he meant Pam or himself, or someone else altogether. 'When I asked her why she said, "We talked about my heart."'

There was a silence, as if everything had flowed away out of the line, leaving it empty and transparent between us.

Lucas had time to say: ' – taken up into the Coeur.'

Then the surf of interference rolled back in, and I had a sudden, clear, agonising memory of Pam describing her first epileptic fit, and the vision she had had along with it –

'It was very clear. A seashore, steep and with no sand. Men and women lying on the rocks in the sunshine like lizards, smiling at the surf as it exploded up in front of them – huge waves, that might have been on a cinema screen for all the notice anyone took of them! At the same time I could see tiny spiders making webs between the rocks, just a foot or two above the tideline. Though it trembled, and was sometimes filled with spray like dewdrops so that it glittered in the sun, every web remained unbroken. So close to all that violence! I can't describe the sense of anxiety with which this filled me. You wondered why they had so little common sense.'

'I saw her in a dream,' Lucas said reasonably. 'Taken up into the Coeur. We're to meet her tomorrow, perhaps for the last time.' A sound like frying drowned everything but the words 'clear instructions'. Then I heard the rhythmic clicking that signals a crossed line, and a woman's voice said:

'Is that you, Alex?'

'Can you hear me?' Lucas shouted suddenly. 'You must be mad if you think I'm saying any more on the phone!'

'Lucas?'

'Alex?'

The other voices on the line went on calling to one another, remote as voices at the small end of the telescope; but Lucas said nothing more, so I rang off, picked up the postcard again and turned it over in my hands.

15

Every Web Remained Unbroken

Carnforth is less a town than a kind of late efflorescence of the old A6 as it hinges away from Morecambe Bay, where you can sometimes hear the seabirds calling sadly in the morning. We met in a bookshop which claimed to have on its shelves a hundred thousand secondhand volumes. Lucas and Pam had visited it regularly over the years in search of texts which would enable them to develop their myth of the Coeur. By the time I got there, it was late on a raw morning, and Lucas – looking along row after row of books with his head on one side like someone who has noticed something missing, though he can't say what – was already puzzled and disappointed.

'Why did we come here?' he asked himself. 'We might as well have met at the railway station.'

'Because you're a romantic, Lucas.'

He shrugged.

'You'd know,' he said.

I laughed.

Lucas looked around him with a kind of amused helplessness. 'This isn't going to be one of my better days.' He offered me a copy of Bruno Bettelheim's *The Informed Heart*. 'Look at that,' he said in disgust. 'He's a saint.'

'Lucas?'

'He's a saint,' Lucas explained impatiently, 'and they want two pounds fifty for him, second hand.' He looked at his watch. 'We've got hours before the train,' he complained.

Over the years the bookshop had been knocked haphazardly into dozens of finicky little rooms: section connected to section – however contiguous – by annex, passageway, steps up and down, often with bewildering changes of direction as each new builder strove to avoid knocking out structural members, so that you always seemed to end up back where you started. 'Two pounds fifty for that?' Lucas would say in a high pitying voice every time he saw the Bettelheim, and glance back over his shoulder, trying to decide what other turning we should have taken. 'It's absurd.'

Two women stood irresolutely on a top-floor landing.

'Oh Christine!' one of them was saying as we passed. 'And it was one of Daddy's favourite plays!'

'Don't touch my arm.'

Lucas glared at them. From somewhere below came a noise like a damp cardboard box full of books bursting as it fell down the stairs.

'Let's get out of here!' he said suddenly. He looked savage and ill. 'This old junk. I – Well, it isn't funny any more.' He wrinkled his nose. He could smell the stifled front rooms, vicarage studies, failed private schools all over the north-west, which had given up all these cramped, affectless, unread collections of *Men and Books, Books and Characters, Adjectives and Other Words.* Eventually we found the main door of the shop and were able to leave.

'If you spent too long in there your spirit would heave itself inside out!'

Lucas stood looking up and down the pavement.

'Let's meet Pam early!' he suggested. 'If we get a bus to Lancaster and then on, we could leave here now, without waiting for the train – '

'We were supposed to wait for this train.'

'Does that matter to you?' he appealed.

'You said it was part of the instructions.'

'Let's go now. Pam won't know!'

I thought about the dreams I had had the night before. I said tiredly, 'Of course she won't. Lucas, Pam's dead. She's dead.'

But he knew I would give him anything when he was in this mood, if only to prevent him damaging himself.

Even so, we didn't get away by bus. For some reason he could only explain by saying, 'I don't like to carry a lot of things around with me,' his briefcase and most of his money were locked in the left-luggage office at the railway station. When he discovered there would be no attendant to unlock it for him until the arrival of the next train down from Silverdale at two o'clock, he could only murmur softly and miserably, 'Fuck it, I always wondered what it would be like to be in Carnforth for more than an hour or two.'

'Now you know, Lucas.'

'There's a whole class of places like this. They wait for you as patiently as Medusa.'

'Come on, Lucas, don't be spoilt.'

Eventually we fetched up in the rain in front of the War Memorial. By that time it was only twenty minutes to wait for the train. Lucas was still tense but I could feel him relaxing. '"Their name liveth for ever more",' he quoted contemptuously. 'I suppose we're lucky it isn't written as one word.' Out of his jacket he pulled the two volumes he had stolen from the bookshop, *Moments of Reprieve* by Primo Levi, and the unexpurgated *Journals of Anaïs Nin 1931–1934*. He threw them down at the foot of the memorial in a wet flutter of pages. 'Forevermore,' he said. 'Forevermoreland.' With this gesture something was finally eased in him. He shivered, then laughed recklessly and pulled me away towards the station, his arm round my shoulder.

'I thought I could hear something on those stairs back there,' he admitted.

Suddenly he began to tell me how, after they were first married, he and Pam had found a wristwatch in the street. 'This will show you something about us, it really will,' he said. He gripped my shoulder and went on anxiously, as if he was afraid I might not be listening: 'We had this thing for six months. No one had claimed it. Neither of us had a watch of our own. But it was one of these modern things – ' He moved his wrist to show me that he had one now, all these years later ' – and we had no idea what to do with it. Every morning at ten o'clock the alarm went off, and we didn't know how to stop it. Every morning at ten o'clock it read eleven, because it was still on BST; and we had no idea how to adjust it. There it was, among all the other stuff – '

I could imagine it, on the sideboard next to the telephone, one of those items carefully picked up each morning so that Lucas Medlar's dwarf could fling them insanely about that night: the mystery novels, the coffee mugs with macaws painted on them, the artificial flowers and silvered pine cones.

' – recording some rhythm of its previous owner!'

'Lucas, you could probably have got an instruction booklet from the manufacturer.'

He shook his head impatiently.

'Listen,' he said. We were halfway across the road in front of the station; further up, some lights had released a thin stream of afternoon traffic. He stood in front of me and stopped and made me look at him.

'Listen, that isn't the point. It was just a tinny metonym of someone else's life. "Peep peep." We thought we'd penetrated the Heart, and we couldn't even work a watch!'

'Lucas, we'd better get out of the road.'

He made a bitter, impatient gesture.

'You, me, Pam Stuyvesant! Together we don't make up one whole intelligence.'

'What do you want me to say? "Perhaps that's the point"? I remember Yaxley telling me, "If you can comprehend the Pleroma you can never experience it." Lucas, please let's get out of the road!'

He looked at me with contempt. He knew that at this point I could never bear his pain.

'Believe that and you're worse than a romantic.'

'What did you expect to find in the bookshop, Lucas?' I asked him unfairly. 'The Library at Alexandria?'

He walked off without answering, and I let him go. The station was deserted. I could see him wandering up and down at the far end of the platform in the streaming rain, looking first at his watch and then up the line. He coughed once or twice. He seemed all right, so I left him to it. At least he was out of the traffic. In case Pam had run out when we met, I got her a couple of packets of cigarettes from the machine on the down-platform. Then I remembered Pam was dead, and threw them one by one across the rails into the waste ground on the other side. Lucas watched this performance and then came up and said:

'I'm sorry.'

'Lucas, you always are.'

'I did expect the Library at Alexandria.'

'Lucas, you always do.'

We laughed.

'Fasten your jacket up.'

Shortly after that the pay train arrived from Silverdale. It was full of children with sore red faces who by the smell had been copiously sick just before we got on; and old men with veins like cables on the backs of their hands who walked up and down in a buckled manner carrying suitcases too heavy for them while their wives changed seats relentlessly. Lucas watched them as if they might be a message from the Pleroma, or from Pam, and then, deciding perhaps that it was impossible to decode, took a copy of *The Tartar Steppe* out of his briefcase and pretended to read it. A few hours later we were stumbling about on the steep windy slopes above Attermire Scar in Yorkshire, looking for a dead woman who had given Lucas the grid reference NGR 842642 but who never turned up there.

It was the last place I wanted Lucas to be. Up on the limestone you feel miles from anywhere, and he was already soaked and cold. It would be a nightmare to get him down again. He raced about in the dark in the big deteriorating amphitheatres and steep hollows above the Victoria Escarpment, putting his feet down rabbit holes and coughing helplessly. 'Pam, you bitch!' he shouted. 'My feet are getting wet!' But after an hour he fell asleep suddenly in the mouth of one of the bigger caves, whose cracked, water-polished walls went above him in the moonlight like something made. I put my coat over him and poked about at the foot of the Scar until I heard him call out in his sleep, 'Yaxley! Yaxley!'

By morning the whole of the Ribble Valley was under mist. Like the cloud you see from an airliner above the Atlantic, it was white, impeccable, solid-seeming. It shifted restlessly, though, against the sides of the hills.

Reluctant to go down into it, we sat on some clints above Settle in the bright horizontal sunshine. Every tussock of grass had a rich luminousness. Every shadow pointed into the mist – which, where it encountered the east wind blowing down the defile between Attermire and High Hill, advanced a little, retreated a little, boiled over a stile, lay there curling back on itself and pushing out faint wisps close to the ground, exactly like the mist in a Sixties film. You had no idea whether it loved or hated the things it covered; you had no idea what they might be. Eventually it began to ebb, leaving a boulder which looked like a lamb, grassy slopes glowing like sun through a bottle. Across the valley the ridge leading up to Smearsett was revealed as a long, mysterious-looking island. Behind that Ingleborough, the ancient continent, inexpressibly bleak and far away.

Lucas who had got to his feet suddenly said in a savage voice:

'It was a real nightmare for her, you know. Fuck your common sense. Fuck it. You were in the Pleroma too, all those years ago!'

'Lucas – '

He stared intently out over the mist and said quickly so that I couldn't interrupt:

'Gallica, who called herself "the Slave of God" but who certainly loved Michael Neville, may not after all have died at the Carolingian Gate.' Soon he was shouting. 'Many of the wounded claim to have seen her after four o'clock, in the citadel itself, where she brought them great comfort. She was glimpsed several times during the three days of massacres which followed. Michael Neville, who though he lay all that time in the heap of dead and dying in front of the Eastern Basilica never saw her himself, recorded twenty years later: "Wherever she moved among them the smell of blood was transformed briefly to that of attar."'

He shivered and wiped his eyes.

'I made that up for Pam, years ago. It was a real dream. Fuck your common sense.'

'She never wanted to be the Empress, Lucas.'

Lucas looked round confusedly, exactly as he had done in the bookshop.

'She wanted to be the daughter,' I said. 'Let's go down.'

We took a wrong turn in the mist and were forced to walk for some time across rough grazing and moorland. Inside the mist it was silent, damp, cold. Lucas swayed and stumbled; he couldn't stop shivering. I pulled his jacket round him but it didn't seem to help. His shoes were coming to pieces.

'Where are we?' he kept saying. 'We should be down now.' And then:

'I hate it here.'

'I know you do, Lucas.'

Suddenly we were standing at the edge of a deep Gothic ravine in the limestone, at the dry bottom of which a well-defined path curved away between overgrown screes. Half a mile or less to the south white crags rose under the grey sky, their tiers of collapsing rock like teeth in a dead gum. Northwards, the path climbed abruptly into the recesses of the cleft and vanished. Light rain had begun to fall; I could hear it pattering quietly in the little bare larchwood at the lip of the ravine. We walked in silence along the cliff edge and stood in the rain to stare at the long featureless green sweeps of moorland stretching north.

'Christ!' said Lucas. But he seemed more cheerful.

The head of the ravine was a stony cleft hardly wide enough to admit two men. There the path came up to meet us, and we followed it down until we came to a village. Ducks honked from the shallows of the stream. A woman in a headscarf and gumboots stopped gardening to watch us pass, trowel in hand. Out on the main road, we waited half an hour for the Settle bus. When it came it was empty but for one bronchitic old man and his sly red-eyed collie.

Lucas was waxy and vague with hypothermia. I got him off the bus as soon as it stopped and took him into the first café I saw. That was a mistake. Warmth, laughter, and the smell of hot fat billowed into our faces as I opened the door: a New Year party was in progress, with a dozen people from one of the local agricultural businesses shouting, laughing and singing disconnectedly at a long table down one side of the room. They were wearing paper hats quartered in red, yellow and green. They all had red, polished, cheerful faces. The floor round their feet was littered with spent Christmas crackers, crumpled serviettes and strings of dried party-foam. Two or three middle-aged women in waitress outfits – old-fashioned belted black dresses with a severe little white collar – were beginning to clear the disordered remains of a second course of roast pork and apple sauce, in preparation for the pudding. Meanwhile a boy ten or eleven years old had the job of pouring out glasses of Tetley's for the men. A bit drunk himself, he ran about in his white shirt, little bow tie and neat black trousers asking hysterically, 'Would you like a beer? Would you like a beer?' The women in the party, who had decked themselves with tinsel and mistletoe, drank white wine. Lucas stood eyeing it all with horror, while the Muzak played first a xylophone rendering of 'Jingle Bells', then 'The Little Drummer Boy'. He didn't know what to do with himself. His shoulders were hunched under the sodden cashmere jacket, and he was shivering.

'I don't think I – '

'Lucas, at least have a cup of tea.'

I sat him down at a corner table where he turned helplessly away from the fun, his upper body stiff with rejection, while bits of talk floated round his head like strips of print on a clever advertisement –

'Pass us that mistletoe, Harry!'

'Ay, old Tommy Walker. Me brother used to work for him. He lost all his fingers and half his thumb, working potato machine.'

'Cost her twenty pound.'

'No, I think they saved some of his fingers – took them in with him and sewed them back.'

'White bread! Now that'll help your bowels come up.'

'Twenty pound? They're having you on.'

'He needed to. He needed to. Bring it up. He probably needed to bring it up.'

'Sorry, Harry!'

'Ay lad, yer will be.'

A large man in his early fifties who had at some time lost his left arm at the elbow, Harry wore a greenish tweed jacket over a maroon pullover not quite long enough to cover his shirt, which in its turn had popped open over a belly fat, smooth and hard-looking. In his youth his face must have been straight-planed yet heavy, quick to redden in the wind, and to develop broken veins. Now it had thickened under and around the jawline, and his lively blue eyes looked out from a lapping of fat. Harry was the most animated of them all. He liked the other men to listen to him. He liked the women, to whose attention he was always bringing his missing limb, to be a little shocked at the things he said. His idea of a joke was to drain a pint of Tetley's, exclaim loudly 'Ah'm not shuwer ah enjoyed that,' and finish: 'Now then! Ah'll joost av some of that *Perri*er watter. Raght oop mah street.' I saw quite soon that something was going on between him and our waitress: they had some old score to settle, some business unfinished since early adulthood, perhaps even before. He would catch her eye and call challengingly across the room –

'Hey! You! Coom 'ere a minute! Ah've summat to tell you.'

'I bet you have, Harry. I bet you have!'

Then, to considerable laughter:

'I hope it's nowt to do with that arm of yours.' And, with a direct look: 'Because I haven't got it!' Harry enjoyed this a good deal, and so did his friends.

She was a well-built lively woman, thirty or thirty-five years old, dressed in what may have been a Monsoon frock, who in addition to waitressing took care of the till. Her eyes were direct and brown, her hair unruly, her forearms freckled. As she talked she held her body towards you, and her skin had a light, pleasant perfume.

'Somebody's having a good time,' I said.

She looked pleased.

'Ay, we're just this minute picking up the debris. They've only been in an hour and a quarter. To get them in and serve them four courses in one and a quarter hours isn't bad.'

'I think I'll have some tea,' I said, mainly to stop her from staring at Lucas.

She leaned her hip unselfconsciously against the back of my chair and stared at him anyway, with a kind of half-amused concern. 'You've been in the wars,' she advised him, 'and no mistake. What would you like?' Her friendliness seemed genuine, but she had never had to deal with anyone like Lucas Medlar. When he failed to respond she shrugged and told me, 'Well you'll have to order for him, won't you? Just two teas? Nothing to eat? Right.' When she came back with the teas a few minutes later she went on: 'It's been nonstop here all week. Turkey dinners! Every single table was packed.' She paused to shout in the direction of the kitchen, 'They're still waiting at table eight!' The sound of crockery answered her. 'People who didn't even know each other were sharing tables.' She drew my attention to Lucas, who was still staring over at the party. 'Are you sure your friend's all right?'

'Leave us alone,' said Lucas distinctly.

She laughed and returned to the till. There, she fussed with some receipts, changed the Muzak tape for a selection of popular choral classics, then, with a yawn, leaned her elbows on the counter and looked out across the café. Lucas and I drank our tea. One or two old ladies finished their lunch and, complaining about the weather, went out into the darkening air. The party, contemplating an afternoon at work with a bad head, had slid into an introspective mood. Even Harry was looking into his glass, sighing, and saying, 'Ay, well.' The woman behind the counter seemed amused by this. She folded her arms under her breasts and said into the silence, as if to herself but quite loudly:

'I'm sure I don't know what I've done to my neck, but it's ached since Wednesday.'

Instantly, the one-armed man was on his feet and making his way across to her.

'Ah know joost what you need!'

'Harry! No!'

Before she could avoid him, he had taken her wrist and pulled her out from behind the counter. He made her sit down on an empty table, stood behind her, and began to massage the side of her neck with his good hand. At first she laughed like a schoolgirl. Then, as his hand began to move down towards her shoulder, she let her body relax and began a pantomime of sexual arousal, looking up and back at him with large eyes, pushing her shoulder-blades back against his belly like a cat being stroked and whispering in a stage contralto –

'Oh, Harry.'

The blues and golds of her frock glowed like a stained glass window.

'By God!' shouted the one-armed man.

He slapped his hand to his forehead, slid agilely out of his jacket and pretended to undo his braces at the front. He panted loudly. His friends cheered and laughed at this demonstration of how his missing arm had somehow granted him more vigour than ordinary people. She, meanwhile, ducked away, darted round behind him suddenly and massaged his neck in turn. Harry rolled his eyes with appreciation; lolled his head; and let his tongue hang out comically. The waitress leaned forward; gave him a quick kiss near the mouth; then, before he could recipro-cate, put the counter between them again. Further cheering broke out, and while Harry was bowing to the applause she slipped away into the kitchen.

What did this exchange mean? All you could say was that it was their party piece. Harry and the waitress knew one another of old, and they had done it before, and probably other things too. I was reminded of Ward Three at the cancer hospital, where among all the other wasted, wayward old dears (like a lot of moulting but cheerful parrots driven to testify at random from their smelly cage) there had been a woman called Doris. Against the odds of that place – indeed against all odds – Doris, seventy-eight years old, no hair and no teeth, pink flock dressing gown which shed all over the ward, radiotherapy implant and all, still enjoyed a rich and colourful fantasy life. 'I'll do most things,' she would carol out at the top of her voice in the middle of visiting hours, 'but I won't be buggered or bitten.' Or, 'Christ, that finger's been up two arses today. Look at it!' It was always unclear to me whether these were actually sexual memories of Doris's, or just some kind of loosening of the internal censors in the proximity of death. Much of the time, Pam told me, Doris irritated or upset the other women on the ward. 'It spoils their own memories.' But on occasion, especially in the middle of the night, when the building was full of their quiet, inturned, lunar despair, she actually seemed to give them an obscure comfort.

On balance, Pam had found her liveliness contagious. 'I think in the end the women did too, although they never joined in.'

I thought this might cheer Lucas up, but all he said was:

'Jesus Christ'

He finished his tea and walked out. I wanted to stay, but in the end followed him wearily.

Outside it was heavy snow. The air was flurried with it, and there was a thin, milky skim upon the setts. Whenever the wind catches falling snow, you seem for a moment to be rushing forward, as if your life has accelerated. Snow has been magical to me since as a child I stayed up late to gaze out of a downstairs back window and watch it fall through the night on to the dark lawn – soft, silent, huge as pennies. (It's easy to tell yourself: 'Memory is the great mythologiser. You were small. It was the first snow you had ever seen. Images like that become magnified out of proportion.' Now I wonder.) Pam Stuyvesant loved snow too. 'Yet if it falls for any length of time,' she used to say, 'I get the

202

sense I'm watching something in slow motion which shouldn't be. It's very unnatural.'

Trying to find the bus stop, Lucas had become disoriented and was walking across the old Settle square – now a car park – towards some narrow lanes on the north side, where Castlebergh rises steeply, wooded like a Chinese rock, above the town. He seemed intent on something: NGR 842642 perhaps, and the image of Pam drawing him back. Halfway across the square, though, he stopped as if puzzled, a gloomy, stooped figure in the poor light. I could see him moving his head from side to side. He gazed up into the whirling snow. He put his hand out to gather some of it, suddenly dropped what he had caught as if it had scorched him. I stood in the shelter of the café doorway and called –

'Lucas!'

He didn't seem to hear me.

'Lucas!'

When I stepped out into the square, I found that it wasn't snowing at all. White rose petals were falling out of the sky. Their thick, Byzantine perfume filled the air.

We were folded into the heart of a rose. The heart of a rose! The whole square beat with it. Lucas Medlar stood distraught and lonely, lapped in attar. He shouted my name: and then, 'Someone's here!' Attar! We were in the heart of the rose, and it was already occupied. People say of someone, 'She filled the place with her personality,' without a clue of what they might mean. Perfume was like a sea around us. If we could not learn to swim in it we would drown. I was gripped by the panic of irreversible events. 'Hello?' I whispered. No one answered, but Lucas called again, more urgently, 'Someone's here! Someone's here!' Now she walked out of the great soft storm of rose petals, the goddess herself, the green – the grown – woman, the woman made of flowers. Her outline was perfectly sharp, it seemed to have no surfaces, and flowers came and went within it as she turned her head deliberately this way and that. She was like a window opened on to a mass of leafage after rain, branches of blackthorn, aglet and elder interwoven, plaits of grass and fern, all held together with rose briars, over and between which went a constant trickle of water. Her eyes were a pitiless chalky blue, without white or pupil. They were flowers, too. She knew we were there. She stretched her arms, standing with one leg bent and the other stiffened to take her weight.

'You are never simply yourselves,' she whispered.

This time she had brought for us a glimpse of her own place, the envelope of her eternal fall, which is perhaps of the Pleroma but not yet the Pleroma itself (thirtieth Aeon beloved of God, she cast herself out and fell into mirrors in Alexandria, Rome, Manchester, Birkenau): roses blooming in a garden. Between the lawns were broad formal beds of Old China Blush – 'China's in the heart, Jack. China's in the heart!' – with lilies planted between them. Burnet and guelder spilled faint pink and thick cream over old brick walls and paths velvety with bright green moss. White climbing centifolias weighed down the apple trees. Two or three willows streamed, like yellow hair in strong winter sunshine. Beyond this garden spread an intimately folded arrangement of orchards and lanes, of sandy eminences and broad heathland stretching off to hills. There, late afternoon light enamelled the leaves of the ilex, briars hung over the grassy banks, clematis put forth great suffocating masses of flowers. Everything was possible in that country beyond. A white leopard couched among the hawthorn; other animals paced cagily along its lanes – baboons, huge birds, a snake turning slowly on itself. I heard a voice not mine or Lucas's say: 'The Rose of Earth is the Lily of Heaven.' The scent of attar was as heavy as a velvet curtain: but through it, from the café behind me like flashes of light through a veil, came piercing human smells – hot fat, brandy sauce, perspiration, beer. I could feel the heat, see the yellow lights. For a moment it might have been possible to go back inside –

But the green woman!

She stared down at Lucas Medlar in his loneliness and offered him the whole garden.

To have it he must first accept her attendants. These creatures, denizens perhaps of the Fullness itself, have power over all transitional states, all re-drawing of borders, all human change. They are always with her:

Around her feet runs the dwarf which haunted Lucas for so long, poisoning the central experience of his life. In the air beside her, naked and joined, hover the white couple. I saw now that under the Manchester street lights I had been mistaken. The dwarf was only a child, a toddler full of delight and charm one moment, full of rage and frustration the next, trying to eat up the world but hampered by some old coat of Lucas Medlar's he forced it to wear. It was only Lucas's own unruly future, made futile by too much longing. As for the white couple: they are five million years old. Sustained by their tao on the perpetual edge between desire and release, they never sleep. Their faces are transitory, yet do not change. They are Harry's stump and the waitress's Monsoon frock; the unfastened buttons of the blind woman in the quarry, the sudden sweet smile on the face of her crippled boy. For a brief moment as I watched, they were Katherine and myself: 'Touch me here, then.' For an even briefer one, like a promise of some admission not yet ready to be made, they presented themselves as Lucas Medlar and Pam Stuyvesant. In such moments, perhaps, out of delight and disorder, the Coeur – if there was ever any such place – is finally brought forth.

As if in earnest of this, the green woman seemed to melt and shift and grow huge, until she towered above the town and Lucas Medlar found himself hardly a speck beneath her. Slowly, and with vast grace, she knelt before him and sat back upon her heels, the palms of her hands flat on her vast open thighs. Lucas fell down before the rosy door, then recovered, pulling himself slowly to his feet again. In response, wavering above him like water, the green woman became his Empress, Gallica XII Hierodule, her plate armour shining through the smoke at the gates of the Coeur: 'When the smoke cleared you could not bear to look directly at her. There is no escape from inside the meaning of things.' Immediately, she became the Empress's daughter Phoenissa, running through the cool rooms of morning to meet Theodore Lascaris by a fountain. 'Fuck me Theo oh fuck me now.' Now that the goddess is in the World, she is searching too. She sways on her heels above Lucas Medlar's silent figure. Is it here? No. Panicked, she becomes the Roman prostitute Eudoxia, wife of Mathaeus; then Godscall St Ives, then Godscall's sickly daughter Liselotte, then Alice Sturtevant, caught in a moment of yearning she can never express. 'Something burns within me,' Alice once imagined shouting as she stood looking in at her father who lay ill, 'but I am never consumed!' She felt a terrible emptiness, and ran to John Duck. Now the goddess has fallen into the world, where is it? Michael Ashman's gypsy prostitute offers Lucas the cards, brings herself off in the air above him with a quick, limping flick of the pelvis. Is it here? (Floodwater was frozen in lakes, forty miles up and down the river.) For a terrified moment, the goddess finds herself as Lawson's twelve-year-old daughter, lying across Yaxley's table beneath Yaxley's pictures and her father's eyes. Then, with bewildering suddenness, she was Katherine; and Kit; and at last, leaping into stability and focus, Pam Stuyvesant as I had seen her that summer afternoon in her rooms at Cambridge, twenty years before, laughing up at me from the floor and whispering, 'This room reeks of sex.' Is it here? 'Don't let him in!' It is never anywhere. It is everywhere at once. The goddess is all these women and none of them, we seek her, she seeks us, less mater than matrix – the bitter world we know, the Pleroma we desire, the Coeur which intercedes. We are wrapped in the heart of the rose. Pam's face, now clear and specific, ages before us in the sky, after the divorce she is dyeing her hair, smoking fifty cigarettes a day, staring out into her garden. She has forgiven the world for not being ideal, and now bequeaths it to Lucas. The grown woman throws back her head in joy. A great open pink blossom fades like fireworks in the night.

I waited for a long time, just outside the café door. The winter air was dark. After a while the falling roses turned to snow again, the scent of attar faded, and Lucas Medlar was left standing in the middle of the car park with his head bowed.

'Lucas?'

'Someone was here.'

'Lucas?'

'I'll come back in.'

Pam's funeral took place a week later.

'A scent of roses,' I remember her saying once. 'How lucky you were!'

'It was a wonderful summer for roses anyway,' I answered. 'I never knew a year like it. All June the hedgerows were full of dog-roses, with that fragile elusive scent they have; I hadn't seen them since I was a boy. As for the gardens, they were bursting with Hybrid Teas and variegated Gallicas, great powerful blowsy things which gave off a drugged smell into the evening air. It was like a tart's boudoir. How can we ever say that Yaxley had anything to do with that, Pam? It would have been a good year for roses without his interference!'

But I sent some to her funeral anyway, though I didn't go myself.

What did we do, Pam, Lucas and I, in the fields of June, such a long time ago? I wish I could remember.

I don't think it was 'wrong' or 'evil'. Why should it have been? I think now it was one of those things that life offers you, from which you take the value you expect, or have been encouraged to expect, rather than some intrinsic goodness or badness. This is what Yaxley, in his corrupt way, might have been trying to tell us. If so, he forgot, and, though he sneered at Pam and Lucas for their lack of self-confidence, came away in the end with less than either of them.

'It is easy to misinterpret the Great Goddess,' writes de Vries in his *Dictionary of Symbols and Imagery*:

'If She represents the long slow panic in us which never quite surfaces, if She signifies our perception of the animal, the uncontrollable, She must also stand for that direct sensual perception of the world we have lost by ageing – perhaps even by becoming human in the first place.'

Lucas and I continued to correspond, although we never met each other again.

Shortly after Pam's death, he claimed he had remembered what it was we did to bring all this on ourselves. Indeed, it was Pam's death, he thought, which had somehow freed him to remember. He thought that in this sense her death was a redemption. The dwarf no longer haunted him. He had begun to write a book. He would not talk about what had happened to him in the snowy square in Settle. He did not remember a green woman, or a scent of roses. What he did remember, he believed, was his own affair. I agreed, although – from the hints he dropped, the obsessions he still had – I thought I could guess what it was. The search for the heart occupied him until his disappearance a year or two later. His letters are full of it. They glow like stained glass.

'The Coeur negotiates between the World and the Pleroma. It controls the dialectic between them. When it is in the Pleroma it cannot be in the World. When it is in the World it cannot be in the Pleroma. But it is never for long in one at the expense of the other.

The fact that it has withdrawn from the World is the surest indication that it will return. Its presence in the World is the clear sign that it must Fall. It is less a country, or even a state of mind, than a counter which the World and the Pleroma must constantly exchange between them to maintain some balance we cannot understand.'

After he gave up teaching and went to Europe, I heard from him less regularly. He would spend a couple of weeks here, a couple of weeks there, moving erratically from Spain to Norway, then back down to the Adriatic. He stopped off at Arles to see the Romanesque cathedral there, perhaps because he remembered what Van Gogh had written. 'We must not judge God by this world. It's just a study that didn't come off.' Or perhaps simply because its cloister reminded him of the one at Cuxa, and the postcard which had begun it all. He wrote twice in a week from Amsterdam; after that not for a year. In the east, governments were going over like tired middleweights – saggy, puzzled, almost apologetic. At first he was unimpressed. Watching TV pictures of East Berliners pouring into West Berlin, he had the sudden impression – from their cheap, dated clothes, their pinched rather unhealthy faces, the way they tilted a bottle of wine greedily to their mouths – that it was in fact people from the back streets of Bolton or Tyne and Wear who were being given their liberty.

Then came the fireworks at the Brandenburg Gate. The fall of Ceausescu brought lyrical footage of Moldavia: 'Ox-carts, bright peasant clothes and broken shoes, a near medieval society coming out from under the snow!' All this was accompanied by a terrible sense of risk, perhaps of guilt: 'At any moment it might go down like a card-house and take us all with it.' Aided more than hampered by a growing sense of his own inadequacy, he determined to re-enact the pre-war journey of his own invention, the travel writer 'Michael Ashman'; and after six months more in Western Europe crossed the border into Czechoslovakia, then Hungary. 'Things are quite different here now,' he wrote to me from a room overlooking Wenceslas Square. 'You can feel a real excitement, an extraordinary sense of something to be rediscovered.'

Budapest was less impressive. He had always wanted to see

the tomb of Gul Baba, a Turk who was supposed to have introduced roses to Central Europe some time in the sixteenth century –

'I wandered about in the old Turkish Quarter. On Frankel Leo all that remained was a ruined mosque with a rusty dome, and, almost opposite, a flower shop. Eventually I found him, quite low down on the Hill of Roses, on a bleak hummock of earth and railed concrete. A few children were playing football on the worn-down grass round the shrine itself, which is a neat sunken garden laid out in squares, with a path of stones leading to the little domed turbe. The roses were tall and sad, covered in huge pale hips. The garden looked as if it would never flower again. But suddenly a thrush sang, the declining sun shed a gold light across the litter and broken-down houses on the hill above, and you could see how it might look in summer, if summer came again. Two or three other Western tourists were grouped about the railings. I heard one woman say clearly:

'"They don't seem to be any better at growing things than they were at socialism."

'It was an unfair comparison to make in February in Budapest. Nevertheless the only flowers I have seen are in the windows of shops, where they look as if they have been injected with wax.

'"Who would want to be Father of this?"

'At the Palace Hotel the night before, a flautist had been practising in the room next door to mine, repeating each phrase of a quite complex piece slowly three or four times, then running them all together in an amazing fluid gesture, as if his failures and infelicities had never happened. You would never get that in a British hotel. Somehow I had expected to hear the same music on the Hill itself.'

A few days later he wrote, 'I'm having difficulty with the frontiers.' But he was determinedly pushing on down the Danube into East Croatia. Things were difficult there, he said. The West was still trying to broker a truce between factions. He would be in touch again as soon as things stabilised. I should take care of myself.

And then:

'Sometimes I think I understand it all so clearly!'

I never heard from him again.

As to my own search:

Shortly after Pam's funeral, I experienced a sudden, inexplicable resurgence of my sense of smell. Common smells became so distinct and detailed I felt like a child again, every new impression astonishing and clear, my conscious self not yet the sore lump encysted in my own skull – as clenched and useless as a fist, impossible to modify or evict – as it was later to become. This was not quite what you could call memory. All I recollected in the smell of orange peel or ground coffee or rowan blossom was that I had once been able to experience things so profoundly. It was as if, before I could recover one particular impression, I had to rediscover the language of all impressions.

But nothing further happened. I was left with an embarrassment, a ghost, a hyperaesthesia of middle age. It was cruel and undependable; it made me feel like a fool.

Katherine had learned to drive quite late in life, and like most people who discover a new skill in their forties, took to it with enthusiasm. Her first car was a little black Peugeot 205 GTi, with engaging plastic 'sports' trim and wheels so wide it looked exactly like a roller skate. By then we had moved out of London proper, and were living in Coulsdon, in a pleasant detached house on the northern edge of Sussex. She was soon whipping along the narrow Wealden lanes like a racing driver, redlining the rev-counter and tapping the clutch at just the right moment to slip from third to fourth gear without any loss of power. 'I love it!' she would say, laughing at herself. 'I love it!' Kit and I were less certain. Kit liked to sit in the back of my Volvo and look graciously out at the woods and flint-faced garden walls; she liked me to slow down for horses.

Sometimes the three of us would go down to Tunbridge in the Volvo after Sunday lunch, to walk on the downs; increasingly, though, Katherine preferred to drive herself, and meet us later. On a sunny Sunday, Coulsdon haemorrhages its BMWs and Jaguars into the surrounding tissues of Redhill, Reigate and Dorking, which flush and bruise suddenly under the strain. She hated to be in queues. One afternoon, following her at a leisurely pace down the M23 just south of Salfords, Kit and I found lines of stationary traffic winking in the sun. All three lanes were jammed solid. A police Land-Rover, a small ambulance and a rescue vehicle raced down the hard shoulder. Every so often a kind of peristalsis shuddered through the lines of cars, a ten- or twenty-yard gap which opened and closed to give each driver the illusion of movement. A quarter of an hour later we were still inching our way towards the accident. Up ahead we could see a tall black plume of smoke, its base somewhere near Outwood or Wasp Green; and once or twice we got a confused glimpse of flames through a hedge.

'There's a church near it!' cried Kit, craning her neck out of the open window. 'I can't see anything else!'

'Why would they be burning a church, Kit?'

'They're a funny lot in Wasp Green.'

But when we finally crawled past the base of the column, we found that a small black car had left the motorway and gone through the hedge into the churchyard, where it had shed its bonnet and one door then fireballed itself among the grave-stones. A disgusting smell blew in through the windows and Kit threw up suddenly across the back seat. I stopped the car and shut her in it. She had begun to scream and kick. I walked back up the hard shoulder and said to the first policeman I saw, 'Does anyone know what make of car it is?' They weren't sure, but I was. The goddess gives, the goddess takes away.

A few weeks later, clearing up Katherine's papers, I came upon some letters, addressed to her from the Chelsea Arts Club, sympathising with her feelings of being 'stifled' by marriage and speaking of 'our long sexy afternoons together'. They were about ten years old. I didn't recognise the man's name. Kit and I drew apart in the following years. After she left home I couldn't seem to be bothered with the house, so I sold it. Bereavement numbed my hyperaesthesia. Then a year or two ago, for a few minutes one afternoon in May, it returned:

I had been sorting books all day. I still have a lot, some of which I have owned since Cambridge. They look their age now, browned by the tobacco smoke, gas fumes and evaporated cooking oil of the places I have lived in since things fell apart. By the shelf load they have a faint smell of dust. It is a cured odour, as if my way of life had been designed to preserve them by bringing about organic and chemical changes, in one-roomed flats like a chain of smoke-houses across London. I was thinking about that, and looking through an old paperback copy of *War in Heaven*, when up from it came a smell like cornflour, or even vanilla, so strong I thought a door had opened and someone I once knew had come in. It was the smell of the individual book – not dust, not decay, but cornflour and vanilla, some transformation of the glues and inks and paper: cornflour, vanilla, then hawthorn blossom like a drug!

I sat there on the floor and burst into tears.

It will soon be fifteen years since Katherine died. Kit has moved to New York, from where she sends me letters I don't understand, about politics and Aids. Pam and Lucas walked away from me somehow, that scented, dew-soaked morning in Cambridge. I remember them all with such happiness.

M. John Harrison

Climbers

In retreat from his failed marriage, Mike heads for the Yorkshire Moors, where he joins Normal, Gaz and Sankey on their obsessive quest for the perfect crag.

Through climbing, Mike discovers an intensity of experience – pain, fear and adrenalin – that obliterates the rest of his world; and for a time, a genuine escape. But it is gained at a price . . .

Harrison's observation of modern Britain is incisive and disturbing. This dark, witty, poetic novel is not so much about climbing as the channels of escape people desperately seek in order to make their lives bearable.

'Why aren't there more novels like M. John Harrison's wonderful *Climbers*?'   *The Times*

'The way he handles the sport and social background bears comparison with that of David Storey in *This Sporting Life*. I know no higher praise.'   *Independent*

'A vivid, restless, deeply cunning novel.'   *Sunday Times*

'Sheer brilliance.'   **Iain Banks**

The only novel ever to win the Boardman Tasker Prize for Mountain Literature.

ISBN 0 586 09065 7

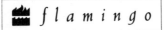 *flamingo*

M. John Harrison

The Ice Monkey

The world of *The Ice Monkey* is a dangerous place, which steals over you like a dream. It is a twilight world of stark cities, doomed humanity, bizarre rites and psychic horrors. Powerful and unsettling, this stunning collection of stories displays the astonishing range of a British writer whose wit and imagination has established him as one of the most original and distinctive voices in contemporary fiction.

'Stylish, accomplished, evocative short stories, exemplary fictions of unease shot through with poetic insights and most beautifully written.'
Angela Carter

'This collection puts Harrison in the company of Ian McEwan and Peter Carey, but he is grittier than Carey and wittier than McEwan.'
Times Literary Supplement

'A curious and accomplished writer . . . the stories in *The Ice Monkey* display his talents quite remarkably. A brief review can only serve to indicate the richness of this book. Mr Harrison's progress becomes fascinating.'
Robert Nye, *Guardian*

'Writing of remarkable resonance and power.'
London Review of Books

'A haunting series of portraits. There's no denying this collection's compelling narrative power.'
Publishers Weekly

ISBN 0 00 654578 5

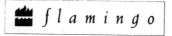
flamingo

Cristina Garcia

Dreaming in Cuban

SHORTLISTED FOR THE AMERICAN NATIONAL BOOK AWARD

'A dazzling first novel'   *New York Times*

Set in Havana and Brooklyn, *Dreaming in Cuban* takes us into the heart of the del Pino family, introducing four wonderfully various, strong-willed women. In Cuba: Grandmother Celia, a loyal Communist with a passion for Castro; and her youngest daughter, mad Felicia. In New York, Felicia's sister, Lourdes, fervently capitalist proprietor of the Yankee Doodle Bakery; and her daughter, Pilar, the sweet, sceptical artistic punk. Visited in her dreams by Grandmother Celia, Pilar longs to return to Cuba, the hot, sultry paradise of her swiftly fading childhood memories.

'Cristina Garcia stands revealed in this novel as a magical new writer. She has produced a work that possesses both the intimacy of a Chekhov story and the hallucinatory magic of a novel by Gabriel Garcia Marquez. Fierce, visionary, and at the same time oddly beguiling and funny, *Dreaming in Cuban* announces the debut of a writer blessed with a poet's ear for language, a historian's fascination with the past and a musician's intuitive understanding of the ebb and flow of emotion'   *New York Times*

'*Dreaming in Cuban* is a rich and haunting narrative, an intricate weaving of dramatic events with the supernatural and the cosmic, the language evocative and lush. A remarkable first novel'
San Francisco Chronicle

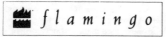

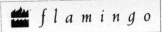

Flamingo is a quality imprint publishing both fiction and non-fiction. Below are some recent titles.

Fiction

- [ ] The Naked and the Dead *Norman Mailer* £6.99
- [ ] The Kitchen God's Wife *Amy Tan* £5.99
- [ ] A Thousand Acres *Jane Smiley* £5.99
- [ ] The Quick *Agnes Rossi* £4.99
- [ ] Tropic of Cancer *Henry Miller* £5.99
- [ ] The Cat Sanctuary *Patrick Gale* £5.99
- [ ] Dreaming in Cuban *Cristina Garcia* £5.99
- [ ] The Golden Notebook *Doris Lessing* £6.99
- [ ] True Believers *Joseph O'Connor* £5.99
- [ ] Bastard Out of Carolina *Dorothy Allison* £5.99

Non-fiction

- [ ] The Proving Grounds *Benedict Allen* £7.99
- [ ] Long Ago in France *M. F. K. Fisher* £5.99
- [ ] The Female Eunuch *Germaine Greer* £5.99
- [ ] C. S. Lewis *A. N. Wilson* £5.99
- [ ] Into the Badlands *John Williams* £5.99
- [ ] Dame Edna Everage *John Lahr* £5.99
- [ ] Number *John McLeish* £5.99
- [ ] Tangier *Iain Finlayson* £7.99

You can buy Flamingo paperbacks at your local bookshop or newsagent. Or you can order them from Fontana Paperbacks, Cash Sales Department, Box 29, Douglas, Isle of Man. Please send a cheque, postal or money order (not currency) worth the purchase price plus 24p per book (maximum postage required is £3.00 for orders within the UK).

NAME (Block letters)_____

ADDRESS_____

_____